"Cut your engines—now!" the man in the head mask shouted.

Ganja had dealt with pirates before, and these looked like big trouble. Lying in wait for the Caribbean Dream yacht around Ram Head, the Grumman hydrofoils armed with antiship missiles and .76 cannons surrounded the boat quickly. Ganja cut his engines down to a slow idle and waited.

Head Mask pulled close on the starboard. He pulled a gun from his belt and fired twice in the air. "Get your fat asses on the deck. Move it!"

The party of tourist fishermen hit the deck immediately, covering their sunburned heads with their hands. Ganja Grant stood behind the helm, one hand raised, one on the throttle.

"That's right, boys," Head Mask said as he boarded the yacht, his gun ready. "You, Dredlocks. Get down here and collect my bonus from your guests. And no bullshit stunts or Mr. LaCoste gets it." He kicked the nearest tourist hard.

"Don't wan' no trouble, man," Ganja said, as he descended the steps to the deck. He walked over to the prostrate men and began taking their jewelry and wallets and sliding them over.

Suddenly, a flare went off from the other hydrofoil. Head Mask turned quickly to see another charter yacht fast approaching.

And the man behind the machine gun didn't look friendly.

Other books in the **KANE'S WAR** series:

#1 KANE'S WAR

KANE'S WAR

#2 THE ASSASSIN

Nick Stone

IVY BOOKS • NEW YORK

Ivy Books
Published by Ballantine Books

Copyright © 1987 by Butterfield Press, Inc.

Produced by Butterfield Press, Inc.
133 Fifth Avenue
New York, New York 10003

Library of Congress Catalog Card Number:86-91837

ISBN 0-8041-0015-2

Manufactured in the United States of America

First Edition: May 1987

CHAPTER 1

"You've tried physical persuasion, of course?"

"Of course," Willoughby said. "But since Kang Sha, pain is no longer a viable option."

Weaver nodded.

They were teaching Kang Sha in the States now at both the CIA training center in Virginia and the top-secret location two hundred feet below the Pueblos in Colorado. The rediscovered methods of the old monk who had lived during the fourth century enabled one to separate mind from body and made torture a time-waster and rather pointless.

The two men were a stark contrast in the narrow, dimly lit passage; Willoughby, short, anemic, with bulging eyes and protruding front teeth, his hair matted by sweat despite the chill in the air, wearing a khaki shirt and shorts over high brown socks and brown shoes; and Weaver, immaculate in a white DeLaurentis suit, tall, regally thin, every blond hair standing straight as a soldier in a military brush cut. His eyes, which were not in Weaver's case "the mirrors of the soul," were a cool gray reflecting exactly what Weaver wanted to project at the moment. At this time it was mild curiosity.

The call had come at an inopportune time for Weaver. He'd had the technicians at Ultratech synch the huge satellite dish in such a way that he was able to pick up network feeds of pro football games in the States. His beloved Dallas Cowboys had intercepted a pass on their own twenty and were in the process of marching down the field for a touchdown. It was first and goal on the three-yard line when Suzy rapped lightly on his office door and let herself in. His secretary screened every call with even more scrutiny than usual during football season.

This call was from Willoughby and couldn't wait for Dorsett to find a hole behind his blockers and scramble into the end zone for a score. Suzy had already ordered a chopper to transport Weaver from Charlotte Amalie to the British Virgins.

Although he wouldn't reveal much on the phone, Weaver knew that Willoughby would not have asked him to come to Windsor House on Britain's Tortola Island unless it was extremely important. Willoughby played his role as personal secretary to Lord Philip Carlisle flawlessly. Only Weaver and Lord Philip knew that in reality Willoughby was the ranking field officer for M16, the British Intelligence Agency.

Windsor House was the seat of British power on the largest island of the British Virgins. The sprawling eighteenth-century mansion, located near Wickham's

Cay and Saint George's Church, had been rebuilt after a fire in the early nineteen hundreds. Weaver had been in the well-appointed mansion several times over the past few years, but this was the first time that Willoughby had shown him the subterranean wing that had survived the fire and was reached through a false bookcase in the library and down a dank stairway.

At the end of the passageway, a formidable steel door stood before them. Willoughby looked up at a camera suspended from the ceiling and gave a half wave. The door opened.

Immediately Weaver felt the difference in temperature due to the air conditioning. They were in a bright modern room, the hum of large electric motors filling the air. Weaver counted four men and three women seated at desks punching in data at computers or monitoring screens.

"Communications?" Weaver asked.

"Yes. We also monitor ship departures and arrivals in the area. We don't have all the spy-in-the-sky satellites that you have at your fingertips, so we make do." Willoughby smiled to take out the sting.

Weaver ignored the dig. The sharing of satellite data had been a bone of contention between the two governments.

"When you need something, ol' buddy, we'll be there for you," Weaver said.

"Of course," Willoughby agreed too abruptly. "Our prize specimen is in here."

He opened a door marked PRIVATE and held it for Weaver.

The man was lying on a table strapped down spread-eagled. He was bare chested but wore the bottom of a frogman or seal suit. He was Oriental—Japanese, Weaver guessed. The man gritted his teeth and strained to break out of the leather restraining straps. He was

3

well muscled, about thirty, his face contorted in a mask of rage. Weaver moved closer, which caused the man on the table to toss his head back and forth. The President of Ultratech, a CIA cover company specializing in sophisticated electronics, grabbed him by the hair and yanked his head down.

"Let's have a look at you, pal," Weaver said. "Yeah, I know you. I've seen your face on tapes. You have Mr. Tsufura here, Willoughby. *The* Mr. Tsufura who participated in the Tokyo Airport massacre that killed twenty."

"He's a big fish for our little pond," Willoughby said, somewhat surprised.

"Indeed! What are you doing here? Not talking, eh? That's not very friendly, is it, Willoughby?"

Tsufura's eyes rolled in his head, and his body went limp.

"He's employing Kang Sha again. We won't get anything from him," Willoughby said.

"I have something here that might stop him from being so shy."

Weaver took a small case from his pocket. Inside there were hypodermic needles and vials containing a red liquid. "We've had some success with this."

"Yes, please go ahead."

Weaver loaded a needle and plunged it into the man's right arm. Tsufura's body tensed. His arms and legs began to spasm, his head started banging against the table, his whole body began to vibrate. The convulsion reached a peak and then slowly subsided.

"He'll be talking in a few moments," Weaver told Willoughby. "I can call for a translator. . . ."

"That won't be necessary. He's an American, born and raised in sunny California. The poor boy hates us, among other reasons because Roosevelt shipped his parents to a detention camp during World War II.

4

How'd you happen to land him?"

"Bit of luck. He washed ashore on Brewers Bay, with what was left of his dinghy. We don't permit anchorage there because of submarine cables, so it would be easy to slip in unnoticed. From the looks of him and the wreckage when we picked him up, I'd say his mast must have been struck by lightning during that squall we had last night. the day before yesterday, a Soviet Class-4 submarine, the *Iskra*, sailed out of Puerto Manotti, Cuba. My guess is this chap was dropped off in international waters with instructions to land at Brewers. We also found a standard assassination kit, Czech, high-powered rifle and scopes, and Uzi, mercury grenades—the usual array."

"Yes, it had to be the lightning. He never would let himself be taken alive. Not this one. Where did you find the cyanide? They keep changing their spot."

"It was surgically implanted under a flap of skin on his left wrist."

"That's a new one. I'll have to let Washington know. I think we're about ready. . . . What's your name?" he asked the man on the table.

"Tsufura." The voice was mechanical and hollow.

"Fine. What are you doing here on the Islands?"

"Assassination . . ."

"Who?"

"The American . . ."

"What American? How about giving us a name, pal?" Weaver asked patiently.

There was no answer.

"It's stopped working," Willoughby said.

"No. He might not know the name. Do you know the identity of this person?" Weaver asked Tsufura.

"No . . ."

"Why is the American to be assassinated?"

"To affect the election . . ."

"What election?" Weaver and Willoughby exchanged glances. "The presidential election?"

"Yes."

"He's talking gibberish," Willoughby said. "You won't have an election for another year, and besides, what does the Virgin Islands have to do with that?"

"We'll soon find out. Where was the American to be killed?"

There was no answer.

"Who was to give you the information on the American?"

Tsufura's mouth opened but no sounds came out. His face went into violent contortions. He began moaning as if in terrible pain.

"What's happening?" Willoughby wanted to know.

"He's in conflict. All his defenses are straining to protect his contact, but the drug is forcing him to speak. This is kind of unique. I may have to increase the dosage."

"You people are far ahead of us in chemical science technology. I could have used this serum many times in the past and changed the course of a mission," Willoughby said wistfully.

Weaver was preparing another needle. "Sorry, buddy boy, this stuff is classified. It isn't really perfected yet. It has flaws."

He plunged the needle once again in Tsufura's arm. This time there were no spasms. Tsufura's face no longer reflected the conflict going on inside his brain.

"Now tell me. Who is your contact?"

Tsufura's mouth opened slowly. He began to breathe heavily. For the first time since being under the drug, his eyes opened. Wide.

"He's still fighting it. Give him another dose," Willoughby suggested.

"WHO IS YOUR CONTACT?" Weaver repeated

6

more forcefully.

The name came out in a whisper. "Gregor."

"Good lord! Did he say Gregor?" Willoughby gasped.

Weaver's eyes opened wider. "Where were you to meet Gregor? Where is this rendezvous with Gregor?"

Tsufura's eyes closed. His body went limp.

"Come on, pal. Talk!" Weaver grabbed him by the neck and shook him. He stared at Tsufura, shrugged, and then let him go.

Willoughby placed his fingers on Tsufura's carotid artery. "He's dead," he told Weaver.

Weaver stood up slowly. He straightened the lapels of his suit. "That's one of the flaws I mentioned before, ol' buddy."

CHAPTER 2

After commanding a submarine in World War II and seeing the majestic beauty of the islands, Mike Mulhaney had had the foresight to purchase the U.S. Navy dockyard facilities when they were declared surplus. When the tourist boom arrived, Mike's property was worth millions. Since then, at one time or another, every developer south of Georgia had made a pitch for the idyllic harbor known as Barracuda Reef. Next to his daughter, Michelle, Mike's primary concern in life was to preserve the reef from being spoiled by the hordes of tourists who were rapidly turning the U.S. Virgin Islands into a Caribbean Coney Island.

Mike paid plenty under the table to be sure Barracuda Reef maintained its expensive exclusivity. He also saw to it that the people who came to the reef were people who "deserved" to be there and joined him for some brew at his Rainbow Keg Inn—an "oasis of fellowship," as Mike called it. He and Michelle ran the yard from the second-story offices of the inn. The main floor was dedicated to good beer, salty tales, and friendship.

"Okay." Mike laughed. "That takes care of two of you. Who wants to try the old captain again?"

His large, pleasant, brown face was covered by a snow-white beard that matched the regulation crew cut on the top of his head. He placed his elbow down on the table in an arm-wrestling stance.

Ganja Grant got up and rubbed his wrist. "The man's an animal. I think he broke my damn wrist!"

This brought another guffaw from Mike and good-natured kidding from the rest of the people around the table.

"Why don't you give him a try, Miles?" Ganja said to the gaunt, silent man on his left. "What you doing, man? Thinking about your love life? That don't take long."

Miles, as usual, had not been joining in with the rest of them. He was somberly staring into his glass. The more morose he was, the more Grant rode him. He would only take ribbing from Grant, or from Ben Kane. Grant because he was "too dumb to know better," and Kane because he owed his life to "the skipper."

"I don't like to play games," he said finally.

People who met Miles for the first time tended to underestimate him because of his silence. In actuality, he was a seething volcano, always one short fuse from blowing sky high. Very few knew of his exploits with Kane, Grant, and the Chief in the Riverine Forces of the brown-water navy. He was haunted by the thirty-six hours he had hidden up to his nostrils in the Mekong

Delta mud while the Viet Cong, who had wiped out the rest of his unit, searched for him. Ben Kane had saved his life then and Ben Kane was the only man Miles trusted and respected now.

"That's enough, Mike. You shouldn't be arm-wrestling and drinking anyway," Michelle told her father sternly.

"First you take away the yard from me, and now you want to take away my ale, too. Just like a woman!" Mike grumbled.

Mike's mild heart attack a year ago had made Michelle the Mulhaney who took care of the day-to-day running of the yard. Like her father, she was tough and knowledgeable and eventually gained the respect of the tough captains who entrusted their vessels to her.

She was a curvaceous little spitfire with brown hair and green eyes who could curse with the best of them but was still treated like a lady without making a point of it. A prime topic of conversation around the reef was how she would be in bed. Rumor had it that Ben Kane knew for sure, but he wasn't talking.

"Your turn, Ben," Chief Bukowski said. Bukowski, like Miles and Grant, had served with Kane in Nam. He was a chief petty officer and a handy guy to have around. Whenever Lieutenant Commander Kane had needed something that was vital for his men but couldn't be obtained through regular or legal channels, Kane gave the job to the Chief. Bukowski had yet to fail him.

Bukowski had been lost when the Navy mustered him out after thirty years of service. When Kane started his enormously successful Caribbean Dream Charter Company, he asked the Chief to join him. Back with his old buddies, the Chief felt like a new man.

Ben Kane thought it over. He took a long drag from his cigar and eyed Mike's big paw of a hand. The Chief, built like a beer keg and strong as an ox, hadn't been able to budge Mike. Seeing that, Ben really didn't think he could take Mike at his own game, but it was a challenge and challenges were what Ben Kane was all about.

"I'll take a crack at you, Mike," Ben said, moving up his chair and placing his hand next to Mike's.

Kane was about six-foot-three and weighed one hundred ninety pounds. Mike was his equal in height but outweighed him by fifty pounds. If Ben were to win, he'd have to do it by guile and not strength alone.

They clasped their hands, and Ganja tied a leather strip around their wrists. The two men stared at each other. Ben's aqua eyes bored right into Mike's. His bronzed stubborn jaw was jutting into the face of the older man.

Michelle knew them both so well. Neither would give up. They were two stubborn grown men acting like children.

"If you people will excuse me, I think I've seen about enough of this foolishness. The only one with any brains is Miles."

Miles looked up at her for a moment and then went back to staring into his beer.

She got up to leave just as Grant slapped the table, signaling the beginning of the contest. Michelle tried not to turn back, but at the door she stopped briefly to see who was winning. The Chief was looking at her and grinning. He had been like an uncle to her over the years since her mother had died. Other than her father, Chief Bukowski had raised Michelle and knew her better than anyone. Smug bastard! she thought to herself. He knew she couldn't stand to see either of them lose . . . especially to the other.

Five full minutes later, the two of them were still locked in combat. Mike's face had turned beet-red, and

Kane's brow was covered with sweat.

"I call it a draw," Ganja said. "That's it now . . . a draw!"

The two men relaxed their grips.

"You're lucky, Kane. Another moment and I would have had you," Mike boasted.

"I think you've been sitting too close to Ganja. Some of that funny weed he smokes has a tendency to go to people's heads," Kane replied.

Mike threw his head back and laughed. He pounded Kane on the back and ordered another round for everyone.

"You're in a good mood tonight, Mike," Chief Bukowski said. "You look like the third man in a *Lucky Pierre*."

"Do I? Well, now that you mention it, I guess I do feel pretty happy. I got a call today from an old friend in the States. Seems he's coming down to the reef to do a little fishing. We've seen each other now and then over the years, but it'll be good to spend some real time together. This codger was with me when we rammed that German U-2 boat right outside the Hurricane Hole. He'll be arriving in a couple of days."

"If he's a Navy man, we might know him," Kane said.

"Oh, you'll know him all right, but I want to surprise you."

"Why? What is it, a mystery or something?"

"Something like that," Mike said with a smile. "Now don't push me on this, boys. You'll find out about him soon enough."

"I don't care about him," Ganja said, "but maybe he'll bring a secretary. These girls from the U.S. get out of their neighborhoods and fall all over the island black men."

"Shit, Ganja! You forgetting that you're originally

13

from Harlem?" the Chief reminded him.

"No, I no forget, mon. An' you better not be the won to tell them that, mon," he said, affecting a broad West Indian accent.

"Uh, oh, here comes trouble. Everybody look the other way and maybe he won't see us," Kane said. He was facing the door and was the first to see Weaver enter the bar.

"Too late—he's got us spotted. Looks like he'll be setting anchor," Mike said.

Weaver walked over to the men at the table, pulled up a chair, and nodded hello to everyone, flashing a broad smile.

"Good seeing everybody again. Mike, tell your barman that the tab for this part goes on the Ultratech account."

"Say what you have to, and then shove off," Mike told him. "You don't have any business parking yourself in the middle of my inn."

Weaver feigned being insulted. "Mike, come on, lighten up. We've got some mutually important things to discuss." He looked around, "Maybe we should find a spot that affords a little more privacy. Why don't I go upstairs to your office and wait for you and Ben up there?" he said, rising. "Don't keep me waiting too long. We've got a lot to talk about." He gave a half salute and made his way to the stairs.

"Slimy bastard!" Mike muttered.

"Come on, Mike. We'd better see what he wants. He *is* a slimy bastard, but he's got ways to bog my charter company and your shipyard in enough red tape to keep us cooling our heels through next season."

"I guess you're right," Mike said, rising.

"For him to come down from Charlotte Amalie, this has to be pretty big. What the hell did you do, Mike?"

"Nothing. Av least, nothing that I can remember

when I'm as sober as I am now!"

Weaver had planted himself behind Mike's oak desk. He leaned back in Mike's swivel chair, lacing his fingers behind his head. "Hey, you guys look great," he said affably.

"Come on, Weaver. Cut the crap and tell us what you want," Mike said.

"You know, Mike, that's one of the things I like about you. You don't like to make small talk . . . and neither do I. Both of you know my position here in the U.S. Virgins. It's to our mutual advantage that if something is going down, I'm made aware of it. Ultratech has a very large investment down here, and we have to protect our backsides."

"When you say Ultratech, you're really talking CIA," Kane offered.

"What's in a name?" Weaver shrugged. "At any rate, it is my function to be sure that my company is in a position to best serve the people who depend on it."

"Sure." Kane and Mulhaney smiled at each other.

"Yeah. Well, it's embarrassing as hell to find out something from my Washington office that you should have told me."

"Namely?" Mike asked.

"Namely your house guest . . . Senator Alan Mason. I don't like to be the last to know."

Mike shrugged. "What's the big deal? Why the hell do I have to tell you if Alan is coming down to do some fishing?"

"Let me explain it to you, Miguel. I know you folks don't listen to the radio or see newspapers in this island paradise, but Alan Mason is a United States Senator with seniority on some very important committees, including the Foreign Relations Committee and the Intelligence Committee. He's taken some very tough

15

stands against our commie pals. He called for the bombing of Iran when our hostages were there. He supported the President's tough stand on Libya. He's pushed for better intelligence and death to terrorists."

"He sounds like your kind of guy," Kane said.

"He's a damn sight better than some of the wimps who've been running the country," Weaver agreed.

"I still don't—"

"Look, Mike, Senator Mason is on the hit list of several fanatical governments. We think there's a master assassin known by the code name of Gregor who's coming to the islands to kill him."

"Shit! I'll tell him not to come," Mike said, standing up.

"He's already been warned; but he's coming anyway. The company can't prohibit a senator from going anyplace he chooses. I'm told that he'll be a candidate for president in the upcoming election, and he's said that he won't be intimidated by anyone."

"That's Alan, all right," Mike said. "He's right, too. You can't let those bastards push you around."

"That's very patriotic of you, Mike, and maybe I agree. But the senator's stay is going to be in my area, and if anything happens to him, my ass is in a sling."

"Good, earn your money," Kane said.

"That's no problem, Ben. You're going to give me a hand, too!"

Kane shook his head slowly. "No way, Weaver. I told you last time, after that drug-smuggling operation, that I was through. You're not getting me to do your dirty work anymore. I'm retired from spook service for good!"

Weaver ignored him. "Let me tell you about Gregor. He's no ordinary international hit man. He's been operating for at least twenty years. He seems to be able to go anywhere and get away without leaving the slightest clue. For years we were convinced that Gregor was a generic name for assassination activities. It was inconceivable that one man could personally kill with such skill and so often, or plot the murders of so many, and see the plans reach fruition.

"Last July, a top Soviet KGB man defected. He had been a contact man for Gregor in Eastern Europe. It seems that all along, the havoc has been caused by *one brilliant individual*. We have no idea what he looks like, his age, or even if he's a man or not. We *do* know that he's coming to the Virgins presumably to assassinate Senator Mason, whose election to the U.S. Presidency would be a disaster for the Soviet Union.

"I can't have him running around the islands unescorted, Ben. He insists that he be assigned no protection. He feels that as a representative of the American people, he's entitled to nothing more than what every other American would receive."

"He's still got spunk!" Mike said, beaming.

"Or, it's a clever move to win votes," Ben said. "But that's his problem . . . and yours, Weaver. I'm out of this for good. Get that through your head! I don't work for you people anymore."

"Come on, ol' buddy. He'll want to charter a boat for his fishing. Your boats are seaworthy. Your guys have shown their stuff in Nam. The pay will be worth your while. All I'm asking is that you take him out fishing and keep your eyes on him for the next week or so. What do you say?"

"No way, Weaver! I've got a business to run. I *haven't* got time to spend with one customer, even if he might be the next president," Ben said.

"I know all about your business, Ben." Weaver's eyes narrowed. "I know all about the million bucks that disappeared while you were making a buy for us nine years ago, and how all of a sudden you had enough money to go big time in the charter business."

"Do you also remember that the backup team you promised me didn't show up? I even began to think you were looking to retire me permanently back then, Weaver. If I did take—I repeat, if—you could write it off as severance pay," Ben snapped.

Weaver ran his fingers through his hair and smiled. "That's all water under the bridge," he said. "The fact is, I need you now. Your country needs you to do this!"

Kane stood up. "This is where I came in. See you later, Mike."

"Then you're saying no?" Weaver said incredulously.

"I think you've finally got it!"

"That's too bad. I thought you would want to do me a favor in light of the favor I've just done for you."

"What the hell are you talking about? You've never done a damn thing for me, Weaver, except to rob me blind and nearly get me killed!"

"It seems the newspapers called one of my contacts this afternoon to ask about the trouble Caribbean Dreams was having with pirates."

"What?"

"Two of your yachts north of Jost Van Dyke were boarded. Nothing serious, as I understand it—a couple of the passengers were roughed up but nobody really hurt. It would seem to me that if your charter boat outfit was being singled out by pirates, that would hurt your business a hell of a lot more than a week or two of protecting Alan Mason. Hey, but that's your decision. I've done what I could to save your neck," Weaver said.

"You son of a bitch!" Kane lunged at Weaver but was held back by Mulhaney. He had a sinking feeling in his gut that Weaver had him back on the string—Weaver the puppet master, making him dance to his tune.

"Just be sure that not one hair on the senator's head gets mussed, Kane. We all want to do the right things and keep our asses intact. Right, fellas?" Weaver asked.

CHAPTER 3

Kane sat back in the brown leather chair and frowned as Bukowski made his report. He tapped off the ash from his Cuban-made panatela, and his eyes hardened.

"They came aboard and pushed some people around," the Chief said. "Nothing happened that got anybody really hurt, but Mr. Bradley got slapped around some. They took his watch, a six-hundred-dollar Movado, and they took a ring from his wife, a two-carat diamond, estimated worth thirty-two hundred dollars. There were two women aboard besides Mrs. Bradley—her daughter and daughter-in-law. The pirates made some remarks and leered a lot, but that's about it."

"Our pirates sound pretty genteel."

"They were definitely under wraps, I'd say. They took the boat's radio and some other electrical equipment, but that was about it. Bradley and his wife are shook up, of course, but I bet they'll talk it up like an adventure, something to impress their friends back in Portland."

"See to it that Caribbean Dreams replaces the watch and the ring," Kane said. "If the Bradleys want to continue their vacation, everything is on the house. If they want to go home, give them back their money and pay for their plane fare."

"Will do, sir."

"What kind of boats did these so-called pirates use?"

"Grumman hydrofoils armed with .76mm cannons and antiship missiles," the Chief told him.

"Very sophisticated. They sound just like Navy patrol boats that operate out of Key West."

"Looks to me like Weaver contacted one of his admiral friends and hoked up this pirate scare. He was careful to board only 'bareboats.' If our crews had been hired, there would have been a hell of a lot of bloodshed."

Kane nodded. "He still took a chance with the lives of innocent people. What happened aboard the other charter?"

"Just about the same. They were coming around Ram Head, and the boat was waiting for them. This time they grabbed the Loran navigational system and the Satnav radio. The two couples on board weren't hurt."

"Give them anything they want to make it up to them," Kane said grimly, grinding out his cigar.

"What about Weaver? Maybe we oughta have Miles pay him a visit with his stiletto."

"No way! They'd just send down another Weaver from Washington, and we'd be up to our asses in new problems. Weaver's got a job to do—unfortunately, his way of doing it stinks. In the meantime, make sure that every charter we send out has a surveillance craft nearby. I also want you to have our people monitor the Navy Grummans around here. If they change crews, or head toward one of our 'bareboat' charters, have the coast Guard send out the *Bertha* and blow them out of the fucking water!" *Bertha* was the Guard's 300-foot cutter, equivalent to a destroyer.

The Chief nodded. "I ran into our friend Gordon. Seems that Weaver also warned him about baby-sitting the good senator."

Walt Gordon was the district marshal for the United States Virgin Islands, a tough-talking retired New York City police captain who got along well with Ben and represented the local law in Barracuda Reef.

"Gordon's probably beating the bushes for this Gregor. Tell Ganja to spread the word among the natives. There's two thousand dollars waiting for anyone who gets a line on this guy. Anyone who's new to the island is a suspect: man, woman, or child. I want to get Gregor fast so we can go on with running the business," Kane said.

"Aye, aye, sir."

"Just one more thing, Chief. I want the *Wu Li* to have a complete overhaul before Mason comes on board. And have the boys rig up the .35mm cannons, just in case."

"They're going to bitch like hell, Ben."

"Tough shit. Get it done anyway."

The yard workers hated the *Wu Li* because of its Oriental construction, and its history. It was a fifty-foot, two-masted Asian-type sailing junk that had appeared adrift in the Caribbean one day. The boat had been owned by a wealthy Chinese importer who had sailed into the feared Bermuda Triangle with a party and crew of ten, and had apparently vanished into thin air. When the vessel was boarded, there was no sign of

21

any of them. For days, the local papers branded the *Wu Li* the "devil boat." There was speculation that the junk had fallen briefly into another dimension, or that unidentified flying objects had spirited the people to an alien planet.

Kane's guess was that a fierce storm had forced the *Wu Li*'s passengers and crew to abandon the craft and try their luck with the life boats. Either that, or real pirates—not Weaver's imposters—pillaged the *Wu Li* and got rid of all witnesses. At any rate, he was able to buy the teak-planked beauty for a song.

The *Wu Li*'s lug rig made it easy to handle if Kane had to sail it with just a few crewmen, or even alone, if need be. Below, Kane had a walk-in engine room with powerful auxiliary diesels; a communications room with the latest state-of-the-art computers and communication gear that kept him in touch with the fleet of Caribbean Dreams, and two entirely self-sufficient living spaces with full electrical power and all modern conveniences. Between the staterooms was the salon, Kane's main meeting room, furnished in mahogany of Oriental design and combining simplicity with luxury. The galley, set aside from the main flow of traffic, was appointed with a refrigerator, freezer, microwave, double sinks, and stove. And yet, the efficient weight-saving design of comfort and storage weighed in at less than eighteen thousand pounds, which made it one of the fastest vessels of its size on the water.

When Ben Kane left the Navy's riverine forces, he promised himself that the rest of his life would be spent blotting out the years of hell he'd gone through in Nam. He parlayed his severance pay into a partnership with a Virgin Islander who owned two charter boats. Eventually, Ben bought one of the boats and started Caribbean Dreams.

He was just managing to earn a meager living with

the boat when Weaver had contacted him. Weaver had served in Nam and had headed up some spook operations that had involved Kane. He offered Kane a chance to make some real money and sold him a bill of goods about being a patriot. So Ben Kane reluctantly became a free-lance operative for the CIA, appearing on paper as an employee of Ultratech. At first, Weaver used Kane for intelligence-gathering operations and transport missions. Then he graduated to hairier stuff. Kane had become tired of the play acting, the double crosses, the secrecy . . . and the killing. Maybe Weaver had sensed it, felt that he had outlived his usefulness.

Kane was supposed to run a shipload of guns to Cuban-financed Central American rebels. He'd delivered the guns and picked up a million bucks. Weaver and his people were supposed to swoop down, capture the rebels, and take the money. At least, that's how it was supposed to go down.

Somewhere along the line, Kane smelled a rat. All Weaver had to do was not show up on time and let Kane buy it. But Weaver hadn't counted on Kane getting a drop on the rebel amateurs and tucking the case with the million in U.S. currency in a safe place to be retrieved later. Weaver and his men finally put in an appearance, and the president of Ultratech almost lost his cool when Kane told him he had no idea where the money was. Maybe if Weaver had arrived on time with his backup, they might have found it.

With that stake behind him, Kane was able to finance one of the most prosperous charter operations in the Caribbean. He had made a name for himself with vacationers by providing a boat that could fit anyone's needs. Included in his armada were very expensive high-speed luxury cruisers, as well as small sailboats for the budget conscious.

After the Chief left on his assigned tasks, Kane

poked through the mess on the top of his desk until he found the embossed invitation that had come in the mail. Lord Philip Carlisle, and daughter, Jessica Spencer, requested the honour of his presence at Windsor House for dinner with the honourable Alan Mason, United States Senator, on the occasion of Senator Mason's arrival in the Virgin Islands.

Lord Philip was the Crown Commissioner of the British Virgin Islands. A tall, silver-haired Englishman with a striking resemblance to the late FDR, Lord Philip, OBE, ME, had been sent to BVI as a sort of reward for his many years of devoted service to Her Majesty's government. The braintrust of Wilson's Labour Government had intended to "put the old boy out to pasture in the balmy tropics." Lord Philip, after all, knew the area. He had been commander of the Royal Navy Corvette, *Bramble*, and had sailed these waters during the war. No one foresaw at the time that the islands would become a hotbed of political activity and, because of their geographical proximity to Cuba and Puerto Rico, a major pawn in super-power confrontations.

Ben knew that behind the facade of "old school" Englishman, Lord Philip was a formidable gent with considerable ability.

Lord Philip resided at Windsor House with his daughter, Jessica Carlisle Spencer. Jessica, a statuesque, unflappable blonde, had been on Ben Kane's mind a lot in the past two years. She had joined her father in BVI after a disastrous marriage to a philandering stockbroker in London, and Kane had been available to offer aid and comfort. He was drawn to her, as any red-blooded male would be. She possessed a cool, British charm which Kane had considered an open challenge to his prowess. But he soon found out that, as in the case of her father, appearances were deceiving.

24

Jessica had proved to be as passionate a lover as Kane had ever known, and he'd know quite a few.

Jessica would invite Weaver, of course. As president of Ultratech, a major U.S. company in the Virgins, he was a VIP whom Mason could relate to.

Kane figured that Mike Mulhaney would be sitting next to Mason, the guest of honor, and along with Mike would be Michelle. Michelle and Jessica didn't get along. Ben had known Michelle since she was a gawky teenager, and over the years they had shared some rough sailing along with the calm. They had been thrown together even more when Michelle took over the yard. There were times when they fought each other like junkyard dogs—and other times when they wound up expending their passions in bed.

Kane teased Michelle that the only reason she disliked Jessica was because she was jealous. "Of that bitch? Hell, she belongs in a wax museum," Michelle scoffed. "Don't flatter yourself, Ben!"

Kane smiled to himself. What a difference between the two women! Petite, dark-haired Michelle, who cursed like a sailor and had a temper that varied with the weather; and Jessica, aristocratic and superficially cool. There would be sparks flying between the two of them at the dinner, he imagined. It might even be worth suffering Weaver, and wearing a monkey suit. . . .

CHAPTER 4

Archie Potter walked out of Windsor House and squinted up at the sun. It was close to 6 P.M., but the thermometer in the window of Bacco's Drugstore still stood at over ninety degrees.

Archie hoped he'd get a new bus. There were two of them on the line that ran from Windsor House to the Spanish Town ferry, six in all, but only the new ones had air conditioning. The other four, relics of the sixties, were stifling, with broken shocks and peeling paint. The odds were one in three that he'd get one of the new Macks, but he resigned himself to the fact that the way his luck was running lately he didn't have a chance.

Yesterday, he had missed by only one number in the

football pool. Some lucky sod collected twenty-eight thousand pounds, and all Archie got was a collection of pasteboards and an argument from Veronica for spending their hard-earned money on that "foolishness."

He checked his watch. He couldn't even wait until a new bus came along. Veronica had warned him that he'd better be home on time tonight. Yesterday he had bent his elbow a bit too much at the Lion's Den and had staggered home after midnight. What a row!

She had cooked him one of her island specialties, *moros y cristianos*—rice, meat, and beans—and had invited a girlfriend and her husband to dinner. She told him at great length how embarrassed she'd been. Like most of the native women on the islands, Veronica had a fiery temper but usually, like the storms that lashed the beaches this time of year, it was short-lived. When Archie had arrived from England ten years ago, a mixed marriage was relatively rare. Today, it was fairly common. Archie felt in his pants pocket for the small box Miss Jessica had given him. He had told her about the fight, and Lord Carlisle's daughter had said she had just the thing to make things right. She'd disappeared into her room for a moment and come out with a beautiful pair of small gold earrings—*real* gold, Archie was sure. He had tried to say no, he couldn't accept such an expensive gift, but Miss Jessica had brushed him off. "I virtually never wear them, and if they can bring peace to your house, it's well worth it. Just tell Veronica that you bought them for her. You'll see. She'll forgive you."

That was the way Miss Jessica was. All the servants at Windsor House adored her. Archie had worked there for a good six years now, and ever since she'd arrived, he had never had a cross word from her.

He started thinking about the dinner they would be having for the senator from America. He had gone over the menu with Miss Jessica and Lord Philip, and they had agreed on a native menu—an assortment of fritters with prawns, marinated fish (*escabeche*), and avocados for the hors d'oeuvres. The soup course would be a choice between turtle (*sopa de tortue*) or black bean (*sopa de frijol negro*). The guests would also be treated to Archie's two main-dish specialties: stuffed plaintains (*piononos*) and his own favorite, *gombo*. The last time he had cooked gombo for the houseguests of the Carlisles, the Duke and Duchess of Albemarle, they had asked their host if they could take Archie back to England with them. He would never leave, of course, especially to go back to cold, damp, foggy England, but it was flattering.

Veronica had originally taught him how to cook the island dishes. She was a pretty good chef herself, Archie thought. Perhaps he would ask her to prepare the dessert for the dinner. She could go to market and buy fruits, and together they would think of something that looked and tasted out of this world. As long as it was a dish that didn't require pepper or curry, she could be trusted.

The bus clanked down the street. It was one of the old ones, of course, shivering and wheezing to a halt in front of Archie. He climbed aboard, not paying particular attention to the European who followed and sat down three seats behind him over the hump of the rear wheels. There were several whites on board and four coloreds. Most of the riders were people Archie saw every day, including the enormously fat island woman in a bright flowered-print dress who always nodded to him. The rest of the passengers were men, staring blankly out the window or engrossed in thought.

Archie noticed his window was closed. With his luck, he probably was sitting next to a stuck one. He tried opening it, and it grudgingly moved upward. The bus

29

began moving and a welcome breeze cooled Archie's brow and cheeks.

Behind him, the dark-skinned European watched with cold, calculating eyes. He was a very thin man of medium height, with a face that looked like a skull painted over with a thin layer of flesh. His hair, gray and black, was combed straight back, exposing a high forehead. He could have been from anywhere, but the sunken eyes and prominent cheekbones gave his features a definite Slavic cast. His eyes never left the unsuspecting Archie as the bus jounced its way from the affluent interior of the island to its more rural native district.

The paved road now gave way to a pot-holed dirt road that was difficult to navigate when dry, and an impossible sea of mud when it rained. By now, all the whites had left the bus, except for Archie and the man behind him.

Archie had dozed off but awakened himself with a start. It wouldn't do to miss his stop today. Veronica would have his head. If he knew the driver, he could fall asleep and know that the driver would wake him when they reached Du Bois Point. But he didn't recognize this fellow. That wasn't too surprising. The turnover rate for bus drivers was very high. That's how it was with many of the natives, Archie thought. They would try a job on for size like a hat or a coat. Once they got their first paycheck, they spent it all on rum and then tried their hand at something else.

Archie reached up and pulled on the frayed cord that signaled the driver to stop at the next road crossing, patting the pocket that held the earrings to be sure they were still there. Then he walked to the exit door.

He noticed the thin man rising from his seat at the same time. He was a strange-looking fellow, Archie thought. He couldn't remember ever seeing him around before. What was he doing on this deserted part of the island? The man got off the bus behind Archie, and the two of them began walking down the road in the same direction. The thin man fell into step with Archie. "Excuse me. You work at Windsor House, don't you?" he asked. There was a slight accent in his deep voice. It definitely wasn't British, but Archie couldn't place his nationality.

"That's right. Do I know you, sir?"

"No. I'm new on the island. I'm looking for work. I thought perhaps there might be something for me at Windsor House."

"Did you follow me all the way out here just to ask me that?"

The thin man shrugged. "I had nothing else to do, and one place is as good as another. I arrived a couple of days ago and lost all my money in a card game. I have not eaten anything all day, and I could very much use a job."

"I know how it is to be down on your luck. I missed the football pool by one number myself the other day. . . . Look, I'm the chef at Windsor House, and I do the hiring. You come over there, toward the end of the week, and I'll see what I can do for you. I'm not making any promises, mind, but if you're a good lad and down on your luck, you can depend on old Archie to give you a hand."

"But I need to work tomorrow," the stranger said nervously.

"Oh, no! Can't help you out there. We've got a big dinner party tomorrow. I can't use a new man right off the streets for something like that, now can I?"

"I'll work hard. Besides, you use colored help, and you know how they are. Not too dependable, or so I understand. You might need a backup, just in case."

Archie felt his temper rising. Who the hell was this

fellow to tell him how to run his kitchen?

"Look, man, how about if I lend you a few to keep you going until Friday? You come around then like a good lad and we'll talk."

"No! You've got to put me on for tomorrow!"

Archie stepped back from him. The chap didn't look daft, but sometimes you just couldn't tell.

"I happen to be married to an island woman, so I don't need your advice on the habits of the coloreds. As a matter of fact, I don't need your advice about anything. Like I said, I'll talk to you at the end of the week about a job, and if that's not good enough for you, buzz off, mate. Now, good day to you."

Archie turned away and walked on down the dusty road. His house stood three hundred feet away, past the sugar-cane field and on the slope of a small mountain.

He was still thinking about the strange man with the gloves when the piano wire was slipped over his head and around his throat. It was over quickly without a sound. His legs kicked out, and the wire left a line of blood as it severed Archie's windpipe.

The man put the piano wire into his pocket and carried Archie's body from the deserted road into the field, where he rolled it into a ditch. He then covered the garroted corpse with vegetation, stood back to admire his work. Unless you knew where to look, the body was virtually invisible. It wouldn't be discovered for at least a couple of days, and that would be all the time he needed.

He removed his gloves and walked back to the spot where he would catch a return bus to Road Town.

"Good Lord, how this place has changed!" Alan Mason said, shaking his head. "Mike, when you and I played tag with the Japs, there were no phones, no roads, no damn electricity."

"Sometimes I think the Virgins were better off then," Mike replied. "Now you've got every land speculator south of Maine trying to carve out a few acres for time-sharing condos."

"Well, can't say as I blame them. This has got to be the Garden of Eden." The senator put his hands on his hips as he surveyed the harbor of Barracuda Reef from Sugar Mountain. Lush, scarlet bougainvillaea and coconut palms dotted the shores of the sandy, white beaches that rimmed the almost perfect crescent of the cay. The harbor itself, with its fleet of sailboats and yachts, each sporting billowing sails of different hues, looked from the distance like a brilliantly colored garden.

"I always thought the islands were just St. Thomas, St. Croix, and St. John. I wonder how many people know about the little islets like this one?"

"Not that many, and we want to keep it that way," Mike said. "Actually, Alan, there are about fifty reefs and islands that make up the archipelago. I'm prejudiced, of course, but I think this one is the best of the lot."

"And look at that water! It's been a long time since I saw water so blue and clear," Alan marveled. "There's only one thing wrong with this place."

"What's that?"

"You're all United States citizens, but you can't vote in federal elections." Mason laughed.

"Thank God for that!" Mulhaney retorted. "We'd be spending all our time ripping down campaign posters from the coconut palms!"

The two men walked back down the slope, heading for the Rainbow Keg. Mike was pleased with the way this reunion had turned out. Often when people from the past turned up, the memory far outshone the reality. His friendship with Mason, forged in battle, had been

33

like a prized antique locked away in a special vault and fondly remembered but little examined. Now it had been taken out once again and studied in the light of modern day where any flaws couldn't be glossed over by time.

To Mike's relief, he found no flaws. He and Alan had meshed together like the cogs of a well-oiled machine. They both felt the bonds of friendship to be as firm as ever. It was as if it were only hours ago that they'd seen each other last, instead of years.

Mason had filled out quite a bit, Mike noticed. During the war, he had been slim; now he was a little on the heavy side. But his hair was more brown than silver, and Mike wondered if there was some "youth in a bottle" at work on it. He made a note to ask him about it later on, after they'd had a couple of drinks. Politicians were a vain bunch, he'd heard. Mike guessed they had to be. Mason was deeply tanned, with a movie star's nose and teeth too white and even to be real. A pair of mirrored sunglasses concealed his brown eyes. Mike wondered if they were prescription. He decided that if Mason had a vision problem, he'd probably wear contacts.

"Hey, Alan, you serious about running for president?" Mike asked. Instead of replying, Mason laughed.

"What's so funny?"

"Nothing, I guess. You know, no matter where I go in the States some reporter is always asked me that. I just found it funny to be the same question walking down a mountain in the Virgin Islands with you. You know what I tell them? Something like it being a long time until the next presidential election, or I'm just interested in being a good senator, or there are a lot of fine men to choose from in our party and I'm flattered that someone might include me among them. . . . "

"Cut the bullshit, Alan. What do you really think?"

Mason smiled faintly. "Naturally I want to be president. You don't go into politics thinking that when you're elected to one public office, that's as far as you can go. We all have terrific egos, or we wouldn't be in politics in the first place. However, *if* I run, I want to be sure I don't get my brains beat out. The only question is if I have a real shot to win. My people tell me I'm the greatest thing since sliced bread, but they're all politicians, too . . . and on my payroll to boot! I've got to give myself a chance away from all the hype to really weigh the pros and cons."

"Is that why you're here?"

"Among other things, yes." He paused. "There's something else, though, that brought me to the Virgins. Something I have to talk to you about. I'm going to need your help, old friend." He stared at Mike. "It's something very important to me—even more important than becoming President of the United States."

Mike Mulhaney met his gaze. The years seemed to melt away. They were standing side by side once again, officers on the deck of a torpedoed destroyer, two men amid the panic and fire who relied on each other's clear head and loyalty.

"Whatever it is, Alan," Mike said, "I'll help you."

CHAPTER 5

On the second floor of the Rainbow Keg Inn, Ben Kane was holding a bill for maintenance work done on the *Wu Li*. He was fuming.

"This is double what it usually costs!" he told Michelle.

She sat behind her father's oak desk and read over her copy, ticking off each of the items with a pencil. Then she looked calmly up at Kane.

"Everything seems to be in order."

"In order, my ass!"

"I've already told you that the *Wu Li* poses special problems for the dock workers. In order for us to guarantee our work, we have to attract able people . . . and they cost money! In addition, there was a special

37

fee for installing arms on your vessel."

"I only did that to protect your father's houseguest!"

"Well, maybe you should take that up with Mike."

"When I talk to Mike, he tells me to see *you!*"

Michelle shrugged and smiled sweetly. "Tough shit!"

Kane slammed the desk with his fist. "I won't pay!"

"Okay. I'll just sell your boat for my money."

Ben laughed. "Over my dead body!"

"Don't tempt me," Michelle said, leaning back in her chair and putting her hands behind her head.

Kane took in the fiery eyes, the perfect mouth. When she sat that way, he could make out the curves of her full breasts beneath the light cotton fabric of her T-shirt. And she wasn't wearing a bra—she never did.

"Tell you what I'll do. Let's you and me stretch out on top of that big desk, and if I can't bring you to three sensational orgasms in five minutes, I'll pay double. If I do, we'll call it even," he said, grinning.

"You'd lose."

"Try me."

Michelle scowled. "Not in a month of Sundays!"

"No guts, Mulhaney. You know that the minute I lay a hand on you, you go crazy. You're a hot-blooded bitch underneath that tough exterior."

"Stop flattering yourself, Kane," Michelle snapped. "You don't turn me on in the least."

"I think you're suffering from amnesia. I seem to remember that I've lost my sea legs with you quite a few times. Don't tell me you've forgotten about our last moonlight swim at Commodore Cove?"

Michelle shrugged elaborately. "I guess I did. You know how it is with trivial things. Besides, that's ancient history. You know what it says in all those greeting cards—today is the first day of the rest of my life. Now pay your bill and *shove off!*"

Kane stood and walked around to Michelle's side of

the desk. "Come on, Michelle. What's eating you?"

"Absolutely nothing."

"I'll raise my bid to *four* sensational orgasms."

He put his hand on the nape of her neck, but she stood and brushed his hand aside.

"No games today, Ben. I have a lot of work to do, and you're taking up my time. If you want a roll in the hay, go see your good friend, Jessica. I'm sure she'll be more than happy to oblige."

"Ahh," Ben said knowingly. "The green-eyed monster rears its ugly head!"

"I couldn't care in the least what you do with that ice cube. If she's your type, then you certainly wouldn't want to have anything to do with me."

She got up and held the door for Ben. "Like I said, shove off, Mr. Kane."

He shrugged and started to walk past her, then suddenly turned and clutched her to him, his hands like steel bands trapping her arms at her sides.

"Bastard!" she hissed.

Because he knew it was coming, he was able to turn his body aside and dodge Michelle's well-aimed knee to his groin. He pressed his legs on top of hers, pinning them against the door as she thrashed to get away.

"You know how a sailor survives a storm? He holds on until it blows itself out," Kane said, smiling.

"I *hate* you!" she snarled.

"Do you?"

He yanked her hair back and kissed her deeply. One of her hands was free now, and she tried pushing him away, to no avail. He crushed her to his chest and felt her anger start to turn to passion as she returned his kiss.

"You hate me?" he whispered when they came up for air.

"Shut up," she said, putting her arms around his neck

39

and kissing him again. When they broke apart this time, they were both breathing heavily.

"On the desk or standing up?" Kane asked, unbuckling his pants as she lifted her T-shirt over her head, revealing her perfectly formed orbs.

"You're still paying full price for the boat," she gasped.

Ben was nuzzling one naked breast when they heard the sound of heavy feet pounding up the stairs, and Mike's booming voice.

"Shit!" Michelle said, hurriedly pulling down her shirt.

They barely had time to rearrange their clothes before Mike and Alan appeared in the doorway.

"Ben, just the fellow I wanted to see! Shake hands with United States Senator Alan Mason," Mike said, stepping into the office. "Hey, where you going, Michelle?"

"I'll have to check on that new hydraulic lift that we spent a fortune on because *you* liked the saleswoman's low-cut blouse!" Michelle said.

Mike winced, then exchanged smiles with Alan as Michelle slammed the door behind her, flashing Ben a look.

"I've heard a lot about you, Mr. Kane," Mason said, extending his hand. "Your Caribbean Dreams is quite an operation, Mike tells me."

"I got lucky," Ben said modestly.

"I've always believed that what people call luck is actually the result of hard work and determination."

"That's nice of you to say, Senator. What brings you to Barracuda Reef?" Kane asked.

"I thought it was time to get away for a little R and R. Mike informs me that you've been booked to be my bodyguard over the course of my stay. Well, I guess you're about as thrilled as I am at the prospect." He gave Kane a dazzling smile. "I hope you know that's not said on a personal basis. It's just that I've never had a baby-sitter before, and I think it's a little late for me to get used to the idea."

"Frankly, Senator, there are a few things I'd rather be doing myself—like running my business."

"Okay then, it's settled!" Mason said briskly. "You go your way, and I'll go mine. If we're asked, we'll cover for each other."

Mike shook his head. "You don't know Weaver," he said.

"Weaver?" Mason's brows knit together as he tried to place the name. Then he nodded. As a member of the Senate Intelligence committee, he knew all about the CIA's Ultratech operation.

"Yeah, Weaver." Ben sighed. "Nothing gets done unless he gives his approval, and he's got dozens of tricks to make sure that he controls everything that goes on. Right now, he's made me responsible for your well-being, and I've got to make sure you leave our friendly islands in the same shape you arrived."

Mason shrugged and looked over at Mike Mulhaney. "He talks like he can handle himself," Mason said.

"He's Navy like us, Alan. He's a fellow that could have served on our bridge," Mike said seriously. "Different war, that's all."

"That's high praise from Mike, Kane."

"I know it is, and I'm honored. And surprised," Kane added with a grin. "Usually the things Mike says about me can't be repeated in mixed company."

"Well, I'll stick it out as long as you will," Mason said. "But one thing I *don't* want is for anybody else to become a target. I won't let these commie bastards intimidate me. If they can force a United States Senator to run scared, then what chance does the average American have? I believe that terrorism has to be faced

41

head on. You in Nam, Kane?"

"Four years, nine months, and six days," Kane replied grimly.

"I ran for the Senate to make sure that if we ever had another shindig like that one, our boys would have everything they needed to finish the job. We lost a lot of good men in that dirty little war."

"We sure did," Mike answered.

"That's the way this Gregor operates. Like the Cong, he never comes out and looks you in the eye. A bullet in the back is his style."

"You know him then?" Kane asked.

"As well as anyone does, and that's not saying much. He's a goddamn phantom. He seems to disappear into thin air just when you think you have him cornered. He was in Brussels when he killed Helmtax of Norway. I caught a piece of shrapnel in my right shoulder. They said another two or three inches, and I would have bought it. He had explosives hooked up to a transmitter under the prime minister's car. I was supposed to accompany Helmtax to the palace but at the last moment, I went in a second car. I watched them blow up in front of us. It was horrible. I'd love to get my hands on that bastard for just a few minutes!

"He's already killed a half dozen cabinet-level officials in Europe. A few years ago, he missed Chancellor Schmidt of Germany by inches. Then there was the minister of trade in France, the Japanese director of internal order—hell, he's even managed to plant bombs in Buckingham Palace!"

"Weaver suggested that Gregor might be a woman," Mike said.

"Maybe, but I doubt it. He's an expert climber, and that takes strength. He's gone up a side of a building using rubber suction shoes, and that's no easy task. I think it's unlikely that Gregor is a woman, but we can't rule out any possibility, no matter how remote."

"Hey, Alan, can you imagine the splash we'd make if we caught him?" Mike said. "You'd have a damn good shot at the nomination then!"

"Now you're talking like a campaign manager." Mason laughed. "I'll concentrate on staying out of Gregor's way, and leave the credit of capturing him to Weaver and his friends."

"This is one time I'll be rooting for him," Kane said.

CHAPTER 6

Jessica Spencer was sitting in her boudoir, sipping her tea and thinking about the evening's dinner party. Much of her thoughts had to do with Ben Kane. She was excited at the prospect of seeing him again. The arrival of the American senator was a tailor-made excuse, and she was glad that her father had agreed that a dinner in his honor was the correct thing for Her Majesty's representative in BVI to do.

She and Kane had begun a torrid affair, and although she had been timid at first (so soon after Kevin), Kane's expert lovemaking had left her breathless. Her father certainly liked the American—he was good at chess, and a Navy man to boot.

Jessica's former husband, Kevin, had been a horse of

a different color. He had attended all the right schools and was a member of all the right clubs. His partnership in the London brokerage house of White and Courtenay had virtually been assured at Kevin's birth. She had believed him when he told her that he was working late night after night, never dreaming that respectable, punctilious Kevin would ever lie to her.

She believed him when he told her that he had business meetings in Switzerland and Amsterdam. Kevin was, after all, a gentleman and gentlemen did not lie.

She went on believing him right up to the day she came home early from a matinee and found respectable, gentlemanly Kevin in bed with her good friend, Jean Hastings. Later, when she had calmed down enough to call Jean and ask, "How could you?" her friend had replied, "But my dear, Kevin told me you two were getting a divorce, and I believed him. After all, he's been with every woman in our crowd at least once and he's been so open about it, we were all certain that you had some sort of arrangement." What a fool she had been. . . .

But being her father's hostess at Windsor House had kept Jessica busy. Since her arrival, she had taken over the running of the household, relieving Lord Philip of a major burden. She soon recovered from the shock of Kevin's philandering, ably assisted by Ben Kane. If Lord Philip suspected there was more than casual friendship between them, he gave no sign of it.

Jessica wished it were possible to invite Ben and Mike Mulhaney to the dinner without also having to invite Mike's horrible daughter, Michelle. She had learned to tolerate coarse language and rowdy behavior among the men of the islands, but Michelle Mulhaney was simply scandalous. But there was no way out of it—after all, the senator was Mike's friend. The entire situation was most distressing.

Jessica knew of Kane's relationship with Michelle, and it made her very jealous. She had once asked him about it, and his reply was that a gentleman doesn't kiss and tell. Only the word he'd used wasn't *kiss*.

Lord Philip had insisted that they invite Weaver, the president of Ultratech, and Gordon, the United States Marshal. A mixed bag, Jessica thought. How they would all get along was anybody's guess.

But perhaps sometime during the evening she would be able to steer Ben Kane off by himself. . . .

There was a knock on the door. "Yes."

Carla stepped into the boudoir. She was a young island girl who polished the silver and did general cleaning.

"Miss Jessica, no one have seen Archie."

"Really? Has Mr. Parsons called his house?"

"He do that, ma'am, straight off, but there be no answer."

"Oh, dear. How very odd."

Archie Potter had never been late before. His wife, Veronica, might have had her complaints about him, but Archie had always made it to work on time. Jessica wondered if the fight with his wife had anything to do with it. Surely the earrings must have sweetened Veronica's mood.

"Have Mr. Parsons send one of the lads over to Archie's house just to be sure everything is all right." Jessica sighed in frustration. Whatever was she going to do about the dinner party without Archie?

"Also, ask Mr. Parsons to call the Skytop and have them send one of their chefs over here right away just in case Archie is ill."

"Yes, ma'am."

"You can go now, Carla."

But the girl didn't leave. "There be one more thing,

Miss Jessica. Mr. Parsons say there be a man down-stairs that Mister Archie promised a job. He want to know if you want to see him now? He waiting down-stairs."

"Yes, I'll see him."

Jessica rose and followed Carla. Perhaps this person could shed some light on her chef's whereabouts.

He was sitting in the drawing room, a bone-thin man, passably dressed. He stood when Jessica entered the room. Although he was obviously European, he averted his eyes as was the custom of the native Virgin Island-ers.

"I understand you're looking for work," she said pleasantly.

"Yes, madam, I am," he said.

"Is it true that my chef, Mr. Archibald Potter, asked you to come by?"

"He did that, madam."

"When was that?"

The man's eyes opened in surprise. "Yesterday after-noon, about six, I would say. Perhaps you would prefer to ask him yourself. He said I should come by in the morning and he would have a job for me."

"I see." Jessica was lost in thought.

"Is everything all right, madam?"

"What? Oh, yes. It's just that Archie is a bit late today; and that's not at all like him. He knows there's a very important dinner party this evening."

"Yes, madam. He said he wanted me to take on a bit of waitering." The man lowered his voice. "I gather he did not have much faith in the colored lads."

Jessica smiled. That was Archie, all right. "You do have references?"

"Certainly, madam. I gave them to Mr. Potter. He said he'd be going home to his house on DuBois Point. He also said he would go over my letters and let me

48

know about a job this morning."

"Hmm. Well, I haven't seen the references—"

"Please, madam, I've had a run of bad luck and lost what little money I had in a card game. I haven't eaten in a day, and I need this job very badly. I just want to earn enough money to get back home to my wife and children. If I do not get my references back, I will never get another job."

Jessica thought it over. If Archie had taken the man's references, she was duty bound to see that they were returned to him.

"Tell Mr. Parsons, our butler, that you are to be given breakfast. We'll try you out at the dinner tonight. Mr. Parsons will supply you with a uniform. If things work out well, you may stay on. Carla will show you the way to the kitchen."

"Thank you, madam."

"What is your name?"

"Nicholas, madam. I am Greek."

"Really? I would have taken you for a Russian."

Nicholas smiled faintly. "Yes, I hear that all the time."

She turned to leave, but Nicholas followed her.

"Oh, Miss Jessica . . ." he said diffidently.

"Yes, Nicholas?"

"I just remembered something. Your chef, this man Archie Potter, when I spoke to him at the bus stop, said that before he went home he was going to stop off at a bar. He asked me to join him, but I do not drink, so I refused. Perhaps Mr. Potter overindulged."

Jessica nodded wearily. "Yes, that's what I was afraid of."

CHAPTER 7

"Mike, have you seen Alan?" Michelle called, knocking on the door to her father's room.

"Come on in, Michelle. Here, give me a hand with this goddamned tie!"

Frustration and anger showed clearly on Mike Mulhaney's face as he wrestled with the strip of cloth that was supposed to turn into a bow tie.

"I'll do that for you." Michelle stepped up to him and expertly finished it off. "There," she said with a final pat.

She had never seen her father dressed in a tux; and the transformation was startling. He looked positively elegant.

"Well, girl, don't stand there gaping. What do you

think of your old man?"

"I can't believe it's you. You'll have every woman's heart fluttering."

"Damn foolishness, these monkey suits. A man doesn't have any room to move around." He sounded annoyed; but Michelle knew he was secretly pleased.

"Okay, let's have a look at *you*," he said.

Michelle was wearing a white chiffon dress, fitted in all the right places. The only ornamentation to her natural beauty were the pearl-and-white coral earrings dangling from her earlobes.

"You're a knockout!" he told her, giving her a peck on the forehead. "You'll have Kane eating out of your hand, girl."

"Who cares? she said nonchalantly.

"Oh, that's right—this week you hate him."

"If he pays any attention to that Jessica Spencer, I'll brain him!"

Mike shook his head. "Let's not do anything to spoil the party for Alan."

"Where *is* Alan? He wasn't in his room."

"I wouldn't worry about him. Ben's got Miles watching the front of the Rainbow Keg, and Ganjas's around in the back. No one is going to get by those two. Let's take a look on the back porch. I saw him sitting out there earlier."

Mason was indeed sitting on the wooden porch, smoking a cigarette and swaying gently in a walnut rocker. He stood up when he saw Michelle and Mike and made a courtly bow to Michelle.

It was obvious that Alan Mason spent a lot of time in formal wear. They were as much a politician's working clothes as denim jackets and dungarees were Mike's. Michelle thought that if Alan Mason ran for president, there would be a lot of women voting for him on looks alone.

"It's nice to be able to look up at the stars without the smog of the cities. I bet you folks take that for granted," Alan said.

In the background were the sounds of the harbor—creaking planks, a bell clanging out a warning, the swish of water on a hundred slippery hulls.

"I think I'd like to come back here to live once I'm finished with my political career." He glanced at his host and gave a sad smile. "It would be nice to have someone to share it with. That's probably my biggest mistake, Mike. I should have gotten married and had a family. I wonder if you realize how very lucky you are."

"I do, Alan. Indeed, I do," Mike said softly.

Mason took a long drag and blew the smoke out in a shimmering cloud.

"Wasn't there ever anyone, Alan?" Mike asked.

Mason sighed. "Yes, there was, Mike . . . but I lost her."

It was obvious he wanted to say something that he was holding back. Michelle started to feel uncomfortable. "Look, fellows, if you want to talk, I'll just come back in a little while," she suggested.

"Please don't go, Michelle," Alan said to her surprise. "I want you to hear this, too. I just don't really know how to start. I guess when I saw you and Mike standing there together, it kind of . . . got to me for a second."

"What do you mean, Alan?" Mike leaned against the white porch railing and watched his friend.

"Do you remember I told you I needed your help, Mike?"

"Yes."

"Well, I want you to help me find my daughter."

Mike and Michelle exchanged astonished glances.

"Let me explain." Alan sighed again and ran his hand through his hair. "Twenty-five years ago I had an import business. Those were the days when the American dollar was worth a lot and you could buy items overseas for a song and make a darn good profit in the States. I had a partner then, a fellow named Larry Stapleton. Larry was always interested in politics, and he was the one who finally persuaded me to run for Congress. It was a hard campaign, and Larry and I were thrown together a hell of a lot. I practically lived in Larry's St. Louis home and . . . well, I really got to know Christine, Larry's wife."

"How well?" Mike asked, raising his eyebrows.

Alan smiled weakly. "We found ourselves falling in love. Oh, we both tried to fight it. We made excuses not to see each other. Christine even told Larry that she wanted nothing to do with the campaign, but Larry insisted. It seems that we were always thrown together. I was torn, Mike, I really was. Larry was my best friend. He would do anything for me, and here I was making time with his wife behind his back. At one point I even thought I'd forget about the campaign and just go away . . . get away from everything, including Christine."

Mason seemed lost in thought, as if he were reliving those days.

"What happened?" Michelle prodded gently.

"We realized we were kidding ourselves. It wasn't just a casual affair—we were really in love. I told Christine we couldn't go on like that. I begged her to leave Larry. I think she would have, too, but she told me to wait under after the election. She felt there would be a scandal and I wouldn't be able to win. Maybe I should have insisted. I guess I felt that another couple of months wouldn't mean anything in the course of a lifetime. I wanted to be elected and I suppose to my eternal regret, my career took precedence."

"Did she leave him for you once the election was

over and you won?" Michelle asked.

"Yeah. She left him . . . and she left me, too. She disappeared on both of us."

"What do you mean, *disappeared*?" Mike echoed.

"Just what I said, Mike. The night of the election, she was gone. I stood on the podium thanking my workers and looking out over the audience, and she wasn't there. I asked Larry where she was and he had no idea. Later, we found a note in the kitchen. It was addressed to 'My Love,' but I knew it was meant for me. Larry never even suspected. The note simply said that things had become too difficult for her and she had to leave, that it would be better not to look for her."

"And that was all?"

"Yes. Of course, Larry and I both did everything possible to find her. They had been having their troubles but I know he loved her, too. I used every means I could think of, including bending a few rules as a congressman. Larry didn't know how to thank me. I thought I was helping him because of our great friendship, But, if I *did* find her, I was determined to marry her, and I think that would have finished poor Larry for good."

"He never found out?"

"No. I never found Christine, so there was no reason to destroy his faith in his wife and his best friend. About a year later, one of the private detectives I hired told me that a woman fitting Christine's description was seen in New York. Her landlord confirmed that the woman who recently moved out of his place was Christine—with her baby daughter."

"A *baby*? You mean she'd given birth to your child?" Michelle wanted to know.

"It might have been Larry's," Mike said. "That would account for her deciding to leave so suddenly."

"It wasn't Larry's child," Alan said, shaking his

head. "I know that for a fact. One night Larry and I got together for a consoling drinking bout. We were both putting the juice away on a regular basis in those days. I must have been some kind of a glutton for punishment, because all Larry would do would be to talk about Christine, and I'd just have to keep my mouth shut and listen, even though his strolls down memory lane would tear my heart out. Anyway, there was this one time that Larry got polluted and started telling me that the reason he thought Chris had left him was because he wasn't able to father children. He said Christine always wanted to have kids and because of some illness he'd had as a child, he was impotent.

"I went back to Christine's doctor and I confronted him with what my detective had told me. He confirmed that Chris had been pregnant when she left town, and he also knew that Larry couldn't have been the father. That answered a lot of questions in my mind. She knew that if she had the baby, people would know it was mine. It would have ruined my career, and destroyed Larry.

"I suppose she might have had an abortion, but even if they were easy to get then—which they weren't—I guess she wanted to keep the baby. I'd like to think it was because that little girl was a part of me, a reminder of our love. I never gave up hope of finding them. I've never stopped thinking about Christine or my daughter. Mike, I've tracked down every lead, every clue. I know I can never love anyone the way I loved Chris. Any relationship I've ever had has soured because of the feelings I still hold for her."

"But, Alan, it's been over twenty years," Mike said gently.

Alan stared out at the harbor. "I know."

There was a long silence. Mike and Michelle waited for Alan to continue. He lit another cigarette.

56

"A couple of times I thought I *would* find her. I traveled all over the country, mostly on false alarms. When I did have a legitimate lead, just as I would be closing in, she would move to another city or even another state."

"How did she earn a living, with the baby and all?"

Alan nodded. "That's how I was able to get so close. You see, Chris was an artist, an absolutely brilliant artist. She could make money anywhere just by doing some paintings and selling them in a gallery. She used her maiden name Christine Elvey. All I had to do was track down her paintings. In the corner of all of Chris's works she had her own little logo—a circle with an *L* and a *V* inside it, for Elvey. I sent letters to every gallery in the country to be on the lookout for any paintings with that mark."

Michelle shook her head. "It's just so *weird* that in all these years she never tried to get in touch with you, or see you."

"In the beginning, I guess she felt it would hurt too much, and she was right. Later on, maybe she felt that we were better off, especially with Larry still around and actively a part of my staff. She had no way of knowing that I knew about the child. Perhaps she was trying to protect me, since I had become a prominent senator by then," he said bitterly.

"You can't blame yourself," Michelle told him gently.

"I can't help thinking that had I lost that election, my whole life would have been different. Maybe I'd be standing here with my daughter, just as you are with Michelle, Mike. Anyway, I had just about given up when two things happened. Larry Stapleton was killed in an auto accident. It made the obituary columns of a lot of papers last year, and I was hoping that perhaps Christine would see the notice and contact me."

"But she didn't?"

"No. Another false hope."

"What was the other thing?" Mike wanted to know.

"I was attending a party. It was one of the usual round of Washington affairs where you stand with a drink in your hand and pontificate to the political groupies. I turned around and saw one of Chris's paintings on the wall."

"Where was it bought, and when?" Michelle asked excitedly.

"I spoke to my hostess, who told me that she had bought the painting from the artist at a showing on the Caneel Bay Plantation on St. John's Island a month ago."

"Are you sure it was Christine's work?" Mike asked him.

He nodded. "There's no doubt about it. The L and V were in the circle, and besides, I've become an expert on her style."

"All those years"—Michelle sighed—"and she's right here somewhere on the island!"

"There was one more thing. The subject of the picture was a young woman. A young woman about your age, Michelle. The painting's title was a girl's name—'Alana.'"

"That's why you came," Mike said.

"Yes, and that's also why I can't be scared off now by Gregor. I'm getting so close, Mike! If I can't have Chris, if she's made a new life for herself, I still want to find my daughter."

"Couldn't this be used against you when you run for president? Your opponents might try to create a scandal."

"I don't care anymore, Michelle. I've lost so much because I've been concerned with what people might think. The public will have to take me, warts and all. And if not . . . *c'est la vie*."

CHAPTER 8

Nicholas finally had finished setting the Windsor House dining table for the guests, placing the napkins and silverware according to the precise instructions of Parsons. He'd done it three times because the first time, the forks were in the wrong place, and the second time Parsons had decided the damask napkins needed to be refolded.

Parsons enjoyed giving orders and pointing out what he thought were interesting tidbits of information to Nicholas. "Do you see the crystal glassware on the table? I do the ordering, along with Miss Jessica, and we only buy Waterford. When you buy well, you buy cheap, regardless of the cost. Did you know that no Waterford design has ever been discontinued? Each piece is blown by a master and contains so much lead that it couldn't possibly be machine cut."

"That is most interesting," Nicholas said, sounding bored.

"You, my man, don't seem to have much appreciation of the finer things in life," Parsons said with a sniff.

"I like nice things, but to me, glass is glass."

"My good man, Waterford chandeliers are hung in Westminster Abbey!"

"I have never been there."

"How unfortunate. But certainly you can appreciate works of art like this Biedermeier dining table and chairs." Parsons ran his hand lovingly over the smooth mahogany. "And hanging above us is a very valuable chandelier, more than one hundred years old."

Nicholas shrugged, his face impassive.

Parsons finally stalked off, mumbling aloud about the insensibilities of *some* people.

Far from being unimpressed by the opulence of Windsor House, Nicholas had already inventoried the large dining room. It was paneled in rosewood, which served as a rich backdrop for the table which could seat twenty-four comfortably but was now set for twelve. A beautiful Aubusson carpet covered the parquet floor. There was a large French breakfront filed with fine china and more crystal, and paintings in elaborate gold frames hung on the walls. Over the windows hung brocade draperies in a hue that matched the velvet upholstery of the chairs. Nicholas had noted that it would be an easy leap from a window down to the garden below, and then to his motorbike hidden near the servants' quarters in what used to be the carriage house.

Nicholas wondered how many starving people could be fed by selling these bourgeois spoils of the filthy imperialists. He would like to show Parsons the beautiful craftsmanship of his Baretta that was strapped to a holster on his calf. He would ask Parsons as the bullet entered his body if he had placed it on the right side. It was a fantasy that gave him pleasure for the moment as he adjusted the huge flower centerpiece. Killing Parsons would be a nice finishing touch, but it was someone else who was his primary target.

Nicholas was looking forward to the arrival of Lord Philip Carlisle's distinguished guest, Senator Alan Mason.

Archie's wife, Veronica, her eyes swollen with tears, sat at her kitchen table telling her mother about the fight she had had with Archie the night before he disappeared.

"He was drinkin' agin, and I said I would leave him if he ever come home like that," she sobbed.

"Well, that's the answer then, girl," her mother said. She was a molasses-colored woman of fifty who had buried one husband and wished she could do the same to her present one. "They all the same when it comes to drinkin'. Black or white, all the same. They can't control their cravin'. Your Archie got drunk agin and then he afraid to face you. You'll see I know what I'm a'talkin' about. You'll see. He be sleepin' it off somewhere with no care in the world, not even knowin' the fuss he's causin'."

"But, Momma, they came to me from the Windsor House. He never missed work before. In all the years, he never missed a day."

"This be the beginnin', girl. You see, that's how it starts. None of them ever miss a day until they start. They got to start sometime, and this was his time."

"Maybe he's hurt."

"Stop talkin' foolishness! If he's hurt, your brother an' his friends goin' to find him. 'Sides, when they

61

drunk like that, they don't hurt theyselves. They bounce around like rubber."

"Momma, that ain't like Archie," Veronica insisted.

There was a knock on the door.

"Maybe that be him now," her mother said. "Now hear, you wait 'til I leave befo' you hit him, girl."

"He don' have to knock, Momma. He's got a damn *key*!"

She opened the door and let her brother John into the small, neat home.

"I jus' come back to see if you heard anythin'," John said. "The boys are lookin' for him in the fields and near the ferry. We spoke to the driver of yesterday's bus. He say he think he let Archie off at his stop. When he was pullin' away, he saw him talkin' to a man that looked like a skeleton."

"Oh, my! My Archie been talkin' to *Death*!" Veronica wailed.

"Oh, hush up!" her mother said. "Was he drunk?"

John shrugged. "The driver didn't know. He wasn't payin' too much attention. He only noticed the man Archie was with because he had a skull face."

Veronica wailed again.

John walked over to the refrigerator and looked inside. "How come if yo' husband is such a good cook, you got nothin' to eat in this 'fridgerator?"

"You jus' remember, brother, that he put plenty of food on yo' table when you was out of work at the refinery!"

John grunted.

"How many boys out there lookin' for him?" their mother asked.

"Six, not countin' Sidney who said he'd poke around soon as he had his late supper. We also got a couple dogs that Arthur Murphy lent us."

John took a couple of mangoes out of the refrigerator,

juggled them, and when he saw he wasn't entertaining his audience, sat down at the table.

"Stop frettin', Ronnie. We find him. He didn't get picked up by no spaceship. They don' want those bleached white, old bones."

His mother flashed John a look to be quiet, but it didn't matter. Veronica was still picturing poor Archie's conversation with Death.

There was another knock on the door, and Domingo stuck his head in. "They want you to come with them, John," Domingo said, looking nervously at the two women.

"You found him?"

"Jus' you come, John," he said.

John stood up, and Veronica followed him. "I'm going with you," she said.

Her brother shrugged.

Domingo had walked away from the door and was heading down the path to the road. Veronica saw two men by the sugar field waving at them as a brown mutt barked its head off and ran around in circles off to the side. The men were looking down at something, and when they saw Veronica, one of them told her to go back to the house. She brushed past him and tried to get into the cane field to see what the men had found. Domingo grabbed her about the waist and started pulling her away, but she broke free—and saw the body of her husband.

She screamed and thrashed and wouldn't stop until finally her mother slapped her hard across the face. Then she moaned, quietly put her head on her mother's shoulder, and began sobbing.

"John," Veronica's mother said, patting her daughter's back, "go down to the Windsor House and tell them what happen to Archie. Tell them to send the police, and tell them 'bout that man you saw before who look like a walking skeleton."

"I'll also tell Miss Jessica there's no money to bury the po' man," John said sadly.

He walked down the road to the bus stop and turned once, to see his mother and sister embracing as they stared down at Archie's murdered body.

CHAPTER 9

Parsons greeted each of the guests and announced them to Lord Philip and Jessica Spencer. Aside from the American senator, there were Mr. Kane, the Mulhaneys, Willoughby, Weaver, Mr. Gordon, Sir Thomas Parker Whitehouse, Officer in Charge of Customs and Excise Enforcement, and an American couple who owned Calico Sugar, Jack and Phyllis Reilly.

Parsons saw to their drinks personally and was pleased to see the evening get off to a good start. He had some reservations about the new man, Nicholas, but thin as he was, he looked good in his livery and he served the drinks without spilling them all over the guests' clothing.

Miss Jessica looked smashing in a mauve off-the-shoulder silk gown. Parsons knew that Jessica had set her cap for young Mr. Kane. He had walked into the library once and had found them kissing. He had knocked, of course, but they had been so involved that they hadn't heard him. He had been able to back out and close the door without their knowing he had witnessed their indiscretion.

From the way Mr. Kane was looking at her now, it was obvious that his ardor hadn't been extinguished. Kane was a nice chap, for an American, not like Weaver with his darting eyes and incessant impatience.

Sir Thomas was explaining to Lord Philip that he needed to have more ships under his command. Lord Philip listened with only half an ear—he had heard Whitehouse's arguments dozens of times in the past.

"I expect a very large problem this year, Philip. You must inform the ministry that we need a larger fleet to handle the drug traffic," Sir Thomas said.

"Drugs? I had always believed the islands didn't have that much of a problem," Mason put in.

Lord Philip sipped his rum and nodded his head. He had an air of command about him even in a white dinner jacket with a drink in his hand. Behind that imperturbable demeanor was a first-rate mind, a fact not lost on the Foreign Office.

"I'm afraid our little oasis has become part of the pipeline to your Miami," he told Mason. "With the increased surveillance around Jamaica, we've gotten more than our share of drug smugglers using the islands as a base. It's perfect for their nefarious purposes, with all our coastline and hidden cays. A ship the size of the *Queen Mary* could be hidden in the harbor of one of our uncharted islands. I believe the American Virgins are experiencing the same problems. We could ask our friend Gordon about that—he's a United States Marshal and has jurisdiction in those waters."

"He does the same thing I do here," Whitehead explained. "We call out the coast guards of our countries and chase the smugglers back and forth."

"Why don't you *catch* them instead of just chasing them?" Mason wanted to know.

"The fact of it is, sir, their boats are faster and better equipped than ours. Take a man like Kane over there"—he nodded his head at Ben Kane, who was talking quietly to Jessica in the corner of the room— "He's got all kinds of superchargers and advanced speed designs. He's got equipment on his bridge that makes the Royal Navy's equipment appear positively antediluvian."

"Certainly you don't mean to imply that Mr. Kane is a smuggler, or rents his boats to smugglers?" Mason said, raising an eyebrow.

"Careful now, Whitehead," Lord Philip warned. "You wouldn't want to cast aspersions on Mr. Kane, who happens to be my guest and friend."

Several years ago, Lord Philip had sponsored a chess tournament between the British and American Virgins. He and Kane had found themselves on opposite sides of the board and had enjoyed the game so much that they sought each other out for further competition. Lord Philip had introduced Kane to Jessica, and he was certain that a spark of romance had been kindled between the two. Jessica needed a diversion after her divorce from that rotter, Spencer. He wasn't sure that he fully approved of young Kane, but he certainly found a lot to like and admire in the Vietnam hero. As it stood now, after almost a hundred games, they were about even in victories on the chessboard.

"I am just saying that Ben Kane certainly has the capability to be a smuggler. Good Lord! The man has dozens and dozens of boats, both sail and motor yachts, a score or more of unsavory captains and crew who were all old Navy buddies and have found their way to Barracuda Reef. He has the money to bribe officials, contacts throughout the Caribbean, and you know as well as I do that Caribbean Dreams didn't materialize out of thin air. That requires a good deal of money. As a matter of fact, I understand he recently bought the *Little Miracle*."

"Is that a boat?" Mason asked.

"A millionaire's yacht that's been sailing around here for the last two seasons," Lord Philip explained. "One hundred and twenty feet of pure luxury."

Whitehouse nodded. "With a helicopter and a 6000psi dive compressor. One doesn't buy that kind of vessel with conch shells."

"I believe Kane told me a rich uncle of his had died in the States and left everything to him," Lord Philip offered, smiling slightly.

"Of course, Crown Commissioner," Whitehouse said with clipped sarcasm.

Off to the side, Weaver was talking in a hushed voice to Willoughby and Gordon. Willoughby was staring at the floor, his ferret face a noncommittal mask. Gordon, square jawed and silver haired, wore a deeply troubled look as he listened to Weaver.

"I don't want to start a panic around here," Weaver was saying, "but I'm pretty damned concerned. I've got these little hairs at the back of my neck that are standing on end. That is my infallible warning system. I want to tell you gentlemen to get on the stick, because something is definitely in the air. Two of my agents are missing. I've gotten reports of rubber raft landings of mercenaries along the coast of St. Croix. There is an increase of seaplane landings on Ram Head. I want to know what the hell is gong on."

"What you're talking about sounds like an invasion force," Gordon said, "with Gregor in the thick of things coordinating the action."

"Yes, it's Gregor, all right, but Gregor has failed to take into account that Mason is under *my* personal protection."

Willoughby flashed Gordon a look, which was subtly acknowledged. Weaver could be a pompous ass at times, Gordon thought.

"We're getting similar readings in BVI," Willoughby told them. "It's not precisely an invasion because they're not meeting in any one place to join forces. It's rather like a fanning out of people all over the islands."

"Try to get one of them in your net, Gordon. If we can break even one, we'll get a better idea of the whole picture," Weaver said.

Ben Kane was off by himself holding his favorite drink, a screwdriver, in one hand and one of Lord Philip's Havanas in the other. He had been exchanging glances with Michelle most of the evening, glances that held the promise of an interesting night later on. Jessica, on the other hand, had been friendly but cool. Ben knew that was her way in the presence of her father and his guests. She was always the perfect hostess, but Kane well knew that underneath that cool "wax museum" facade was a lusty, flesh-and-blood woman. He marveled again at the contrast between the two women and how he could find both of them so damned attractive.

"Refill, Mr. Kane?" Parsons asked, interrupting his thoughts.

"Yes, thank you."

"Mr. Kane, sir. Something here for you from Miss Jessica."

Parsons placed a small piece of folded pink stationery into Kane's hand. Kane looked at the butler, but his face was totally expressionless and gave no insight into his private thoughts.

"Thanks," Ben said. He looked around the room to see if anyone had noticed Parsons's action.

Michelle was busy conversing with Phyllis Reilly. The Reillys were among the largest employers on the British Virgins, having moved the family business from Cuba after the fall of the Battista government. They were a pleasant enough couple who had chartered several boats from Kane over the years. Jack Reilly was the strong, silent type, while Phyllis was a prattler. Usually her conversations centered on illness and symptoms that struck her and her circle of friends. A person could make a good living, Kane often thought, renting her helicopters to hopscotch to doctors' offices all over the islands for her mostly imagined afflictions.

When Ben was sure that Michelle was occupied with Phyllis and Jack, he stealthily opened the note and read it in his cupped hand. The message was simple and direct: "The garden . . . fifteen minutes."

Kane smiled. Jessica had her back to him as she pointed out to Senator Mason a sculptured bust of Napoleon, a work commissioned by Lord Philip and executed by the Australian artist Harrison Todd. Mason bent to get a closer look at the piece, and Jessica used the moment to catch Ben's eye. A hint of a smile played at her lips, and Ben gave her a furtive nod.

A waiter dressed in the Carlisle's livery distributed hors d'oeuvres from a silver tray. There was something about him that seemed different from Lord Philip's other servants, and it wasn't only because he was white. Ben tried to put his finger on it, but the only thing that he could come up with, aside from his subjective uneasiness, was that the man seemed to be too interested in the guests, almost too willing to please. A good waiter should be practically invisible, Kane thought. This one sticks out too much.

He walked over to Parsons and took him aside.

"You've got a new man on board, I see," he said.

"Yes, sir . . . Nicholas. Is there any problem?"

"No, I was just curious about him."

"He began work this morning. Apparently Archibald Potter hired him. He hasn't had much experience, I'm afraid, but we'll soon whip him into shape."

"He seems awfully eager, if you know what I mean."

"Hmmm. Well, the fellow says he's down on his luck. He's all skin and bones—claimed he hadn't eaten in a couple of days. Probably wants to make good and is overdoing it a bit. I'll speak to him about it, Mr. Kane."

"No, forget it. Guess I'm imagining things."

"Very well, sir."

Ten minutes later, Ben walked casually out of Windsor House, past Lord Philip's security men, and down to the front gate. He whistled three times, each whistle slightly higher pitched and slightly longer than the one preceding it. As if by magic, Ganja Grant appeared out of the shadows.

"What's up, Skipper?" Ganja asked.

He was wearing jeans and a loose-fitting black overshirt that concealed the .32 in his waistband.

"Everything secure?"

"Dead calm."

"Good."

He didn't have to tell Ganja to keep alert. The man's reflexes had been legendary in Nam. Kane had been amazed at Ganja's expertise as a gunner on the *Swift*, Kane's Mekong patrol boat. Ganja could do twice the job with half the firepower. He was a natural-born gunner, Kane had said, but Ganja's prowess extended to all weapons. He was just as proficient with a stiletto as with a .35mm cannon.

Kane walked around the side of the building and approached the tall hedges that enclosed the garden. He repeated his three-whistle call and waited for Miles to appear. In seconds, the quiet, intense man stood next to him.

"Ganja says it's quiet."

"Yeah," Miles answered.

"Take ten and keep Ganja company for a while. I'll hang around the garden."

"Okay, Skip."

The garden at Windsor House was Lord Philip's pride and joy. Kane had lunched several times with Jessica and the crown commissioner on the balcony overlooking the garden and had been impressed with the abundance of tropical blooms. Now, bathed in the Caribbean moonlight, it was even more impressive.

There were fragrant frangipani, or *plumeria acuminata*, as the little card Kane had seen at the foot of the flower bed stated. There were also pink-and-yellow *poui* with their trumpet shapes. The *cassia fistula* was evident with its attractive gold petals, the Pride of India and its roselike flowers, and many flowering trees. Among them was the immortelle with its crimson blossoms, also known as the *madre de cacao* because of its use throughout the Caribbean as shade for cacao plants. In addition to the landscaped walks through the luxuriant vegetation, there were a number of hothouses where Lord Philip grew hundreds of species of lilies and orchids.

Ben heard a rustling sound and turned, to see Jessica moving toward him. She had just come through a side door off the dining room. It had been several months since they had seen each other. The last time, they had picnicked at a farm in the mountains of Tortola. It had been a beautiful day, and they had planned to make love for hours under the warm, tropical sun.

It was then that the bullets started crashing around them. Jessica's chauffeur, Hutton, had been hit and

72

only because of the intervention of Waiting Fox, one of Weaver's agents who had tailed them, had they been able to escape with their lives.

The memories came back to Kane—memories of the old man, Victor, and Cy and the one they called Detroit. After Kane and Jessica had been captured, Victor, smiling, had gloried in showing them video tapes of the brutalization of some poor woman by his thugs, in order to make her husband cooperate in a business merger. Kane was told that the same thing was in store for Jessica if he didn't agree to transport large quantities of cocaine into the States.

So he had agreed—temporarily—and when he saw his chance, was able to turn the table on their captors. The only thing he regretted was that Jessica had seen him release his fury on the evil old man. He had the big .45 in his hand, and the next minute he was mindlessly pumping bullet after bullet into the cancer-riddled old hoodlum, overcome by ungovernable rage.

Jessica had said she understood—but he wondered if even *he* knew why he had felt the need to empty the chamber into the deadbody . . . or why he felt so comfortable doing it.

The kicker, of course, came later when Weaver showed him that he had a tape of the whole incident. It could be construed as murder, Weaver implied smoothly—just another blackmailing device that Weaver tucked away somewhere to pull out whenever he needed Kane to dance to his tune.

Jessica ran into Ben's arms and kissed him passionately on the lips. He felt her tongue probing his mouth, and he answered by holding her tightly to him.

"Of all the flowers in this garden, you're the most beautiful," he told her softly.

"Oh, Ben, I've missed you so much." She sighed.

His kisses trailed down the side of her neck and onto

her bare shoulder. The silk rustled softly as he eased it down to her waist, exposing her beautiful breasts, tanned and lovely. The hard, pink nipples seemingly strained to feel his touch.

"Oh, God!" she moaned as his strong hands circled the pliant flesh.

His thumb and forefinger teased her nipples in a rubbing, pinching motion. He felt his cock grow rigid, and he let her feel his need for her by trapping her thigh between his legs. His erection was like a burning poker radiating heat through the thin shield of material.

"Ben . . . Ben, we can't," she said breathlessly. "Not here . . ."

He wasn't listening. His head was buried between her perfumed breasts. His tongue licked its way sensually down to her already inflamed areoles. He seized a pert nipple and sucked it into his mouth.

"Ohhh!" she groaned, and he felt her body trembling.

He knew how it excited her when he touched her breasts. She was one of those women who were "connected," which meant that the sensation from her breasts went directly to the smoldering cauldron of her vagina.

"Ben, we can't stay out here too long—we'll be missed," Jessica gasped. "As I was leaving, Michelle was looking all over, trying to see where you were."

"Don't worry about it," he told her breathlessly.

His hand was between her legs now, lifting the gauzy material as it moved toward her sex. He felt her whole body stiffen. Her arms tightened around him.

"Jessica!" he said in surprise, as his fingers touched the warm, damp fur.

She didn't answer at once. She had to wait for the spasming of her body to stop.

When she could speak, she said, "Has my lack of

modesty shocked you? One can't wear any undergarments with this kind of dress. The material is too thin. Everything shows and it looks terrible."

"Believe me, honey, I'm not complaining," Kane replied.

His fingers probed the dewy insides of her hot flesh and then found the protruding clitoris. He rubbed it against the folds of her labia. She was reaching peak after and peak and mumbling his name over and over in the throes of her passion.

"To hell with the party," he said gruffly. "I've got to have you!" Her hands darted to Kane's erection. She held him tightly as her breath came in small gasps.

"Yes, Ben . . . Yes!"

He led her behind a high hedge and stood her up against a gnarled tree. They broke their kiss for just a moment as Kane unbuckled his belt and lowered his pants and shorts. She reached out with one hand and drew him toward her. Kane hunched his hips, sweeping away the silk of her dress and then he was inside her. He felt the moist heat of her enveloping him, and thrust himself into her. She responded by arching her pelvis until he had her fully impaled.

"Ben . . . Ben . . . You feel so good." She sighed.

He braced her back against the tree and lifted her legs so they were wrapped around his waist. Her arms entwined around his neck. He made love to her then in long, hard strokes that fanned the fires of their lust and sent them hurtling into unbridled passion.

"Oh, Ben . . . Come with me . . . Come with me now . . . *nowww!*"

He felt her opening and closing around him like the wings of a trembling bird, delicate and fragile, yet as strong as life itself. He felt himself release as his mouth covered hers and they muffled their cries of pleasure in a kiss.

Nicholas watched the guests as they began taking their places around the dining room table. Lord Philip was seated at the head of the table. There were two empty chairs where place cards indicated Jessica Spencer and Ben Kane were to sit. Next to them were the American couple, then Willoughby. On the other side of Lord Philip, and facing the butler's pantry, were Alan Mason, Weaver, Gordon, Mike and Michelle Mulhaney, and Sir Thomas Whitehouse.

The fact that Mason would be looking at Nicholas would not be much of a problem. He had the element of surprise working in his favor. He could empty his gun into the senator's chest and still be gone before anyone reacted.

Parsons was setting up the silver serving trays in the pantry. The chef, a foul-tempered Armenian brought in from Tortola's finest restaurant, was complaining that if the food wasn't served immediately, the flavor would be lost forever. Parsons at first tried to ignore him, but when the chef grew so boisterous that his voice might have carried into the dining room, Parsons took him aside. "My good man, we cannot serve, we *will not* serve, until Miss Jessica and Mr. Kane are seated."

"Well, where the hell are they?"

"I haven't the foggiest," Parsons replied.

The chef went back to venomously stirring a large pot. "If this dinner is ruined, it won't be my fault," he muttered.

Several more minutes passed. Finally, Lord Philip dispatched Parsons to look upstairs for Jessica and Ben. Most of the guests seemed to be taking the delay in stride—all except Michelle, who had turned a glowing shade of red and had fire in her eyes. When Parsons returned and told Lord Philip they were apparently not in the house, Lord Philip instructed the butler to serve without them.

"Bad form," Parsons mumbled under his breath to express his annoyance.

Nicholas hoped that Jessica and Ben would soon be seated, too. He liked everything to be exactly right when he had a job to do. There was little margin for error if you wanted to do a job the right way. Sometimes seemingly unimportant things had a way of coming back to haunt you. . . .

CHAPTER 10

In the process of brushing the back of Jessica's gown and buckling his pants, Kane heard a noise and then a muffled cry of pain.

"What was that, Ben?" Jessica asked.

"I don't know, he answered.

He took a deep breath and tried to get his body working again on all cylinders. After good sex, nature wanted you to go to sleep. But from the sound of the scuffling, he had better get all his wits about him, and fast!

He gave the three-whistle signal and in a few seconds, Miles and Ganja appeared. They were holding a tall, thin, black man who obviously hadn't given them the correct answers to the questions they had asked.

"Who's that?" Ben wanted to know.

"We found him near the front gate. He looked like he was trying to sneak on the grounds," Ganja reported.

"I was not sneakin' anywhere. I simply lookin' for the servants' entrance. I don't know any of you, and I won't talk to you."

The man tried to move away but Miles was holding his thumb in a police thumb lock. The man winced as Miles increased the pressure.

"The skipper wants you to tell him what you're doing here," Miles said in an ominous voice.

"I have to talk to Mrs. Jessica Spencer," he said.

"About what?"

"I talk only to Jessica Spencer," he insisted.

Jessica stepped forward. "I'm Jessica Spencer. Do I know you?"

The black man looked her over as if expecting a trick. When he was satisfied that Jessica was who she said she was, he nodded.

"I'm John. I'm the brother of Veronica."

At first, Jessica didn't know what he was talking about. Then she realized that this was Archibald Potter's brother-in-law.

"It's all right," she said to Miles. "You can let him go."

Miles looked at Ben, who nodded slightly, and Miles released the lock. The man drew his hand away and rubbed his thumb to get the circulation going.

"John, what happened to Mr. Potter? I've been quite worried about him," Jessica said.

John shook his head. "Terrible news, I'm afraid, ma'am. Archie, he dead."

"What? But how could that be? I just saw him the day before . . ."

"Murdered, Miss Jessica. He murdered when he be comin' home last night."

"Any idea who did it, or why?" Kane asked.

"Why? I do not know. He was talkin' to a mon before he die—a very thin mon that looked like a walkin' skeleton. My sister think he was talkin' to Death . . . or the Devil."

Wheels started turning in Kane's head. *The thin man. The thin man who Parsons said had been hired by Potter.*

"It could be Nicholas," Kane said.

"But . . ." Jessica didn't understand what Kane was getting at. Why would Nicholas want to kill Archie? Just to get his job? Then she remembered Alan Mason. "Oh, dear Lord!" she gasped.

Kane was already running back to the dining room, entering the building through the side door that Jessica had used. Ganja and Miles were right on his heels. Kane could still move quickly, in spite of the wound he had suffered to his right leg in Nam. He had worked the leg so that the limp was almost imperceptible, unless you knew what to look for. When he ran, it slowed him down, but only after a long distance.

Nicholas was in the center of the room carrying a tray in his hand midway between the kitchen and the guests at the table when he heard the noise to his right. Kane and two other men were running into the room. There was no cover, no place to run.

Nicholas could tell from the look on Kane's face that something was wrong. Then he saw the black man, and Jessica Spencer behind them. *They must have found the limey's body*, he realized.

Kane was fifteen feet away from him when Nicholas tossed the tray of hot soup at him. Bowls hurtled through the air and smashed against the wall. Steaming hot soup mixed with broken porcelain, spreading dark stains on the carpet.

Kane was caught off balance—it was the moment

Nicholas needed to crouch and bring out his Baretta. Immediately Kane drew his nickel-plated .22 that he kept wrapped in a handkerchief in his pants pocket. It was a small gun, but the hollow pointed bullets could blow a big hole in a man. Ganja and Miles had also drawn their guns.

Nicholas stood with both hands grasping the Baretta. The gun was pointed directly at the seated Mason.

"Nobody is to move!" Nicholas cried. "If anybody moves a muscle, I will kill Mason!"

"Oh, no!" Phyllis Reilly wailed, clutching her throat.

"Pull the trigger and you're a dead man," Kane growled, training the .22 on Nicholas.

Mason stared at the would-be assassin, his eyes wide as saucers as he focused on the barrel of the gun. Nicholas, his face drenched with sweat, kept the Baretta trained on the senator as he backed away from Kane.

"Drop your guns and nobody gets hurt," he told the three.

"Drop yours," Kane ordered.

"I will count to three. If you do not drop your guns, I will kill him. One . . ."

"You're a dead man, Nicholas!"

"Two . . ."

"Listen to him, Kane!" Weaver called from the table. "Do what he says, for God's sake!"

Defeated for the moment, Kane said, "All right, Nicholas. don't shoot." The .22 dropped to the floor.

"Now the rest of you. Now! AND I MEAN IT!!"

Ganja and Miles reluctantly dropped their weapons.

"All right . . . good. Everyone stays calm and no one will get hurt." He backed cautiously toward a window that overlooked the Windsor House garden. "Everybody just stay calm and nobody will get hurt," he repeated. He put his hand on the window and pushed it open.

The Baretta shifted first to Kane and then to the people seated at the table. No one dared to breathe.

Then Nicholas turned the gun on Alan Mason. The Baretta coughed out two shots at point-blank range into Mason's chest. The senator clutched his heart as the force of the bullets knocked him backwards out of his chair.

Nicholas spun around, intending to leap through the window, but was stopped in his tracks as five shots rang out almost simultaneously. Ganja, Kane, Miles, Weaver, and Gordon blasted almost as one man. The bullets tore into Nicholas, causing him to spasm like an epileptic. He tumbled out the window, blood spurting from his chest and head.

Kane raced to the window and looked down. He was glad he hadn't eaten anything yet. The assassin's remains were a grisly contrast to the moonlit beauty of the garden.

He turned back to the crowd that surrounded Alan Mason. He was sure Mason was dead. The two bullets had been fired only a couple of feet away, directly into the senator's chest. Great bodyguard work, Kane, he told himself grimly.

"Alan! Alan, are you all right?" Kane heard Mike Mulhaney's voice above the others.

Kane couldn't believe his eyes when he saw Mason sit up, shake his head, then look down at his tux. In the center of his chest were two distinct holes the size of quarters.

Mike and Weaver helped Mason to his feet. The senator opened his jacket and shirt, and then Ben saw the green bulletproof vest that had saved his life.

"Thank God you were wearing that," Michelle said.

"Well, I knew they were going to try something,"

Mason said with a smile. "I may be a bit foolhardy, but I'm not altogether crazy."

"Are you sure you're all right?" Lord Philip asked, offering Alan a glass of brandy.

Mason rubbed his chest. "I'll be sore for a week or two but outside of that, I'll be fine. Thanks."

Greatly relieved, Kane took a seat next to Weaver and spoke in a low voice. "This gets me off the hook with Mason, Weaver."

"Think so?" Weaver smiled faintly.

"I don't expect any pirate problems now. If I do, believe me, you'll pay the price!"

"What makes you think Mason is out of danger?"

"Your master assassin, Gregor, is lying in the garden looking like a piece of Swiss cheese."

Weaver dismissed Kane's words with a wave. "That's not Gregor. I don't know who this Nicholas is—or was—but he certainly is not Gregor. This man was a bungling fool. Gregor is much more clever and sophisticated. If anything, what you saw tonight was most likely a ruse to make us relax our guard. No, ol' buddy, I'd say the waters around your Caribbean Dreams fleet are still troubled. I suggest you stay on the job and try to improve the level of protection you're providing for our important client."

Weaver walked away and joined the happy throng of Mason well-wishers. Ben started to rise as well, but was pushed back in his seat by Michelle. The brunette spitfire glared at him.

"Where were you and Jessica before the big show-down?" she hissed furiously.

"Why, Michelle, you seem jealous," Kane said in mock surprise.

Michelle took a deep breath to calm herself. "Not jealous . . . *curious*."

"I went to check on Ganja and Miles," Kane told her.

Jessica came out to tell me that dinner was about to be served when we ran into John, Archie Potter the chef's brother-in-law."

He was telling the truth, at least up to a point.

"Oh?"

"Why, Michelle? What do *you* think happened?"

"Never mind," she said, somewhat mollified.

She turned, to see Jessica putting ice wrapped in a napkin on the bruises Mason had suffered to his chest.

Michelle's eyes narrowed. "I can't stand that cold bitch! Did you see where she seated me? If I had been any farther away from you, I would have been out the door."

"I wouldn't say Jessica was cold," Kane said thoughtfully.

Michelle sniffed. "That's because men are such incredibly poor judges of character."

"Maybe you're right," he said.

"What were you jawing with Weaver about?"

The mention of Weaver's name brought a cloud over Kane's horizon. "Just a small matter of blackmail," he said.

"Blackmail?"

He told her of the bargain he had been forced to strike with Weaver to ensure trouble-free charters for his company. Ben knew that all Weaver had to do was have a few of his contacts plant a story about pirates boarding Caribbean Dreams charters, and he could kiss most of his business good-bye. Every competitive charter company would spread the news faster than a prairie fire. Charter brokers would feel they were doing their clients a favor by steering them away from Kane's outfit. The business lost by the pirate threat could never be regained and might in time wipe out his company.

"What a bastard!" Michelle said, glaring across the room at Weaver.

"I've just got to hope that somebody nails this Gregor character, or that Mason decides to leave the islands."

Michelle seemed to be in deep thought. "Maybe I can

come up with something to help you, Ben."

"How?" He looked at her, wondering what she had up her sleeve.

"I'll talk to you on the way home. It's too long a story to go into now, but I think you'll be interested."

Ben agreed, then joined the others gathered around Mason. Alan was making a joke of it now, and things seemed to be back on an even keel. Gordon had made some calls and was tending to the paperwork that Nicholas's death entailed.

"Weaver doesn't think this character is Gregor," Ben told the marshal, hoping that Gordon would disagree.

The big man shrugged. "I'm not too familiar with this so-called master spy, but based on Weaver's profile, this guy doesn't fit the bill." Gordon scratched his jaw. It was the squarest jaw Kane had ever seen, set on a thick bull neck with equally square shoulders.

"In what way? Weaver called him a bungling fool."

"Well, Kane . . . he worms his way into Windsor House by killing the chef. That's kind of a drastic maneuver which opens up a lot of problems, the first being to get rid of the victim's body. See, if you're going to ice someone, you've got to be sure that the victim's corpse isn't going to surface before the job is done. Next, the perpetrator decided to shoot Mason. If you're able to be in the kitchen where the food is prepared, all you got to do is dump a little quick-acting poison in his soup, serve it to him, and be on your merry way while your victim is turning a beautiful shade of blue."

Kane thought about that. Nicholas had been serving the guests. He could have easily handed poisoned food to Mason alone or, for that matter, poisoned everyone in order to be sure that there would be no witnesses.

"Then there was the matter of how the shooting went down. He was standing a few feet away from Mason and he shot him in the chest. Hell! Nobody who knows what he's doing goes for a guy's chest at that range. If you're far away and you're not sure of your target, then you aim for the broadest part of a man's torso and hope for the best. If you're standing right on top of him, you never shoot for the chest."

"You can never be sure you can get the heart," Kane agreed.

"That's right. People have hearts in different parts of their chests. Some are close to the middle, some further to the left. Hell, I even heard of a guy who had his heart on the opposite side of his chest. As close as this guy was, there was no reason for him not to go for the head. even if somehow you don't kill him, you've got a vegetable, which is the same thing as being dead."

"So you feel this man was just a hired hand?"

"Sure. An independent contractor maybe, hired by this Gregor fellow. He probably was in the bar the night before when Potter had come in drunk and mentioned the dinner for Mason. He hatched his plan, killed Potter, and almost scored. There's probably a standing price on Mason's head of a million bucks. Anybody who pops him can collect."

"A million dollars!"

"If he were already president, it would be ten million. Gregor and his paymasters probably think they're saving money by having it done now," Gordon said with a rueful smile. "Weaver and Willoughby tell me there are twenty to thirty hired guns that have shipped into the islands in the past couple of days. Bounty hunters, I would say."

"Terrific," Kane said sarcastically.

Weaver was holding him directly responsible for Mason's safety and there was an army outside trying to kill him.

"If Weaver knows about these killers, why doesn't he have them arrested?"

"Look, Ben, we get reports from field people all the

87

time. The islands are filled with folks that pick up a hundred dollars a week for information, but that's all they do. They don't do spook work—that's where Willoughby and Weaver use their regular people. By the time they check into the first reports, the mercenaries have melted into the hills."

Lord Philip walked over to them. "Something wrong, Ben?" he asked.

"No. Just some unsettling news from Gordon here."

"I think we're all a bit unsettled this evening. I don't think we'll be finishing the dinner, I'm afraid. Our friend in the garden has cast a pall over the proceedings. I've invited Mr. Mason to stay here this evening, but he prefers to go back to the Barracuda Reef with you and the Mulhaneys. I understand he'll be staying aboard the *Wu Li*."

"Yes, Lord Philip."

"Well, I'd keep a sharp lookout. I'm not sure this is the end of the matter. By the way, good work, Kane."

"Yeah, Kane. If you hadn't busted in here with that Mexican standoff, there might have been a few more people in Her Majesty's Coroner's Office tonight," Gordon said.

"I'm terribly sorry for Archie's family," Lord Philip went on. "I believe Jessica is going to hire Archie's wife, and this John fellow . . . he seems like a nice enough chap. We were talking for a little while." He shifted gears abruptly. "All right then, Kane, let's have a go at it on the chess board one day soon."

Ben could see Jessica over Lord Philip's shoulder. She was bringing a glass of wine to Phyllis Reilly, who was being fanned by her husband. He thought of Jessica and what was under that clinging mauve gown.

"Yes, sir. I would love to have a go at it again real soon," he replied, smiling to himself.

CHAPTER 11

Ben told Ganja and Miles to report back to Chief Bukowski on board the *Delphi*. The *Delphi* was an elegant Cheoy Lee, long-range motor yacht with an extensive customized interior.

Ben frequently liked to use the *Delphi* in the medium-sized hops from Barracuda Reef to Tortola. He enjoyed traveling in a yacht with three elegantly appointed"gues with spacious showers and heads.

Tonight, Kane had left the Chief on board as a safety precaution.

"Go over every inch of the *Delphi*, Ganja. They missed Mason once tonight so they might try again. And check the sides of the yacht for plastic explosives."

Ganja nodded. "No problem, Skipper."

Miles and Ganja borrowed one of Lord Philip's cars and left for Careening Cove. They had docked at Careening Cove, which in years past had been a beautiful mangrove-lined cove with complete shelter in hurricanes. Now, the bird sanctuary was gone and in its place, dredging had begun. There were rumors about a new marina, but Ben had heard that before and nothing had come of it so far.

The Chief liked Careening Cove because of the pub, a cheerful pub and restaurant run by his old mate, George Hendix. George was an expert on everything that went on in the British Virgins. It was too bad that they wouldn't have time on this trip to pay George a visit. The Pub was situated only fifty yards from the agency's maritime office and the extremely hospitable British Virgin Islands Yacht Club. The yacht club ran the BVI spring regatta, which formed one of the legs of the CORC series. The other legs were the Rolex Regatta, the Copa Velasco, and the Antigua Sailing Week. Ben had been thinking about entering a yacht in this year's competition under the urgings of Ganja and the Chief.

Kane, Mason, and the Mulhaneys left about fifteen minutes later in a chauffeur-driven limousine flying the British flag. When they arrived at the *Delphi*, Ganja was standing on the deck and Miles was looking through the cabins below.

"Everything normal, Skipper," he reported.

Ten minutes later Ben was navigating the Sir Francis Drake Channel heading east to Leinster Bay. Barracuda Reef was located on one of a string of pearl islands in U.S. waters that was about equidistant from Tortola on the north and St. Thomas and St. John's to the south.

There was a knock on the bridge door. Michelle was standing at the glass door, and Kane motioned for her to come in.

"How's the water?" she asked.

"A little choppy," he replied, "but don't knock it. The wind keeps the bugs away."

The motors of the *Delphi*, two purring Jensen diesels, gobbled up the nautical miles as Michelle took a seat near Ben and the wheel.

"Everybody tucked away?"

"Yes, Mike and Alan are busy talking in our cabin. I think the Chief, Ganja, and Miles are playing cards in theirs. . . . You know, you look good in formal wear, Ben."

"You're not so bad yourself," he told her.

"Do you think I'm prettier than Jessica?"

"That ice cube?" Kane said, mocking her. "Sure— and besides, you're here now and she isn't."

"Go to hell!" she said angrily as Ben chuckled.

Michelle looked out the port-side window of the *Delphi*, watching the twinkling lights of the commercial boats farther out in the channel. Would this be the kind of life she would lead married to Ben Kane, she wondered? She would be at his side on board a beautiful yacht, and jealous of any woman that looked his way. She remembered the first time they had made love.

It had happened at one of her father's anniversary bashes for Barracuda Reef. The harbor had grown in size to accommodate island boats as well as charters. Mike felt that a monumental party once a year to celebrate his good fortune, as well as touching base with old friends, was in order.

Michelle had made the transition from an awkward teenage girl to a woman with delicately attractive features, long brown hair, green eyes, and a voluptuous figure. Ben always seemed to be around her father, smiling at her and generally treating her like a kid sister. But Michelle had made up her mind that the man she wanted to be her first lover was going to be Ben

Kane. The problem was to get him to stop thinking of her as a little kid.

She had whispered to Kane that she needed to talk to him about something very important, and he had followed her down a winding path that took them some distance away from the lights and sounds of the party into the tropical jungle. They still carried their drinks with them. Michelle stood in such a way that she knew the silver ribbons of moonlight through the trees would spotlight her long, shimmering hair.

"What is it, Michelle? What's wrong?" Kane's strong, handsome face had looked down at her with concern.

"Please finish your drink, Ben. There's something I have to ask you," she said shyly.

She watched as he finished his screwdriver hoping that the alcohol would dispel any reservations he might have. She finished her white wine, then placed both their glasses on the ground.

"I want to whisper something to you," she said. She stepped close to him and wrapped her arms around his neck, pulling him down to her as she stood on her toes, and put her lips against his ear. "Would you make love to me, Ben?" she whispered, as if kissing his ear with every word.

If he had any qualms or misgivings, they were not apparent. He kissed her then, a sensuous, electrifying kiss that almost made her knees buckle. She felt his hands running up and down her body, then unbuttoning her blouse and caressing first one breast and then the other. They had undressed each other in a fever and made love with a fierce passion that had surprised them both.

He had told her that he had desired her for a long time, but she had been too young. As for Michelle, she knew she had always wanted Ben Kane. He had been the focal point of all her most romantic fantasies. . . .

"Michelle? Michelle!"

Ben was calling her, bringing her back to the present. They weren't in a tropical forest now—they were on the *Delphi*, rounding the western point of Tortola.

"Sorry, Ben. Daydreaming, I guess," she said.

"Well, are you going to tell me how to get Alan Mason out of my hair?"

"He's a wonderful man, Ben," she told him.

"I'm not arguing that, but I'd feel better about admiring him from afar, especially with thirty or so mercenaries out to kill him."

Michelle sighed deeply. "He told Mike and me the real reason why he's here, Ben. I know he won't leave until he gets what he came for."

"What's that? A swordfish to hang over his mantle?" Kane asked drily.

"No, you unromantic baboon! He's here to find the woman he loves . . . and his daughter. And I'm going to help him find her!"

Michelle told Ben about Christine Elvey and her daughter, Alana. He listened, asking a question here and there. When Michelle finished, he reached into his pocket and brought out one of Lord Philip's Havana cigars that he had been saving.

"Okay, I understand why he's here, and why he's reluctant to leave. Now you tell me know you think you can help."

"He said that his friend had bought the painting at Caneel Bay Plantation on St. John's. They have a very fancy art gallery there and only invited artists' works are displayed."

"So . . . ?"

"I know the director of the gallery. His name is Jacques Estes. I called him and asked him to look through his files for Christine Elvey's address."

93

"Did you tell Mason about this?"

"No. He's been through so many disappointments already that I couldn't bear to build up his hopes and then risk dashing them again. As it turned out, Jacques couldn't help me. He only had a phone number for her, and that number has been disconnected with no new listing."

"Too bad," Ben said without much enthusiasm.

"Jacques gave me another idea, though. The artists who don't live on St. John's use the Caneel Bay Plantation's helicopter to pick up their paintings or sculptures and delivery them to the gallery. Jacques gave me the address of the pilot. He's sure that he has records of his pickups over the last couple of years. He should have Christine's address. I'm not going to say anything to Alan until I'm sure that we can find Christine and through her, Alana. I'm going to St. John's Island tomorrow morning. If you want to go with me, you're welcome to."

Kane sighed. "Great. Just what I need—a wild-goose chase! But I guess I'd better help him find the lady and his daughter, so he can leave Barracuda Reef, become president, and live happily ever after—if an assassin doesn't get to him first. Then maybe I can get back to running Caribbean Dreams."

Michelle's eyes were shining.

"You know, Ben, if Alan Mason *does* become president, you could advertise Caribbean Dreams as the charter company used by the President of the United States!"

Kane took a long pull from his cigar. "Hey, that's right! The Presidential Charter . . . it has a nice ring to it."

Chief Bukowski knocked on the door, peering through the glass pane.

"C'mon in, Chief," Kane called.

As usual, the Chief was wearing his blue yachting cap. When they had served together in Nam, he'd always worn a woolen watch cap. Come to think of it, Kane had never seen the Chief without something covering his noggin. Ganja had once quipped it must be where he kept his money. Miles, in a rare burst of verbiage, offered that maybe he kept a bottle of rum there.

"Whyn't you take a break, Skip? I'll take the wheel for a while," he suggested.

"What happened to the card game?" Kane asked.

The Chief made a face. "Ah, the Ganja man wins hand after hand. It don't make no sense to play against him. I'd be better off handin' him my money before the game starts and enjoyin' myself the rest of the night. And Miles, he justs stares at the both of us like we're in it together against him. Maybe he thinks Ganja and me split his dough after the game."

Ben turned the wheel over to Bukowski and followed Michelle down the companionway.

They found Mike and Alan sitting in Mason's stateroom with a bottle of Scotch on the table between them. They had stripped to T-shirts and suspenders, incongruous with their formal trousers. Their shirts and ties were draped over the bunks. Lord Philip had given Alan one of his own shirts to replace Mason's bloodstained one. Mason's bulletproof vest was also lying on the bed. It was obvious to Michelle and Kane that the two men were, if not three, at least two sheets to the wind.

"Oh, Ben Kane—just the man I wanted to talk to," Mason said, trying to stand up and then flopping back into his chair.

Mike Mulhaney thought that was funny and broke into a giggle.

"When we dock at Barracuda Reef, I want you to cut

95

me adrift," Mason said drunkenly.

"Why should I do that?" Kane asked.

"I'm to much damn trouble. . . . Don't want anybody else to get hurt. Not right a'tall to do that to anybody."

"You stay with me, buddy. You can stay with me," Mike said, patting the senator's shoulder and groggily shaking his head.

"No . . . no. You've got your lovely daughter, and she's got you, and I'm not going to let anyone hurt either of you. . . . I got a daughter, too, Mike. Did I tell you about my daughter? My daughter's name is Alana. Did I tell you?"

"Sure you told me. You told me a hundred times already."

"Well, now I'm telling you a hundred and one." Mason pushed a finger into Mike's soft belly for emphasis. "And there's people out there gunning for me. Can't let you get involved."

"Well, then you stay at the Rainbow and we'll beat back the bastards!" Mike told him.

"I think the best thing for both of you to do is to sleep it off right here on the *Delphi*," Ben said.

"They'll be out cold by the time we dock," Michelle agreed. "But will Alan be safe?"

"I'll bunk in the next stateroom and the Chief will keep watch on the deck. The *Delphi* might even be safer than the *Wu Li* tonight. At least I know this vessel has been gone over from stem to stern. I'd want the *Wu Li* to be thoroughly checked out before we boarded her."

"What're you two whispering about?" Mike bellowed.

"What're you yelling at them for, Mike?" Mason slurred.

Kane leaned over to Michelle and whispered in her ear, "*He's* going to be our next President?"

Michelle shrugged. "Why not? He's a good man,

drunk or sober. He'll probably make my father secretary of State . . . and you secretary of the Navy."

A slight smile spread across Ben Kane's face as he thought of a few people in the so-called Annapolis Protective Society that he would love to get even with.

"Mike, why don't you get some sleep?" Michelle helped her father up and steered him toward one of the bunks.

"I'm not going . . . not tired," he muttered, but allowed her to ease him down on the pillow.

"'I'm not tired either," Mason protested as Ben helped him to his feet and set him down on the other bunk.

"Well, just rest up then until we get to shore," Kane said diplomatically.

The two men were asleep almost the moment their heads touched the pillows.

Ben picked up the bottle of Scotch and followed Michelle out.

"There's another stateroom not being used," Ben said, leering at her. "The bunk's big enough for two."

But Michelle tossed her head. "I'm going upstairs to sit with the Chief. Why don't you take a rest, too? Your *meeting* with Jessica must have tired you out!"

Kane was back in Nam. He was standing on the deck of the *Swift* and searching the shores of the Mekong Delta for VC. Something moved in the thick underbrush.

"Starboard at five o'clock!" he yelled.

Ganja was sitting in a machine-gun turret. He whirled and splattered the brush with bullets.

"Okay, Ganja, you got him!" Kane said.

He looked up. Grant had stopped firing. He was lying half in and half out of the turret, his face a bloody pulp. The Chief ran along the side of the deck and he, too, was cut down. Kane did a complete three-sixty and couldn't locate the enemy fire.

"Where's it coming from, Miles?" he shouted frantically to the thin SEAL who was taking the bridge. When Miles didn't answer, he knew he, too, was dead.

A bullet ripped up the planks of wood of the deck inches from Kane's foot. He wanted to run, but his feet wouldn't move. The next shot got him in the right leg. He collapsed, grabbed his leg, and felt the gooey wetness of blood.

The shots were coming in regular bursts. He fell to the deck and closed his eyes. Bang . . . bang . . . bang . . . bang . . . closer and closer, and he couldn't move. . . .

The shots turned into a dull rapping, and he wasn't in Nam anymore.

"Ben! Ben, open up. *Open up!*" He recognized Mike Mulhaney's voice.

Sunlight was streaming into the stateroom. Ben shook himself awake and ran to the stateroom door.

Mike, wearing the same outfit he'd had on last night, stood there with panic in his eyes.

"What's wrong, Mike?"

"It's Mason. He's gone! I woke up, and his bunk was empty."

"Shit!" Kane cursed.

He raced up the steps. The Chief was supposed to be on watch. What the hell had happened?

Bukowski was nowhere to be seen. Kane knew the Chief well enough to know that he would never leave his post without a damn good reason.

"Check the bridge, Mike," he ordered. I'll look in the lifeboats."

Ben lifted up the canvas cover of the second boat and found the Chief, bound and gagged.

"What the hell happened, Chief?" Kane asked.

"Mike, over here—I found him!"

He undid the ropes around the Chief's hands and pulled off the gag.

"That miserable dirty son of a bitch! If I ever—"

Kane cut him off. "Who did it? Where's Mason?"

"Mason did it, that's who! He came up in the middle of the night to have a smoke with me. The next thing I know, I'm lookin' down the barrel of a gun."

"Why?" Mike asked, running up to join them.

"Said he was too much trouble, and he didn't want to put us all in danger because of what he had to do. He was very apologetic and all, but that don't make my stiff achin' joints feel any damn better!"

"The fool!" Mike said softly.

"He's a fool, all right, but I'm going to have to pay for it if anything happens to him," Kane said.

"I'll call Weaver and Gordon. He couldn't have gotten too far," Mike said, rising awkwardly.

"No! We can't let anyone know that he's not with us. We'll tell everybody he's holed up on the *Wu Li*. That will keep Gregor guessing, at least for a while. Mason's life won't be worth a cent if they know he's running around the islands without any protection—and neither will my ass!"

Mike nodded. "You're right, Ben. He won't have a chance with Gregor's crew gunning for him."

"I hope they do the bastard in!" the Chief muttered, rubbing his chafed wrists. "I'll tell you this much, *I* won't vote for him."

"You haven't voted since F.D.R.," Mike said.

"That's beside the point!"

"All right! Quit bickering," Kane snapped. "Mike, here's what I want you to do. You and the Chief row over to the *Wu Li*. Mike, make sure your face is covered. You're about Mason's height and wearing what he wore. From a distance someone might mistake you for him. Then put on a change of clothes and leave. If the *Wu Li* is being watched, they'll think Mason is still aboard. I asked Ganja and Miles to check it out for security. They'll be on deck waiting for you. And Mike, not a word to anybody about this."

"Okay, Ben."

"Where will you be, Skip?" Bukowski asked.

"With Michelle. She's got a lead on Christine Elvey. If we find Christine, before long it's a cinch Mason will show up."

"Who the hell is Christine Elvey?" the Chief wanted to know.

"I'll explain it to you while you're rowing," said Mike.

"Why do I have to row?"

"You expect a United States Senator to row a dinghy?" Mike chuckled.

"Damn! . . . Hey, wait a minute. Sure, I'll row." Bukowski began lowering the dingy at top speed.

Mike was puzzled. "What the hell is he smiling about, Kane?"

"He just figured out that if someone's got a rifle with a telescopic lens, you'll be the target, not him," Kane informed him.

"Oh," Mike said glumly.

CHAPTER 12

The main door of the Rainbow Keg Inn was open. Ben walked in and took the stairs two at a time until he reached Michelle's room on the second floor. He banged on the door.

"C'mon in, it's open," she said.

It was a small room, very feminine, done in peach with flowered curtains and a fluffy, white rug. Michelle was lying in the center of the large bed. She threw back the covers and looked seductively up at Kane. She was completely nude.

Kane's eyes feasted on her tanned body, framed by her long hair which fanned out over the pillow behind her head. Her perfect breasts with strawberry-sized nipples caused Kane to feel the stirrings of an erection.

The thatch of soft mink between her legs brought him to full attention.

"I'm afraid I wasn't very nice to you last night," she purred. "You've cooled your heels long enough. I think it's time to make it up to you."

"Hold that thought . . . for later," Kane said with deep regret.

He turned and opened her bureau drawer and took out a pair of bikini panties, which he tossed to her. Her jeans were lying on a chair along with a blouse. He threw them over to her, too.

"We can't play now, angel. Get dressed—we have work to do. Mason's gone!"

Kane and Michelle took the *Delphi* and headed south to St. John's Island. St. John's was two miles east of St. Thomas and connected by a ferryboat that traversed Pillsbury Sound. Unlike its two sister islands, St. Thomas and St. Croix, it had a very sparse population.

The Danes, who had settled St. Thomas, had set up second plantations on St. John's to provide employment for other members of their families. What they hadn't realized was that the fertile land and wetter climate were more beneficial on St. John's than on the original plantations. This caused the island to prosper, and Coral Bay became the main town, fueled by sugar revenues.

Although Coral Bay was a fortified city, in the 1750s the oppressed slaves working the plantations revolted and started to massacre the white settlers. They managed to kill almost everyone except a handful of survivors, who succeeded in making it to the home of Edmund Durloe, who had built his home in the form of a miniature fort complete with cannons. Durloe and his countrymen were able to hold off the slaves until fresh troops arrived from Martinique and St. Thomas, putting an end to the rebellion by routing the insurgents.

Rather than die at the hands of the soldiers, many of the slaves chose to leap off Mary Point, north of Francis Bay. According to local superstition, the moaning noises heard at Whistling Cay in the middle of a cold, windy night are the tormented spirits of the dead slaves.

St. John's never recovered from the onslaught. Estates went to seed. Peace—and poverty—reigned until the area was declared a national park and vast areas developed for the North American tourist. Nevertheless, many of the families who had lived on the island for hundreds of years resented being dispossessed. Even if they were allowed to remain, the land would go to the government at the time of their deaths.

Caneel Bay, north of Cruz Bay, was part of the vast holdings of the Rockefeller family. Caneel Bay Plantation was an elegant resort which the island people described as a place for "newlyweds and nearly deads." The grounds were a swirling riot of Caribbean color and charm set off by magnificent imported marble and filigreed wood and iron gates.

As Michelle and Ben walked past the partially restored ruins of the Caneel estate, Kane made a mental note that someday he would like to come back and check out what remained of the sugar plantation that had been assaulted in the 1750s rebellion. He would have enjoyed the view more, however, if someone hadn't put a snack bar on the top terrace.

Jacques Estes was in his office on the second floor of the Caneel Gallery. Michelle introduced him to Ben, and Kane took a seat opposite Jacques's desk.

Estes was a slight man in a white suit with a red bandana tied around his neck. His hairline had receded considerably, making him appear to be all forehead. What hair he had left was obviously dyed. It looked as though he had used shoe polish on it. He had large expressive eyes and his hands moved with each word he uttered for emphasis. Kane pegged him to be in his mid-fifties, but he might have been older. And he seemed to be very nervous, for some reason.

"Ah, Michelle, it is so good to see you. How is your father, Michael?" he asked in a pleasant voice with a hint of a French accent.

"He sends his regards."

"Now you must make pardon for me. I am in a hurry, and I know you are, too. So what is it I may do for you?" he asked, wiping the perspiration from his upper lip with a large white handkerchief.

"You remember that we spoke about Christine Elvey?" Michelle began.

"Yes, yes, of course!" He slapped himself on the forehead. "I am so *bouleverse*, I forget my own name. I recall her paintings very well indeed. Her name is Elvey, and she makes a circle with an '*LV*' on her paintings. Most distinctive. and she is a most talented artist. I have not, however, had the pleasure of meeting the lady in person."

"And you don't know where she lives?"

Estes shook his head.

"Then how do we find her, Jacques?" Michelle asked.

Jacques's expression indicated deep regret. "I'm so sorry. I don't have that information here. Perhaps I never received it, or perhaps it was lost. But do not fret, I have a solution."

He reached into his desk and handed Michelle a business card. Ben looked over Michelle's shoulder and read it:

HENRY P. BRAND
Helicopter for hire
Licensed Pilot—Individuals or Groups
14 Hawks Nest Street
St. John's 4716

"This man may be able to help you. We use him to fly paintings back and forth from the islands for the gallery shows," Jacques explained. "He keeps very careful records for billing purposes. He will no doubt have the address you need. I think if you leave now, you might be able to catch him. If he doesn't do any business by midday, he goes home."

Michelle thanked him, and he shook hands with Kane.

"Do you know where this place is?" Ben asked as they left Estes's office.

Michelle nodded. "Follow me."

Hawks Nest Street was within walking distance of the gallery. It was a squat, gray building, one story high, that Brand shared with an island doctor. The small wooden sign on the door said HENRY P. BRAND, LICENSED PILOT.

Michelle knocked on the inside office door and was told to come in.

Brand was sitting at his desk. He was a sturdily built man of about forty, with a round face that was fighting a double chin. He looked up and frowned. "Oh, I thought you were the police," he said.

Kane looked around the small room. The floor was covered with papers. File cabinets had been hauled away from the walls and their contents spewed all over the floor, giving the room a two-inch carpet of records and files. Drawers from Brand's desk were also overturned and thrown around. Someone had obviously been looking for something and had completely ransacked the place. Whatever could be broken was. Whatever couldn't be broken had been tossed around or emptied on the floor.

"Unusual filing system," Kane quipped.

"Just what I need—a wise guy," Brand replied with a sigh. "What can I do you folks for? If you've come to rent the chopper, you're going to have to hang around until the cops come and file a report. Two guys walked in here this morning, held a gun on me, and busted the place up. Tough customers, too."

Kane surveyed the damage. "The papers on the floor wouldn't be your company records, would they?"

Brand's eyes narrowed slightly. "You folks sent by Judy?" he asked suspiciously. "I've already told her that I'll send her the rest of the money I owe her when I get it."

"No, we're not from Judy. Who's Judy?" Kane asked.

"Judy's my ex. A real pain in the butt. She gives the best headache in town."

"We wanted to ask you about a client," Kane said, looking around. "Guess we're out of luck."

"What client did you have in mind?"

"Would you know a Christine Elvey?" Michelle asked. "It's very important that we get her address. You took some of her paintings over to Jacques Estes's gallery. By any chance do you remember her? Monsieur Estes said she was a very talented artist. She signs her paintings with the letters *LV* in a circle."

Brand nodded. "That rings a bell. This is a big deal, huh?"

"Better believe it," Kane said. "A life may be in danger. Do you think you could take a look around? If you know what to look for, you might be able to find a card with her name."

"No, I can't do that. I'm not supposed to touch anything until the police come down and dust for prints. You know how that goes. . . . They work on Virgin Island time, which means anytime between now and next weekend, but there's no way I could find what you're looking for."

"How can you be so sure?" Kane asked.

"I'll tell you how!"

Brand took his hand out from under the desk. He was holding a Smith and Wesson .38.

"Now let's stop the games," he growled. "Suppose you folks explain what's going on here."

"That's not very friendly," Kane said, eyeing the Detective Special.

"No, but neither is having two goons come in here and run my records through a blender."

"What do you want from us?' Michelle protested. "We had nothing to do with them."

"What would you call it then, just a coincidence?" Brand said angrily. "What's the story with this Christine Elvey?"

"She's a friend of a friend, and we want to find her. Why did you pull a gun on us?"

Brand looked from Michelle to Kane, searching their faces. "You telling me the truth? You telling me you don't know anything about the two guys who came in here and did a job on my place?"

"Of course not. Why the hell should we?" Kane snapped.

"Because they were looking for this Christine Elvey, too," Brand told them.

Michelle and Kane exchanged surprised glances.

Brand watched them closely. "Hell, you're not kidding, are you? You really *are* in the dark on this thing," he said, slowly putting the gun down.

"I'm glad you believe us. What did these guys look like?" Kane asked.

"One was a white guy, mean face and a voice that sounded like he gargled with razor blades. The other one was an island black. He was big as a house with a pair of hands on him that looked like he was wearing catcher's mitts. The white guy called him Sparky."

Kane scowled. "Sparky Suarez," he told Michelle.

"He's a Cuban who'll work for anyone if the money is big enough. There's nothing, including murder, he wouldn't do—and hasn't done."

"How did he know that I would have the lady's address?" Brand asked.

"Estes?" Michelle said, looking inquiringly at Kane.

"He did seem nervous, like he wanted to get rid of us as quickly as possible. Suarez and his friend may have put a scare into him before we got there."

"Well, I can't blame him. Those two looked like stone-cold killers," Brand said.

"They probably have the same idea we do," Michelle said worriedly. "They'll hold Christine and draw Alan Mason out into the open."

"Alan Mason the senator? What does he have to do with all this?"

"It's personal, Brand," Kane told him.

"They got the address from you, didn't they?" Michelle asked.

"Yeah. I didn't know the woman, and I didn't want to be a hero. They went to the file and pulled out her card. I have to keep flight logs for every trip I make. Until they busted up my place, it was no skin off my nose. They took the card and broke the place up anyway, just for fun."

"There's no way you could remember the address, is there?"

"Nope. I have a lousy memory. Now tell me how Mason figures in."

"Like I said before, Brand, it's personal," Kane said.

"Well then, I guess Elvey's address is personal, too."

"You told us you couldn't remember it," said Michelle.

"That's right, I can't. But who needs the card? I've got all my records duplicated on computer disks. I don't care about this garbage on the floor. Those goons actually did me a favor because otherwise I might never have thrown the crap out."

"Well, come on then! Let's check it out," Kane said excitedly.

Brand shook his head. "Mister, that's classified information that I can't share with a stranger."

"We have to tell him," Michelle said to Ben. She turned to Brand. "Christine Elvey is most likely the mother of Alan Mason's child. He's desperate to find her, and we think these people, this Suarez and his friend, might kill Mason when he tries to see her. They're obviously working for a very dangerous assassin.

Brand digested what Michelle told him. "Come on. I owe those bastards something," he finally said.

They followed him down a small hallway into a room that probably was originally intended to be a closet where Brand had a computer, disk drive, and printer on adjoining shelves.

"I had some high-school kid put all my business records on a disk," he told them. It took the kid most of a month, but now I'm damn glad that I did it. It used to be that the tax man or Judy's lawyer would ask me questions, and I'd sit there trying to bluff my way through. Now all I do is push a few buttons, and there it is. . . ."

He typed *Elvey, Christine* on the screen. There was a momentary pause as the machine searched its memory banks and then it lit up with the information Kane and Michelle needed. Christine Elvey was born in 1928. Her occupation was listed as "painter." She had used Brand's helicopter service in March, and Brand had been paid two hundred and fifty dollars for the taxi service to the gallery. He was paid by Caneel Bay Plantation check #345, signed by Jacques Estes. Her address was 25 Rum Cove, GSJ.

"What's the GSJ stand for?" Kane asked.

"Great St. James' Island. It's about a fifteen-minute chopper ride from here."

Kane knew the area well. It was south of St. John's and St. Thomas, a picturesque island about three miles bigger than Little St. James'.

"How about tearing yourself away from all this and taking us over?" Kane asked.

Brand shrugged.

"Might as well. These cops may never show, and even if they did, they don't do a damn thing," Brand said bitterly. "Hold on while I get my hat."

CHAPTER 13

The big Hughes chopper was on a lot about a hundred yards from Brand's office. It could seat six in a pinch but was actually designed for four people. Brand, now wearing a large straw hat, pushed some buttons, and the large blades began to move. In a few seconds they were airborne.

"You fly one of these things during the war?" Kane asked him.

Brand pulled the headphone off one ear. "What say?"

"You a chopper pilot during the war?" Kane yelled over the whirring of the blades.

"Yeah. You in it, too?"

"Riverine Forces in Nam."

"I hear that was rough duty."

111

"I guess there was worse," Kane said, remembering the swamps and snipers, "but you'd have a hard time convincing me. How about you?"

"Nothing like you, Kane. I was stateside, taxiing generals from one golf course to another. Closest I ever got to action was when I picked up Bob Hope and brought him over to Palm Springs to meet with the Joint Chiefs."

"Sounds like you had it rough," Kane said good-naturedly.

"Like they say, Kane . . . war is hell!"

They were over water now. An occasional yacht appeared beneath them, its sails dazzling white against the blue water backdrop.

"You know the big black guy, huh?" Brand went on.

"Unfortunately," Kane replied. "He's from Cuba. They call him Sparky because he's supposed to have been the executioner at Castro's Ciudad Prison. He was in for murder himself. Every prisoner had a job. Some of them worked the kitchen, some of them farmed sugar in the fields. Sparky did what he was good at— killing people. He strapped them in, and pulled the switch. I hear he enjoyed his work"

"How the hell did he get out?"

"Remember a few years back there was an exchange between the United States and Cuba? Well, Uncle Sam got a handful of its Cuban operatives out of jail, but along with them Castro shipped out all the scum of his society. The first chance they got, Sparky and his brother, Ernesto, left Miami and settled in the Virgins. They started off here by getting a stable of girls and setting up a prostitution ring. That gave them the money to open up a gambling joint on St. Thomas."

"Sounds like you've run into Sparky before," Brand said.

"Yeah. We're not exactly what you might call buddies," Kane told him, as he remembered. . . .

Chief Bukowski had come to Kane with a friend of his by the name of Howard Putnam. Putnam was an independent yacht captain who worked for various charter companies in the Virgins. Kane recalled that the Chief would occasionally hire Putnam to work for Caribbean Dreams. Kane had actually received a complimentary letter about Howard Putnam from a Wall Street executive who had been very pleased by the captain's manner and knowledge of the Caribbean. In the back of his mind, Kane also remembered that Putnam had a small yacht of his own that he and his wife, Marge, took a great deal of pride in.

The Chief's story wasn't a pretty one. He told it to Kane while Putnam stared down at the ground like a schoolboy being reported to the principal.

"Howard's got himself in a kind of a mess, Ben, and I thought I'd tell you about it. Seems he wandered into this gambling club over on St. Thomas about three weeks ago and he lost a bit more than he had. They told him not to worry about it and that he had credit at the club. He finally quit after he lost seven grand."

"It wasn't any more than six, seven thousand at the most," Putnam said. "I would swear to that on a stack of Bibles."

"Well, the fellow who's doin' the tallyin' hands him an IOU for twelve thousand. Howard refused to sign it, naturally. They tell him to step into the office and they'll straighten everything out. There are these two Cubans, the owners, sitting in the office. One of them is named Ernesto, black as the ace of spades with a flat, busted noise and a half-moon scar on his cheek. The other guy, his brother Sparky, looks like King Kong with a toothache. Howard here is shakin' in his boots. He tells them their counting man made a mistake. He'l

113

pay off the seven thousand, but he won't go for the twelve. This guy, Sparky, tells him he can forget about the whole debt altogether. Howard asks, 'How come?' This Ernesto character pulls out a machete from a drawer while Sparky pins Howard to the wall. 'A leg is worth twenty-five hundred,' they tell him, 'and an arm is worth three grand.' They offer to cut off his arms and legs for eleven thousand, and certain other parts of his anatomy will make up the difference. Then they brought out the IOU again and asked him how he wanted to pay it off."

"I signed," Howard said meekly.

"Well, it was a pretty persuasive argument," Kane said.

"The terms were twenty-five percent interest a week until the principal was paid off."

Kane whistled. "You'd have to give them three thousand a week."

"I was able to do it for the first three weeks. I had some savings, I borrowed . . ."

"So you've paid off the nine thousand and you still owe the original twelve?"

"Yes, and the only way I can·pay them the whole amount is if I sell my boat, the *Robin's Egg*. It's my only negotiable asset. If that goes, I'm busted."

"They've already told him that he can pay off his weekly installment with money or pieces of his body. And Putnam's not the only one either, Ben. I've heard of two or three of our people who've been under the Suarez brothers' thumbs. They've also played the same number on a couple of our charterers. It's giving the Virgins a bad name, it's bad for business, and bad for our people. I've also got it on pretty good authority that the games are crooked. I heard they brought in some sharpies from Vegas to show Suarez's folks how to rig the games."

"What's Gordon doing about it?" Ben wanted to know. "He's the marshal for the territories. He could clean it up."

"He can't act unless there's a complaint. Up to now, nobody dared to say anything."

"I'm no hero, Mr. Kane. I've got a wife and a family. If I had the money, I would just pay them and try to forget about what a complete jackass I've been," Putnam said ruefully.

Kane thought it over. "Chief, get three thousand for Howard and let him take care of this week's juice. Then get Miles and Ganja and we'll take a crack at Suarez's establishment. I'm in the mood for a little fun and games."

Suarez's club was fronted by a cheap-looking gin mill. You nodded to an ape at the back door and went down a flight of steps to where the real action was going on. Kane saw three crap tables, five wheels, six card tables featuring poker, and three blackjack tables. All of Suarez's housemen were wearing tuxedos, as were the three beefy islanders who were watching everything that was going on . . . and also served as Suarez's muscle.

One of them stood in front of a closed door marked PRIVATE, which was the obvious domain of the Suarez brothers, and where Ernesto kept his very persuasive machete.

The crowd was mostly well-dressed North Americans looking for a little local excitement off the beaten track. There were a few American women wearing expensive jewelry and smoking cigarettes in long holders. The men, generally pudgy with red faces, drank booze supplied by Sparky and his brother. Hard-looking native prostitutes encouraged the men to keep gambling and teased them sexually.

"I make you win now," one of them said, rubbing the

dice against her crotch as the businessmen types roared with laughter.

Kane drifted from one table to another. The big game was the one-hundred/two-hundred-dollar poker game. You didn't stay in the Navy for too long and not learn a thing or two about games of chance. Kane considered himself a pretty fair card player. He had been taught by pros who had piled up big bankrolls in the service of other enlisted men's money. Like many other pastimes aboard ship, if you watched hard enough, and paid your dues, you got to know what you were doing.

The game was stud poker, and there were seven players. After watching the first deal around the table, Kane spotted two players using the "mechanic's grip." Although they attempted to shuffle clumsily, Ben could tell by the way they moved their hands that they had been around a hell of a lot of card games. The third sharp was more difficult to spot. She was a good-looking blonde who prattled on as if she didn't care about who won the pot. She insisted she didn't know too much about the game, but she was the big winner of the evening. She raked in the money with continued exclamations of "*I don't believe this!*" and "*I can't believe my luck!*"

Kane knew the three were working together in what was called a *wolf pack*. It was the three sharps against anyone else in the game. They had to be working for Suarez, he thought, and they probably alternated among themselves as to who would be the big winner on a given night.

Kane watched as one of them, a thin, pale man with a pencil moustache, raised the pot, setting it up for the blonde once more. A young, well-dressed Oriental balanced one of the local girls on his knee and snapped at the bait. Kane watched as he raised three hundred and was counter-raised five. There were unlimited

116

raises on the last card. The blonde was home safe as Pencil Moustache folded with pretended disgust.

"I don't believe it!" she cried again as her three fours topped the Oriental's aces up.

Bukowski joined Kane as he watched the poker game. "The dice are shaved, and there's a button under the roulette wheel," he whispered.

"They must be taking in fifty to a hundred thousand a night," Kane said. "I spotted three sharps in this game, but I can't figure their code yet."

The code was the way one of the players signaled to the other what his hole cards were. They weren't setting up the deck and cheating on the deal, he was sure of that. Somehow, though, they knew one another's cards and what cards their opponents had. The decks didn't look marked, but that didn't mean anything. The way to check it was to ruffle the backs and look for the marks to go jumping around like old-time movies. But Kane was sure that a marked deck would have been too obvious. There were other tricks, though, some so innocent-looking that they could only be spotted by eagle-eyed pros.

Kane had seen people deal cards over polished cigarette cases, or while wearing mirrored rings. Then there were the "clock setups," where one partner telegraphed his bottom cards by touching a spot on an imaginary clock in front of him and then touching a part of his face . . . the nose was spades, the eyes diamonds, the mouth hearts, and the ears clubs. Sometimes the cards were nicked on the edges, and the dealer could feel as he dealt what the cards were.

Kane couldn't figure out how they were signaling, but he knew they were. Suddenly he smiled. Of course! It was so obvious, once you knew what to look for.

"Have Ganja and Miles ice the bouncers," he muttered to Bukowski. "I think I'll play a little cards."

Bukowski gave a small nod and strolled casually over to Miles and Ganja. A moment later, he watched as they moved behind two of the heavyweight guards and quietly put guns in their backs. Miles seated the two of them down at a table, whispering that he had a gun on them and they should just sit tight. The third bouncer, who was standing at the office door, looked around and saw his two buddies sitting down on the job.

He walked over. "Hey, what's with you guys?" he growled.

He froze when he felt the cold steel of Ganja's gun nudging his backbone.

"Now you join your playmates at the table and no one gets hurt," Ganja whispered.

"I'll kill you, you mother-fu—"

"Sit down, turkey-face! Or I blow your ass away," Ganja commanded.

When the Chief saw that Suarez's men were sitting quietly, he came back to the table and tapped Kane. "Everything squared away, Skipper."

Kane nodded imperceptibly.

They had worked so smoothly that none of the patrons had any idea of what was going on.

"Mind if I join the game?" Kane asked the thin man.

"No room now," the thin man said, not looking up from his hand.

Chief calmly lifted the Oriental man and the hooker off the chair and shoved them away. He did the same thing to a half-drunk German and two American businessmen who had lost a bundle.

"Hey, what's going on?" one of them said.

People around the room stopped playing to see what the commotion was all about. The housemen at the tables looked around for the bouncers to step in, but they weren't moving out of their chairs. They sat stone-faced, knowing there were two men directly behind them with guns aimed at the backs of their heads.

Kane took a seat at the table. "I see there's room now," he said, looking across the table at the blonde, the thin man, and a white-haired man with a white goatee.

"I don't believe I'll play," the white-haired man said with a British accent and started to rise.

"You're in!" Kane said, swiftly removing the .9mm MAB automatic from the ankle holster on his left leg. He placed the gun down on the table. "All three of you are in this game."

"What is this?" the thin man squawked.

"Just a game of stud poke with three excellent card players," Kane told him.

The three sharps exchanged nervous glances.

Kane smiled, his eyes steely.

"Don't worry, I brought money."

He held out his hand, and the Chief dropped two large bundles of one-hundred-dollar bills in his palm.

"Now here's the rules," Ben continued. "We play one game of poker—you three against me. If I lose, you folks get ten grand each. If I win, I get to keep all the money you've got showing on the table. I estimate the little lady here has about sixteen thousand in front of her, and you two gentlemen have about ten grand each. You're putting up a bit more money, but then again, you have three chances to win to my one."

"What's the catch?" the man with the pencil moustache wanted to know. "You going to deal?"

"You can deal, if you want. We'll play it strictly blind. You give each of us five cards facedown and then we turn them over. Whoever has the best hand, takes all the money."

"We get three hands to your one?" the Englishman asked incredulously.

"Correct."

119

The door to the office exploded open, and Ernesto and Sparky came out.

"What the hell is going on here?" Ernesto bellowed. "What are you doing on your asses?" he yelled to his guards.

"He's got a gun on us," one of them said, tilting his head back.

Ganja smiled and waved.

"What is this shit?" Sparky snarled at Kane. "You robbin' me, mister?"

Kane raised his eyebrows. "Just here for a little excitement, like everyone else," he said.

"He wants us to deal out four hands blind, and if any of us beat his hand, we get to split thirty gees," the blonde said.

Suarez looked at Kane. "You loco?"

"Maybe a little," Kane said, shrugging his shoulders.

"Okay, then," Sparky said, rubbing his hands together. "Deal out the cards," he snapped to the thin man.

"I'll get very annoyed if I hear any swishing sounds," Kane said mildly.

It was impossible to see anyone dealing from the middle or the bottom of the deck. The only way that could be discovered was by the slight swishing sound the bottom card made as it came out of the deck.

The thin man ignored Kane, but he dealt fairly. In a minute, there were four hands of facedown cards in front of each player.

"Now, all you want us to do is to turn over our hands and if any of ours beats yours, we get to keep your money?" the blonde said.

"That's right," Kane agreed.

"All right, then. Let's get on with it," the white-haired man said confidently.

"Just a minute," Kane put in. Let's make it a little

120

more interesting. Since this game was my idea, how about if I get to choose which hand I want to play? The cards are all facedown, so it wouldn't matter which hand I chose, right?"

"It's the same three-to-one odds anyway you slice it," Pencil Moustache said. "Which one do you want?"

Kane thought it over. "It's so hard to make a choice. . . ."

He looked around. With the exception of the three tough guys Ganja and Miles were holding at gunpoint, everyone in the club was gathered around Kane's table.

Kane looked up at the Englishman. "You know what I noticed?" he asked suddenly. "All three of you are wearing glasses with a slight pink tint. That's one hell of a coincidence, don't you think?"

"C'mon, pal. You're wasting time," the thin man said impatiently.

"They sure are sharp-looking glasses. Yours are nice, too, miss," he said to the blonde.

"Can we play, please?" she replied. The giggly schoolgirl was gone. She was all business now.

"Mind if I try your glasses on?" Kane said, snatching the pair off the nose of the Englishman.

The smile faded from Sparky's face. He mumbled something in Spanish to his brother.

"I'll play *this* hand," Kane said, taking the five cards that were set before the white-haired old man. "Okay, everybody," Kane said cheerfully, "let's boogie!"

He turned over a pair of jacks. "Anybody beat me?"

The blonde had king high; the Englishman a pair of tens; and the thin man had sevens.

"I can't *believe* I'm so lucky!" Kane said, mimicking the blonde. She wasn't laughing.

The crowd around the table began applauding Kane. He got up and stuffed the money into a brown bag the Chief handed him.

"This was fun," he said. "We've got to do it again."

Ernesto and Sparky were wearing sick-looking smiles. "Yes, come again, *señor, señor* . . .?"

"Kane. Ben Kane. Thanks a lot."

Kane, Miles, the Chief, and Ganja backed their way out the door and up the stairs. But Kane caught the look of unbridled hate that was directed at him from the two Cubans as he left the club.

"How did you know which hand to play?" Ganja asked him when they were outside.

"The glasses were treated with a substance that made them ultraviolet. I got suspicious when I saw that all three of them were wearing glasses with pink-tinted lenses. When I put the damn things on, I could read the marks on the back of every card as if they were highlighted by neon lights.

"Give Putnam back all the money he spent and let him pay off his debt to Sparky. You guys can split whatever's left," he added.

"Aye, Skip."

"Thanks, Skip."

"There's one thing though, Ben," the Chief said. "Did you see the way Suarez looked at you? That was one angry honcho! He sure as hell would like a chance to get even."

"Well, let's not give him that chance," Ben said.

CHAPTER 14

"Yeah, now I remember this Christine Elvey," Brand was saying. "See, sometimes I go over flight patterns, and that triggers my memory. Watch it, there's a little mountain coming up about now, then a forest, and we should be able to see her cabin just about . . . NOW. See it there on the left?" Brand told them. "I'll put the chopper down behind the house. that's what I used the last time I was out here. It's nice, level ground."

Kane noticed that everything seemed very quiet. If Sparky and friends had taken a chopper, they would have snatched the artist and been long gone by now. If they were coming over by boat, however, they would have to hire a car and then navigate the winding roads up to Christine's cabin.

He looked at his watch. If that were the case, they might arrive any moment.

Kane got out of the chopper first, gun in hand. Michelle followed and then Brand, also carrying his gun.

"It's so quiet," Michelle said, almost in a whisper.

They looked around, searching for a telltale sign to let them know if they were walking into a trap. Only the sound of the chopper's blades winding down in slower and slower revolutions could be heard.

Kane walked over to the cabin door and knocked. There was no answer. He went over to a window but couldn't see anything because of the heavy curtains. He tried the door. It was locked.

"What now?" Brand wanted to know.

"Stand back," Ben said.

Brand and Michelle moved off to the side.

Kane kicked the door at the lock's strike level, and it flew open. He dropped to one knee and waited. Nothing. Michelle and Brand waited while Kane entered the cabin. A few seconds later he came out.

"Come on in. Nobody's here, and the place looks like it's been sealed up for a long time."

Michelle, entering, saw what Ben was talking about. The closets were open, and all the clothes had been removed; the bedding was dusty as if no one had disturbed it for a while; and the refrigerator was unplugged, its door standing open.

"She's gone," Brand said, stating the obvious.

Michelle began looking at a pile of letters that were on the kitchen table.

"This last postmark was three weeks ago," she said.

"That's about when she stopped crossing off days on this calendar," Brand said, bringing it over to show Kane.

It was a calendar distributed by a local insurance company—J.K. Honeyball—and like a lot of people, Christine was apparently in the habit of crossing off the days. Kane wrote down the phone number of the insurance company, just in case.

They poked around a few minutes more and weren't able to come up with anything that gave them the slightest clue to Christine Elvey's whereabouts.

"No sign of where she might be," Brand said at last.

"What surprises me is that there's nothing at all to indicate that she's an artist. She must work in a studio somewhere," Michelle said.

Brand stood looking around with his hands on his hips. "Kane, do you think Sparky and that other guy got here first and maybe they have her?"

"No. Christine Elvey hasn't been here for at least a couple of weeks, and neither has anyone else. If the Suarez brothers had been here, they wouldn't have left the place so neat. I'm pretty sure, though, that they're on their way. It would be a good idea for us to get out of here before they arrive."

Kane closed the door behind them. He looked around, then led the way to the chopper in back of the house.

"Where to now?' Brand asked, climbing aboard.

He sat in the pilot's seat as Michelle and Kane entered the cockpit. Before Kane could reply, he heard a distinctive voice behind him say, "Nobody do anything foolish!"

The man had been waiting for them, hidden behind one of the seats. His voice was gravelly, and Kane immediately thought of the character whom Brand had described earlier, the guy who sounded like he gargled with razor blades.

He was of medium height and build with long, matted hair and wearing dirty, wrinkled clothes. He had a protruding forehead which overhung his eyes and cast them in shadow. Kane figured him for his mid-thirties. He had the cool demeanor of a man who didn't have much regard for human life. The sawed-off, twelve-gauge shotgun he was pointing at them tended to

125

confirm the analysis that Kane had made.

"Let's go. Everybody out," the man said, gesturing with the gun.

Michelle got out first, followed by Kane.

The man kicked Brand as he was getting out. "I knew we should have iced you back in your office," he said angrily. "Now, everybody lean against the chopper with your palms touching the paint. The first one of you that takes your hand off the chopper gets cut in half."

He patted Brand down and came up with the pilot's gun. He moved behind Kane and found the .9mm automatic and Ben's wallet, but missed the nickel-plated .22 in Kane's pocket, wrapped in a handkerchief.

He moved over to Michelle. His hands roamed over her body very slowly, between her legs, cupping her breasts.

"Bastard!" Michelle hissed.

He chuckled. "I'll take care of you later," he said, reluctantly releasing her. "Okay, who's going to be number one?"

He leveled Brand's gun and aimed first at the center of his back, then at Kane's. A shot rang out and echoed in the quiet valley. When Kane didn't feel any pain, he thought the man had shot Brand, but the pilot hadn't buckled and Michelle was all right.

Then he realized it was a signal. In a moment there was the sound of a motor and a late-model Chevy pulled up next to the house.

"You've got a great sense of humor, pal," Kane told the man sourly.

"You didn't think that was funny? Well, I got some other fun things to do to you."

Two men got out of the car and Kane's worst fears were confirmed—Ernesto and Sparky Suarez.

"It worked just like you said, Ernesto," Gravel-Voice told him.

"See, I told you I recognized that chopper," Ernesto

126

said proudly, turning to the other two.

"Yeah. But remember, I said we should have taken care of Brand."

"Okay, okay, but who knew he was going to stick his nose into this?"

"I can just as easily stick my nose *out* of this. I'll hop into my chopper and be history," Brand said hopefully.

"You're history already, man," Gravel-Voice said.

"All of you turn around," Sparky growled.

Kane turned and looked directly into Sparky's face. He could see that the Cuban trying to place him.

Ernesto poked Sparky in the ribs.

"*Mamacita!* Look at the girl! She's a beauty, eh, Sparky?"

"Shuttup, Ernesto. Who is this guy?" He nodded at Kane.

"How do I . . . " Ernesto did a double take. "Hey, I know him! He's the one who took our money in that card game. You know, with the blind hand?"

An evil smile spread over the face of Sparky Suarez. "Oh, yes." he nodded slowly. "Today we pay you back, *señor*," he said menacingly.

"Screw you!" Kane told him.

The Cuban punched Kane in the small of his back and laughed as Ben's knees buckled. Kane tried to clear his mind of the pain. He could reach into his pocket and pull out the .22. But with Ernesto and the other guy both holding guns on them, the best he could do would be to get off one shot. They'd mow him down before the second. Kane made a split-second decision to wait and hope that no one else searched him.

He rose unsteadily to his feet.

He heard Ernesto say, as if he were reading his mind, "Did you search them good?"

"Yeah. What do you think?" Gravel-Voice sounded offended.

"I'll search them again," Ernesto offered, leering at Michelle. "Maybe the broad's got something hidden on her."

Sparky cursed him in Spanish. "We got time for her later. Don't forget what we're supposed to be doing out here, Ernesto. Jimmy, you check in the house for the lady. I'll cover them."

Gravel-Voice, otherwise known as Jimmy, came out a few minutes later. "It's empty, man. Looks like she hasn't been around for a while. There's no food and no nothin'."

"Shit!" Ernesto exclaimed.

"All right—everybody get into the house. Move!" Sparky ordered. He was looking through Ben's wallet as he spoke. "Our poker-playing friend's name is Ben Kane." Then he pawed through Michelle's handbag, "and this *chica* is Michelle Mulhaney. Ernesto, go out and get Gregor on the radio. Find out what we should do now."

"Okay, Sparky."

Ernesto walked back to the car while the rest of them went into the neat cabin. Jimmy kept Kane, Michelle, and Brand covered.

"Where's the lady?" Sparky asked them.

"We don't know. We found the house empty, just like you did," Brand told him.

Sparky grunted, then said to Jimmy, "They must know something. Find me some rope."

Jimmy handed his gun to Sparky and went into the kitchen. He came back holding a clothesline, which he cut into strips, then tied Kane's and Brand's hands behind their backs.

"Don't do the girl," Sparky ordered. "I got other plans for her."

"Drop dead, you shit-faced blimp!" Michelle screamed.

Jimmy walked over and slapped her hard across the

128

face. "Have some respect, girlie."

"Bastard!" Kane yelled. He tried to get out of the chair, but Jimmy was a pro. Ben's hands were tied behind his back and his legs secured to the legs of the chair. He was as helpless as a newborn babe. Now he cursed himself for not squeezing off a shot when he had had the chance. "What's this all about?" he asked, giving up the futile struggle.

"Shuttup, Kane. I'll ask the questions. First, tell me who you're working for."

"Nobody."

"Then what are you doing here? Why are you looking for Christine Elvey?"

"Tell him, Kane," Brand said. "It's crazy to get killed because of Mason."

"Mason? Who is this Mason?" Sparky wanted to know.

Michelle and Kane exchanged looks. If Sparky and Ernesto weren't looking for Christine as bait for Mason, what were they doing here?

"Senator Alan Mason. He's an old friend of Christine's," Brand said desperately. "Look, how about if I just get lost? I'm not going to say anything, honest."

Ernesto stormed through the door. "The boss says we have to get out of here. There are cops on the way. It seems our friend here, this crummy pilot, told the police that we broke into his office looking for info about Christine Elvey. They'll be sending up a car any minute."

"I told you this guy was bad news," Jimmy said, cuffing Brand on the top of his head.

"What are we supposed to do with our company?" Sparky asked his brother.

"Boss says to waste 'em." Ernesto shrugged.

"Good, let me do it," Jimmy said. "I'll kerosene the place so there's no prints or nothing."

Sparky ordered, "Ernesto, take the girl to the car."

"The boss said everybody!" Ernesto whined.

"So, we do it, but not all at once. First, we take the broad back to the club and have a little fun, eh?"

Kane strained at the ropes that bound him. He couldn't budge them. Brand was breathing heavily, sweat glistening on his forehead.

Ernesto walked over toward Michelle with a look of animal lust in his eyes. She sprang off the chair and attacked him, scratching, kicking, and cursing.

Sparky threw his head back and laughed as Ernesto tried to fend her off.

"Hey! Hey! Take it easy! Stop that!" Ernesto squawked. "Hey, guys, help me! Get her off me! JIMMY! SPARKY!"

Jimmy pulled her off the Cuban from behind. He pinned her arms in a bear hug while Ernesto took a piece of the clothesline and tied it around her flailing feet.

"*Mamacita,* what a wildcat!" Ernesto exclaimed.

"Get her hands, too," Sparky told him. "She'll scratch our eyes out."

When Jimmy had Michelle tied up, Ernesto slung her over his shoulder. "I'll put her in the backseat. Jimmy, get the kerosene out of the trunk."

Sparky got up and held open the door for his brother. "Good-bye, Mr. Kane. I will think of you when I'm fucking your girlfriend." He laughed.

"Yeah, me, too," Jimmy said, walking out with them.

Kane waited until he was sure they were gone. "Brand, do you have your fingers loose?"

"Yeah, but so what? My hands are tied at the wrists behind my back."

Kane managed to edge his chair over to Brand's and then moved so his right side was near Brand's back.

"Feel around and try to get your hand in my pocket."

"What are you talking about?"

"Just do what I tell you! Jimmy will be back in a second, and we won't have another chance."

Brand began feeling around. Kane tried to help him by angling his body up to Henry's searching fingers. After what seemed an eternity, he was able to get his hand into Kane's pocket.

"Now, careful, damn it. Slowly!"

"What the hell am I fishing for?"

"I've got a .22 wrapped up in a handkerchief. Go slow—if you drop it, we're finished."

"Shit, Kane, we're finished anyway! What the hell good is . . . Hold it! I've got my fingers on it."

"Okay, easy. Be careful you don't lift it by the trigger. I don't want my leg blown off. Come on, Brand! He'll be back in a second."

"Shit, Kane, I can't go slow and fast at the same time. . . . Okay, I got it. Don't move, and I'll pull it out."

They heard the door open just as the gun came free of Kane's pocket.

Jimmy came in, carrying a large red plastic container, and saw the chairs together.

"Go ahead! Try to untie yourselves. If I don't know how to tie a good knot, I deserve you guys getting loose." He laughed. "Neither of you can open that knot," he boasted.

He turned his attention to the red container. "You guys ever see a kerosene fire. It just doesn't *burn* things, it melts them down. They're never even going to be able to identify you by the fillings in your teeth."

Kane tried one last desperate ploy to distract Jimmy's attention. "I'll make it worth your while if you let us go. I own Caribbean Dreams. I'll see to it that you get one million bucks."

Brand transferred the gun into Kane's hand, being careful to hold it between both his own to be sure he didn't drop it.

"Sure, and I'd never have to worry about you or the cops coming after me, right?" Jimmy scoffed.

131

"You'd be able to go anywhere. I could never find you."

"Save your breath, asshole!"

Jimmy poured the kerosene all over the room, saving about a quarter of the container to pour over Kane and Brand.

"You know," Jimmy mused aloud, "a lot of people say that Sparky Suarez is a mean bastard and doesn't have no heart. They don't really know the big guy. He sure is going to be nice to you. Y'know what he told me? He said he didn't like the idea of you guys being burned alive, so he said I could put a bullet in your heads before I torch the place."

"The man's a saint," Kane said somberly.

"Now let's see if we got all the bases covered." Jimmy walked around the room, making sure the kerosene was evenly spread. "Wouldn't it be something if I didn't have a match?" He patted his pockets. "Aw, look here, a cigarette lighter."

"I wish you'd come over and shoot us already," Kane growled. "I can't take your snappy patter."

"Don't worry, pal. You're getting it first."

"Can you just answer something for me before you shot us?"

"What's that?"

"I'm career Navy. I pride myself in knowing knots, but I never saw the kind of knot you tied us up with. What's the name of that thing?"

Jimmy chuckled. "My old man was a farmer. He used to teach us kids different knots. It don't have a name, it's just a variation I come up with on a sheep shank."

"Not bad," Kane said.

"Not bad, shit! *Nobody* can get out of that one, including Houdini."

"I'm practically out," Kane told him. "Another minute, and I would have had it."

"Bullshit!"

132

"Take a look," Kane said. "I'm not going anywhere, not with that gun in your hand."

"This I got to see!"

Kane waited until Jimmy was directly behind him, bending over to get a better look. The .22 coughed twice; the first bullet tore into Jimmy's groin, the second killed him instantly as it penetrated his heart. The gunman spun around crazily and dropped to the floor.

"Holy shit, Kane! You did it!" Brand whispered. "I never thought a .22 could stop a guy like that!"

"Hollow-nosed bullets," Kane told him. "Break the goddamn chairs," he said rocking. "The bastard was right about his knots—we'd be here forever."

Brand's chair broke first. He crumpled to the floor and slipped the ropes off his wrists and legs. Then he helped Kane to get loose.

"Hey, Jimmy. What are you waiting for?" they heard Sparky call out.

"They're coming." Brand crawled over to the window and looked out behind the drapes. "Shit! They're *both* coming back here!"

Kane took his own automatic from Jimmy's belt and slid Brand's .38 across the floor to him.

"When they open the door we'll blast them," Kane whispered.

"Hey, Jimmy!"

Ernesto sounded like he was in front of the door. Suddenly they heard Sparky Suarez yelling to his brother in Spanish.

"What's going on?" Kane whispered.

Brand took another peek out the window. "They're running back to the car."

Ben crawled over to Brand's side. When Ernesto and Sparky had seen that Jimmy wasn't coming out, they must have realized something was wrong. Kane searched for Michelle but he couldn't see her.

133

"Maybe they'll just leave," Brand said hopefully.

Just then Ernesto turned and fired at the window, shattering the glass.

Kane returned the fire, causing Ernesto to flatten out on the ground. The Cuban got off two more shots, blowing holes in the cabin's masonry, then took cover with his brother on the other side of the blue Chevy.

"We can't stay here," Kane said. "If a bullet hits the floor, this place will go up like an inferno."

"Kane, what are they doing?" Brand hissed. "They're opening the back door of the car."

Kane saw some movement, but he wasn't sure what was happening. Then Sparky stepped out from behind the car. He was holding Michelle in front of him as a shield. The girl was hanging over his arm like a rag doll, either unconscious or dead.

Brand aimed his gun, but Kane pushed his hand down. "We can't take a chance on hitting Michelle."

Sparky kept walking toward the cabin as Ernesto laid down a barrage of covering fire.

The small cabin had no back door and Ben knew that if he and Brand tried to get out through the window, they would be picked off by Ernesto, who was now using a rifle. Sparky held his shotgun in his right hand. Kane knew that one blast from the twelve-gauge would set the cabin ablaze. He took a look in the bedroom, hoping to see a skylight that would enable them to get to the roof. No dice.

He turned to Brand. "You'll have to dive through the window and try to get to the chopper. I'll cover you."

"I can't, Kane! I'll never make it."

"It's the only chance we have. Like I sai I'll cover you."

"No!"

"Damn it, Brand, if Sparky ts close enough to get off a shot, we'll be fried! Once you're on the chopper you can cover *me* so I can get out. Come on, Henry. *Move!*"

Brand took a deep breath. He stared at e window and then back to Kane. "I (can't move my legs," he whimpered.

Kane pointed his gun at the trembling man d said between clenched teeth, "Brand, if you don't get out that window, I'll kill you myself!" Then he rned and started firing away at Ernesto, and at Sparky's feet. He couldn't aim higher for fear of hitting Michelle,ut he couldn't let the Cuban get any closer.

Brand covered his face with his hands and leaped headfirst out the side window. He rolled into a somersault, then ran toward the chopper across twty feet of open ground. Ernesto leveled his rifle but Kane was able to get a couple of bullets close enougso that Ernesto had to pull backSparky tried to aim but couldn't manage both the gun and the girl. Kane saw Brand make it to the chopper. For a second it brought him back to Nam. He was with his men on what was supposed to be a simple reconnaissance mission. They had gone into a peaceful village named Mei Po to inquire about "Charlie" and a courle of American prisoners he was supposed to be offering in exchange for a captured "Charlie" major.

At first, everything appeared to be going well. The mayor of the village invited Kane and his men to have lunch while he discussed the situation with the other villagers. Outside the native hut, children were playing and the women were going about their chores. It was Ganja who first noticed how quiet it had suddenly become. Kane's host hadn't returned, and the children's shouts in the middle of their games had abruptly ceased. Kane peered out the doorway. There was no sign of human life. It was as if everyone n the small village had suddenly disappeared. *"Take cover!"* Kane had warned just as the air exploded with rifle fire and rockets.

H.Q. had provided them with a single tank escort

which moved next to the hut and provided some shielding. The tank commander, a green kid named Harrison, whirled the machine-gun turrets around, trying to figure out where all the firepower was coming from.

The VC attack was massive by their standards. Bullets and shrapnel kicked up the dust, making it almost impossible to see. There was no question that in a few minutes they would all be goners.

Then Kane had heard the most welcome sound of his life—the whirr of the rotors of twenty C100 combat helicopters. They circled over the village like giant mosquitoes, raining down payloads of death on the snipers and militia of the Viet Cong.

Kane wasn't a demonstrative man, but he'd cheered like the rest of them when the choppers completely routed the enemy.

Just as a chopper had saved his butt in Nam, he watched Brand's chopper rise into the air. With Henry now able to strike from above and Ben on the ground, they would have the advantage. . . .

Except Brand wasn't staying.

"You son of a bitch!" Kane exclaimed under his breath.

Brand wasn't attacking the Suarez brothers. He had turned the chopper around and he was leaving. Ernesto took a shot at the helicopter and missed.

"Hey, Kane! You don't have a chance now, man. Throw out your gun. What did you do to Jimmy, man?"

Kane squeezed off two defiant shots.

"Your man ran away, Kane. Nobody going to help you now. Throw out your gun and we'll talk. Okay, man?"

"Go to hell!" Kane yelled.

"Let's rush him, Sparky," Ernesto called to his brother.

"No, man. I got another idea. Hey, Ben Kane, you like this girl? If you don't come out when I count to three, I'm going to put a bullet in her head. What do you think of that, man?"

"I'll kill you, Suarez! How do I know she's not dead already?"

"*One* . . . I gave her chloroform to take the fight out of her. She's not dead. I give her my *penga*, she wake up fast." He placed the shotgun on Michelle's temple. "Her head's going to look like a watermelon that fell from the top of a big building in New York. *Two*. . ."

Kane knew that Sparky had him. "Don't do it, Suarez! Okay, I'm coming out."

Kane opened the door.

"First throw out your guns," Sparky ordered.

Kane held the MAB by the barrel and drew back his arm to toss it out when all three of them heard the sound at the same time.

Henry had circled around the mountain and was coming behind the Suarez brothers. He swooped down like an eagle diving for a field mouse. His big .38 fired loudly, forcing Ernesto to scamper under the car for cover. Sparky was caught in a cross-fire. He whirled on Kane and blasted one chamber of the shotgun. It blew down the cabin door. Then he spun again and took a shot at Brand. For one brief instant Kane had a clear shot at the Cuban's head but didn't have a chance to aim and fire.

The cabin seemed to explode as the shot touched off the kerosene. Kane saw the flames darting around the room and then head for him in a straight line. He dove headfirst out the window and hoped Brand was still firing away, covering his flank.

As the pilot had done, he rolled himself into a ball and then leaped to his feet.

Sparkey had thrown Michelle to the ground. In a gesture of futile rage that made absolutely no sense, he threw the spent shotgun at the helicopter and ran for cover under the car with his brother.

Kane was completely in the open now, and Brand saw him. The pilot made a ninety-degree turn and hovered in the air next to Kane, only a few feet off the ground. Kane jumped for the open cockpit, got his arms inside, and pulled himself up.

"We've got to get Michelle!" he yelled over the noise.

Brand nodded and gave a thumbs-up sign. He swooped again over the body of the unconscious girl and hung there as Kane lifted her on board.

It was the chance Ernesto and Sparky had been waiting for. They crawled out from under the far side of the car and ran off into the surrounding jungle.

Brand lifted the chopper and began to give chase but soon realized that it was fruitless. They were completely hidden by the lush, thick vegetation. If he went after them, they would have the advantage of first sight.

"What do we do now?" he hollered at Kane over the noise of the rotors.

"Forget about them. If we get too close to the trees, Ernesto can pick us off with his rifle. Let's just get out of here," Kane yelled. "Set us down near the *Delphi*. It's at Careening Cove."

"I know where that is. By the way, Kane. I get hazardous-duty pay for this."

Kane held Michelle in his arms. She was unconscious but breathing easily. He could stil smell traces of chloroform on her breath.

Brand had done exactly the right thing. By circling around Sparkey and his brother, he'd negated their advantage of using Michelle as a shield. Kane held out his hand. "You got your double time, Henry. You're all right!"

They shook hands briefly. "You're not too bad yourself, Kane," Brand said with a grin.

CHAPTER 15

When Ben Kane wasn't at the helm of Caribbean Dreams, Ganja Grant took charge. Ganja had a way with the charterers, especially the women. To many, he was their first encounter with the Virgin Islands, and Ganja loved to put on a broad native dialect. The outlandish print shirts and faded cutoffs were also part of his repertoire, as was Doxie—a parrot he'd picked up somewhere, which perched on his shoulder occasionally spouting, "Wow! She's a knockout!" No one would ever guess that the handsome black man, speaking the island patois, had been born and bred in Harlem.

The Chief handled the internal workings of the company, making sure that the boats were well stocked, manned, and shipshape. The Chief also had the authority—and ability—to procure whatever was necessary. With his contacts throughout the Caribbean (everyone, it seemed, had either served with the Chief or was indebted to him for some kindness), there was nothing the Chief couldn't supply, legal or illegal.

Kane still told the story of how several years back, when Caribbean Dreams was a fledgling company seeking financing, he had thrown a party aboard the *Wu Li* for a powerful Greek shipping magnate. The billionaire, a dour, colorless man, was known to be a terrific fan of an internationally famous film star. In the middle of the evening, the Chief showed up, resplendent in a tuxedo and escorting the dazzling, voluptuous beauty. Kane had spent the rest of the night speechless and gaping. The terms of the loan were drawn up most favorably to Kane, since the Greek couldn't be bothered by such trifles while in the company of the glamour goddess he'd always worshiped from afar.

Later, a dazed Kane, holding the check in his hand, asked the Chief how he was able to pull off such a coup.

Typically, the Chief made light of it. "I was a friend of her fourth husband way back when. We did some sailing and ballooning together. I try to stay in touch with the lady, Skip, but the fact is, I'm too busy to be writing and taking her phone calls all the time."

Now Ganja and the Chief were at their customary table at the Rainbow Keg. Mike Mulhaney, worried about his missing friend and more than usually unhappy with the way the Chief was preparing lunch, was in the kitchen, swearing up a storm and forgoing his usual midmorning snack.

Ganja was practicing his island accent, telling the Chief of the problem he was having with a landlubber who had tried to convince Ganja that he could bareboat one of the yachts with only his wife as crew.

"No matter what I tell the mon, he don' want to take

140

no for an answer. He offer me one thousand dollars to look the other way. I say, 'No way, mon! This boat cost a quarter-million dollars, and I won't leave it in the hands of an inexperienced captain.' Then he want to show me how good he is. I tell him to turn starboard, and he goes in the other direction. I tell him to make a turn to port, and he turns starboard. I say, 'What you doin', mon?' You know what he tells me? 'Oh, I forgot this was a wheel. I'm used to a tiller.' "

The Chief threw his head back and roared.

"I don't understand the people a'tall."

Ganja took a sip from his Coke. He never touched an alcoholic beverage, preferring to indulge in the local "herbs."

"You had it easy," the Chief told him. "I had to deal with Weaver. The bastard wanted to know where Mason was. I told him that he went with the skipper on a fishing expedition. Weaver chewed me out, but good— said we're *all* supposed to be protecting him."

Ganja shook his head. "Lord! If that man finds out Mason is out by hisself, beatin' the bushes for his old flame . . ."

"He better not find out, or we're going to have Bluebeard and Long John Silver mixing drinks for our North American tourist friends."

The Chief turned serious as he asked, "Did the skipper call in this morning?"

"He stayed overnight on the *Delphi* at St. John's. He told me he ran into some trouble that he didn't want to talk about over the radio."

"Is Michelle all right?" the Chief asked anxiously.

"Yeah, she's cool, but a little shook-up. We can't mention anything to Mike, though."

"Watch it!" Chief whispered. "Here he comes."

Mulhaney strode out of the kitchen, wearing a white apron around his ample middle, with a beer in his hand

141

and a darkly threatening scowl on his face.

He glowered at both men. "*You* did some cooking, Chief. You tell me what goes into a good tomato sauce!"

The Chief thought it over. "Tomatoes, tomato paste, onions, garlic, olive oil, oregano, basil, parsley, a little sugar—"

"What about the potato?"

"What potato?"

"Hell, man! You've got to put in a potato to soak up the acid," Mike bellowed.

"I never heard of that. You're thinking of cabbage. You put in a potato to take away the *smell*."

"You moron! You're just as stupid as Cookie. You put in an *apple* with cabbage!" Mike fumed.

"Don't tell *me*! *Sugar* cuts the tomato acid, and a potato takes out the smell of cabbage," the Chief told him, beginning to get angry.

"You don't know what the hell you're talking about!"

"*You* don't know what *you're* talking about, you white-bearded, pot-bellied, tea-sippin' fool!" the Chief raged.

"*Tea-sippin'*? I never sipped tea in my life, you skin-headed, bloated piece of driftwood!"

"What did they serve you over at Limey House—beer and pretzels?"

"Hell, man they wouldn't invite *you* to Windsor House because you ain't got a damn ounce of class," Mike sneered.

"You're right! That's why I hang out at this god-forsaken bar—where, I might add, the tomato sauce STINKS, and I know why! What fool would ever put a potato in tomato sauce?"

"That's it!" Mike shouted. "That does it. OUT! Get out of my place now, Bukowski. Get out before I throw you out!"

Bukowski rose and stood eye to eye with Mike. "You'd

need the Seventh Fleet to help you throw me out. But I'll go on my own. I'll take my business elsewhere."

"You do that!"

Ganja grabbed at both of them. "Hey, guys, mellow out, okay? You're both acting like a couple of old fools! We have more important stuff going down."

"Who asked you?" the Chief said.

"Yeah, and what's so important?" Mike asked belligerently.

Ganja was looking past them. "What's important is the man who just walked in the door."

They turned to stare at Alan Mason, who stood in the doorway, smiling sheepishly.

Michelle awoke with a start. She gingerly lifted her head, and then dropped it back onto the pillow as the room started to spin. She felt nauseated and thought she was going to vomit, but that passed quickly. In its wake came a dull, throbbing headache.

She took several deep breaths, then looked around her. She recognized the bright, cheery stateroom of the *Delphi*, and the memories come flooding back. . . .

Ernesto and Sparky Suarez were tossing her into the backseat of their car. Ernesto put his hand on her breast, and she tried to bite him. He had slapped her hard, and the next thing she knew, he was taking out a bottle from the glove compartment and pouring drops of some liquid onto a handkerchief. She had tried to turn her head away, but Ernesto grabbed the nape of her neck and eventually covered her mouth and nose with the handkerchief. Michelle knew she was being drugged. She felt herself losing consciousness no matter how hard she tried to stay awake. Finally, she gave in and sank into the warm whirlpool of darkness.

What was she doing on the *Delphi*? Had Ernesto and Sparky killed Kane and taken over the boat? she wondered, suddenly terrified.

Groggily, she made her way to the porthole and looked out. They were still moored at St. John's. She tried the door, fully expecting it to be locked. It wasn't. Her faculties were returning ever so slowly. It took her a few minutes to realize that she had been stripped to her panties. She looked around for her blouse and jeans, but there was nothing in the room.

Had they raped her when she was out cold? She didn't feel any different. God, if she became pregnant by those animals she would kill herself! *Take it easy*, Michelle thought. *Just get hold of yourself. If you'd been raped, you'd know it, all right*. It was morning, which meant that she had slept through the night; at least, she *hoped* it had been only one night.

She opened the door cautiously and looked down the hall. She smelled food—pancakes—and realized then she was starving. Whoever was in the galley was whistlng. When she heard the door of the galley open, she pulled back and frantically searched the room for some kind of weapon. The only thing she could think of was the lamp. She unplugged it and waited by the door, hardly breathing, the lamp raised over her head.

But when the man stepped through the doorway, it wasn't Sparky or Ernesto. It was Ben Kane, holding a tray on which was a plate heaped high with steaming pancakes.

"Oh, Ben!" she gasped in relief.

He turned, saw her standing there holding the lamp, and chuckled. "Come on, Michelle. You haven't even tasted my cooking and you're ready to clobber me."

"I thought . . . I was afraid you were Sparky or Ernesto." Michelle was beginning to recover. "Hey, where are my damn clothes!"

"Being dried after a good washing. You think you can dig into this while I get us some coffee?"

Michelle nodded, set the tray down on the bed, and started eating voraciously.

Ben came back carrying two steaming mugs. "How're you feeling?" he asked as he sat down on the bed beside her.

"I had a throbbing headache, but maybe I was just hungry. I feel better now. Your pancakes aren't so bad, Kane."

Ben grinned. "Thanks."

"So what the hell happened?" Michelle asked. The last thing I remember was that Jimmy character walking toward the cabin with a can of kerosene. I think I missed all the good parts. What happened to Brand?"

Ben filled her in as he helped her polish off the pancakes. Michelle shook her head a couple of times, as if she couldn't believe what Kane was telling her. When he described how he'd shot Jimmy, she responded with an emphatic, "Good!"

Then she sighed. "You know, I thank I'm glad I was out cold. I don't think I could have handled it."

"You would have been worried about me, huh?"

"Yeah," she said reluctantly, "a little. I wish you and Henry had captured those Suarez scumbags. Do you think the police might have picked them up?"

"No," Kane said, staring into the wafting steam of his coffee. One day soon, there would be a day of reckoning when he would deal with Ernesto and Sparky.

After a moment's silence, Michelle said, "You know what I found very strange?"

"Yes, I do know, because I haven't stopped thinking about it either. If Ernesto and Sparky had never heard of Mason, why were they looking for Christine Elvey? Of what importance could an elderly artist be to two gangsters from St. Thomas?"

"Maybe they were lying," Michelle suggested.

"I doubt it. I don't think Sparky has the brains to lie

so convincingly."

"Then maybe it was just a coincidence that they were looking for her at the same time we were."

"That's some coincidence!" Kane said.

Michelle finished off the last pancake and leaned back on the bed. "Now what do we do?"

"The second thing we do is get in touch with the post office and see if there's a forwarding address for Christine Elvey. The only mail around was postmarked three weeks ago, so that means whatever came in afterward was picked up for her, or was sent to another address."

"Maybe no one sent her anything in the past three weeks.

"In this day of junk mail? Highly unlikely."

Michelle made a face. "You said that was the *second* thing we had to do. What's the first?"

Kane gazed at her, half-sitting, half-reclining on the bed. She understood that look in his eye. Until that moment, Michelle had completely forgotten that she was almost naked. Their conversation had been so absorbing that neither had thought about anything else. Now Kane was reminding her in no uncertain terms that she was dealing with a man . . . a man who was ready to take care of their unfinished business. She felt a hot flush spread from her hairline down to her naked breasts, and her breathing got shallower.

Kane leaned over and took her chin in his hand. He moved her face close to his and kissed her passionately. His hand moved to her hand and then to the nape of her neck. She entwined her arms around his neck and kissed him again, more deeply, rubbing her bare breasts against his shirt. Suddenly she was burning with desire.

Kane moved his hands over her body and felt her shiver in expectation.

"God, you're setting me on fire," she moaned.

He paid special attention to her breasts and the ripe cherries that were her nipples. When he put his lips to her taut buds, she laced her fingers behind his neck and pressed his head down harder.

"Bite them, Ben," she gasped. "Hurt me a little!"

His hands moved to the bikini panties, and she raised her hips as he slipped them off her long, shapely legs. Then he stood and took off his jeans and shorts.

Michelle reached out and caressed his throbbing erection.

"Please, Ben," she whispered. "Please, I can't wait."

The moment he entered her, she climaxed. He had to hold on to her squirming body as she reached peak after peak. He began to move with her then. She covered his face, neck, and chest with tiny butterfly kisses as she told him how wonderful he was making her feel. He exploded finally, and she joined him in one more orgasm that left them both exhausted. Then they started all over again.

Later, Ben made several calls to different friends on St. John's until he found one who had the clout to get him the information he needed. Christine Elvey's address had been changed. Kane wrote down the name of the place where her mail was being forwarded—the Caribe Beach Nursing Home and Rehabilitation Center of St. Thomas.

The crackle of the radio broke into his thoughts.

"Skipper, this is Ganja."

"Yes, Ganja, go ahead."

"The big fish has just wandered back into the net," Ganja said cryptically, knowing that the airwaves could very well be monitored.

"That's interesting. Is he in one piece?"

"Absolutely. Plus, we got a promise that there'll be no more foolishness," Ganja told him.

"Ganja, I want you and the Chief to bring the *Wu Li*

over to St. Thomas. Bring Miles, too."

"Will do, Skip."

"And you can tell the big fish that we might have found what he's been looking for," Kane added.

"Hey, that's cool. That oughta perk him up. He's been looking a little green around the gills."

Alan Mason stood on the deck of the *Wu Li* and watched the Chief and Ganja handle the big sailing craft as if it were a toy. They had made the trip from Barracuda Reef to St. Thomas and now were docking to await further instructions from Kane.

Mason noticed that wherever he went on board, the thin, morose man called Miles was close at hand. It was obvious he was shadowing Alan, but in a most unobtrusive way. Mason guessed that Kane was determined not to let him go off by himself again—not even to the head.

"Alan, how are you doing?" Mike Mulhaney asked genially as he approached.

Mike was wearing white deck pants and a striped polo, and he looked more than ever like a sun-bronzed Hemingway.

Mason grinned. "I'm excited, Mike. It's been over twenty years, but I feel like a kid waiting for his first date. Kane *did* say he knows where she is, didn't he? He *was* talking about Christine, wasn't he?"

"Sounds like it to me, Alan." Mike turned away and leaned over the rail.

Mason noticed that he was staring off over the water, lost in thought.

"What's wrong, Mike? There's something on your mind. Something that you're not telling me."

"No, not really . . ."

"Come on, old buddy. Out with it."

Mike hesitated, then said, "Alan we hadn't seen each other for a long time and yet when we met again, I felt the

148

years pass away. I looked at you and saw my old shipmate who'd stood on a burning deck with me while all hell was breaking loose. We stared Death right in the face."

Mason smiled. "We made the bastard blink, too, didn't we?"

"Aye, that we did! What I'm getting at is that it might not be the same for you and your lady. You were the one who said it, Alan—about how it was twenty years ago. A lot of things happen to a person in that length of time. People's looks change. Hell, man, if I put on my dress whites today, they'd fit on my arm. I just don't want you to get your hopes up too high."

"I know. I understand your concern, and I appreciate it, believe me."

"Let's face the facts, Alan. She could have gotten in touch with you at any time. *You* weren't the one who disappeared. She could have let you talk to your daughter."

"Mike, I know what you're saying to me, and don't think the thought hasn't crossed my mind. The one thing you don't get much of when you're a senator is candor. I'm glad you've told me what you think. The way I look at it now, though, is just the opposite. If she *didn't* still love me, then it wouldn't have been important to her to keep the secret of our daughter and of our affair. No, Mike. By continuing for twenty years to protect my name and my political career, she's telling me that she never stopped caring."

Mike shrugged. "I hope you're right, Alan."

"I know I'm right!"

The two men leaned over the rail side by side and looked down at the harbor water slapping gently against the sides of the *Wu Li*. Alan glanced around for a moment and caught a glimpse of Miles just out of hearing range doing something to one of the sails.

"I thought the Secret Service guys were thorough,

but this is ridiculous," Mason joked. "I can't go to the bathroom without Miles handing me some toilet paper."

Mike laughed. "Think of him as a security blanket. That guy knows three hundred and fifty ways to kill a man, most of them with his bare hands and not too pretty. With Miles watching over you, you can rest easy."

"I wonder if he's there to protect *me*, or to protect Kane's interests," Mason said thoughtfully.

"In this case, they're one and the same," Mike assured him.

The two men shared a quiet moment. Mike was deep in thought about the only woman he'd ever loved, whom he had lost to death . . . Janine. He thought of her often in his lonely room on the second floor of the Rainbow Keg. He would have liked her to see what had become of their "little investment" and how the chubby tyke in braids, Michelle, had turned into a lovely woman . . . like her mother. He understood perfectly how Mason felt. There had been other women in Mike's life— he certainly was no monk—but no one could ever compete with the ghost of the beautiful Janine. . . .

Mason broke into his thoughts. "What do we do now, Mike? Just wait here until Ben Kane summons us?"

"You got it, Alan. And let me tell you, there are worse things than being marooned on the *Wu Li*. You've got every convenience you could think of on board— and don't tell him I told you so, but the Chief really does know his way around the galley."

"You know how I feel, Mike? It's like going into battle. If Kane really has a line on Christine, I'd like to know about it and get it over with."

150

CHAPTER 16

It would have been easier to take the ferry from St. John's to Red Hook Bay but that wasn't an option for Kane. What used to be Lagoon Harbor was now the American Yacht Harbor, and Kane swore he would not in any way contribute to that harbor's coffers by riding the ferry. The American Yacht Harbor charged what Kane considered to be an exorbitant landing fee. He called them "money gougers," who anchored yachts halfway across Pillsbury Sound. Since it was difficult to anchor without paying a king's ransom, many boat owners simply took the ferry. It seemed like a good solution until Kane found out that a certain percentage of ferry revenues went to the American Yacht Harbor.

Kane chose to take the *Delphi* into St. Thomas

harbor. He saved himself a beat to windward by passing inside Rupert Rock and around the west side of the West Indian dock. There was still the unlit buoy on the western end of Lindbergh Bay, which marked the shoal area north of Red Point.

He arrived in the West Gregerie channel and stayed north of the red flasher at Sandy Point. Kane knew that many boats had experienced serious trouble by passing on the wrong side of the marker. He entered on the eastern side of Haulover Cut, practically kissing the reef, and around the point of Hassel Island. Kane and Michelle both kept a sharp lookout for seaplanes because they, too, docked at St. Thomas Harbor. They used the same Haulover Cut, and no one had yet figured out who had the right of way in the water—boats or planes.

Most of Kane's customers insisted on making at least one stop at the Free Port of St. Thomas. Charlotte Amalie, the capitol of the U.S. Virgin Islands, was universally known as St. Thomas. The term "free port" was in Kane's view a blatant misnomer. The shops were dazzling, all right, with a selection of goods that could keep one busy shopping for weeks on end, but there was a 6-percent overall duty on everything that came in. In addition, there was an excise tax on goods from the States, plus a nonreceipts tax, and local taxes. It was common knowledge among the islanders that all these levies added more to the price than the standard U.S. duty. Let the customer beware, Kane often thought, if the seller passed on his costs to the unwary buyer.

At any rate, the island had undergone almost miraculous changes. The ramshackle slums of St. Thomas had been replaced by pleasant modern buildings, and upwardly mobile West Indians lived in quaint wooden homes flanked by gardens and American cars.

It was hard to believe that there had been a time not

too long ago when native women would carry one-hundred-pound baskets of coal on their heads and be paid a penny a bag for their labor. There was still a large disparity between the rich and the poor, however, in a place where luxuries were relatively cheap and essentials expensive.

After he had docked the *Delphi,* Kane and Michelle walked three blocks to Vimmelskrafts Gade and Back Street, which had been the site of many of the original slave markets. Today, the bustling streets were filled with natives hawking their goods in front of covered stalls.

Kane hailed a cab and got in after Michelle. American visitors to the island found it disconcerting that cars were driven on the left, British fashion, but Kane had gotten used to it long ago. Their driver, a slim black man without any teeth, gummed a smile and nodded his head when they asked him if he had ever heard of the Caribe Beach Nursing Home. He drove, with frequent bone-jolting stops and much cursing, out of the main area of the city to a suburban section and stopped in front of a well-manicured garden that lay like a lush carpet before a large old Dutch mansion. The brass sign hanging on the mahogany front door confirmed that they had indeed come to the right place.

Kane paid the driver, who mumbled an incoherent "thank you." Between the man's lack of teeth and his thick accent, it was almost impossible to understand a word he said.

There wasn't a bell, so Kane used the heavy cast-iron knocker. It made a dull, heavy *thunk*, but there was no sound of anyone moving inside the house. Kane looked up at the wide windows, which were well shaded from the hot sun. When the door suddenly opened, it gave Ben and Michelle a start.

The woman in the doorway was wearing a white

nurse's uniform and stood over six feet tall. She was probably in her thirties, Kane guessed, and had a long, narrow face with a pointed chin which seemed even more pronounced because of the severe way in which she wore her hair, pulled straight back in a spinsterish bun.

"Yes?"

Kane saw she was wearing a name tag: *Kerchee*.

"Miss Kerchee, my name is Ben Kane, and this is Michelle Mulhaney. We'd like to get some information about one of your patients . . . Christine Elvey."

"I see. You may come in."

Kane could see why he hadn't heard anything and had thought the place was empty. The mansion had Persian-style rugs on the walls, thick carpeting underfoot, and heavy drapes covering the windows that absorbed all sounds.

There were many people around, most of them in wheelchairs, some with walkers. Almost every person had a white-uniformed nurse in attendance. As he and Michelle walked down the long hallway, Kane could see that the old Dutch mansion had a large dining area, kitchen, and a library where a couple of very old people were reading while a nurse sat next to them crochetng.

They came to a door on which was a plaque that said ADMINISTRATION and followed Nurse Kerchee into an outer waiting room.

"Excuse me, please," she said and knocked on another door.

A male voice answered, "Come in," and the nurse stepped into the inner office.

They waited alone, looking at each other, then at the room around them.

Michelle turned to Kane. "This is quite a place. The ceilings look like they're about fifteen feet high. And did you notice the paintings in the hall?"

"No," Kane admitted. "I was looking at the people and thinking how quiet and subdued everythig is. It reminds me of a funeral home."

"You don't see many funeral homes with Van Goghs on the walls,"Michelle said in awe. "They look like originals, too. This place must cost big bucks."

The door opened to the inner office, and Miss Kerchee stepped out and smiled at them. When she smiled, her face softened and she seemed almost attractive.

"Dr. Van Rhijn will see you now," she said, standing by the door. She waited until they were inside then closed it behind her.

Kane and Michelle found themselves in a small room with one window, facing a cherub-faced, balding, middle-aged man hiding a good-sized paunch with an expensive, well-tailored, tropical-weight blue suit. He stood up from behind his desk to shake hands with them. He was short, with pudgy hands and a weak grip. Kane noticed that the desk was covered with papers, envelopes, and assorted clippings from newspapers and magazines.

"I'm Dr. Van Rhijn, the director of this residence. How may I help you?"

Looking at the man, Kane had anticipated some kind of European accent and was surprised to hear none.

"Dr. Van Rhijn, my name is Michelle Mulhaney—" Michelle began.

"Yes, I know. Joann Kerchee, my head of staff, told me. And you are Mr. Benjamin Kane, the owner of Caribbean Dreams, the charter boat people."

Kane looked at him in surprise. "How did you know that?"

Van Rhijn smiled and shrugged. "You see, I have almost nothing to do all day long, so I read. That is the luxury of having such a marvelous staff. I read everything about the islands and I also have what they call a

155

photographic memory. Anything I read, I retain. There was an article about you, Mr. Kane, in the *Island Yacht World* of March a year ago. It dealt with your *Wu Li*, a most unique vessel, and had photographs of the state-rooms and the galley." He proceeded to rattle off the *Wu Li*'s precise dimensions.

"Well, I'll be . . . " Kane said in amazement.

Smiling at Michelle, Van Rhijn went on, "You would probably be the daughter of Mr. Michael Mulhaney, who owns the Rainbow Keg Inn at Barracuda Reef, and who recently attended a dinner party at Windsor House on Tortola in honor of the arrival of his old friend, Senator Alan Mason. That was in the *Tortola News*."

"You're incredible!" Michelle said.

Kane wondered if the paper had mentioned anything about the attempt on Mason's life, and then realized that, with Weaver's connections, any article mentioning it would never have seen the light of print.

Van Rhijn made a waving gesture, "To tell you the truth, I'm a bit of a show-off, and it gives me pleasure to impress people. Aren't I terrible?" He chuckled to himself, holding his hand over his mouth like an embarrassed schoolboy.

"I think you've got every right to show off," Michelle told him, smiling.

"Well, I guess I could go on an American television quiz show and win a car or something. . . . Oh, dear, enough of me talking about me—why don't *you* folks talk about me? Only kidding!" He chuckled again. "Now, who was it Joann told me you were inquiring about?"

"Christine . . . You're kidding again, right?" Kane said.

"Yes, but I had you going." Van Rhijn started his now familiar chuckle. "Christine Elvey is a patient of ours. She was admitted fourteen days ago. May I ask what interest you might have in her?"

Kane thought about how much he ought to say. Van Rhijn seemed to have a screw or two loose in that computer brain of his.

"We'd like to be sure she's all right. We're acting, actually, for an old friend of hers, Alan Mason, who takes an interest in her welfare."

Van Rhijn nodded. "Ah, yes, the charismatic senator who's rumored to be a presidential hopeful. I see."

"Who pays for all this? It looks like very expensive care," Michelle said.

The cherub face turned red. "Well, I guess I do."

Michelle was puzzled. "I don't understand."

Van Rhijn leaned back in his chair, serious for once. "Well, you see, this mansion has been in my family for hundreds of years. My great, great grandfather was one of the most prosperous slave traders on the island. He grew rich on the misery of other human beings, and I learned to hate the Van Rhijn name. You see, I always had this gift for memory, and I could remember very distinctly everything that my father and grandfather told me even when I was very young about the old slavery days. It appalled me that people could be so cold and callous to the sufferings of others. I was determined to leave the islands as soon as I was old enough, because in my mind, I felt burning shame to be associated with the Van Rhijn name.

"Of course, others did not feel about it the way I did. I was rich, and nobody seemed to care where the money came from. In a way, that made me even sadder. I was determined to do something constructive with my life, and so I entered the field of medicine in order to be of help to mankind. I guess, in my small way, I was trying to atone for my ancestors' misdeeds. I achieved some success and I already had more money that I could ever need, so when my parents died, I moved back into this mansion and converted it into a home for the aged and infirm. I pay for everything, and I spend my time helping people and reading. A useful life, yes?"

"I think it's wonderful!" Michelle said.

Dr. Van Rhijn beamed.

"There must be a lot of people who need your help, Doctor. How do you choose?" Kane asked.

For the first time, the doctor's bright blue eyes clouded. "That is the difficult part. There are so many to help. I try to do something for those who have in the course of their lives made contributions to the betterment of others. That contribution might be in politics, or in medicine, or in the arts . . . like your Christine Elvey and her paintings. I think it is most sad when people who have given of themselves grow old and find that they're reduced to loneliness and obscurity, having nothing and no one. I feel these people should not have to suffer simply because the world has forgotten them, and I provide the means for them to live out their last years in dignity.

"I read my papers and magazines and come across names of people whom others have forgotten but I still remember. Those are the ones I invite to the Caribe Beach Home. Here is the article about Miss Elvey."

He handed Kane and Michelle a small clipping from the *St. John's Post.*

Worried neighbors who had not seen Miss Christine Elvey in over a week went to her home in Brathwaite Township and found the sixty-year-old artist unconscious. She was taken to French Town Hospital where she is in serious but stable condition.

"What was wrong with her?" Michelle asked him. "Is she all right now?"

"Well, she's out of danger, but . . ." The doctor stood up. "Why don't we go see her?"

Dr. Van Rhijn led the way from his office down another carpeted corridor to a rear doorway. As they walked, Kane could look into half-opened doors of patients' rooms. They were well appointed and clean. The staff seemed competent and caring and the patients, most of them very elderly, smiled and nodded to Van Rhijn as he passed.

He stopped for a moment in front of a gnarled old woman the color of ebony. Her hair was white and as wispy as a puff of cotton, but she walked by herself, although she was accompanied by a burly male nurse who watched her every step.

"We can't talk you into a wheelchair, can we, Miss Flowers?" Van Rhijn shouted, beaming.

The woman cupped her hand around her ear. She looked up and smiled, toothless, with wrinkled leathery skin. "No, sir! I can still get around by myself. Don't want to be an old lady."

"All right, then. Just go slowly so Walter, here, can keep up with you," Van Rhijn teased.

The old lady digested that, then cackled. She shook her head. "God bless you, Dr. Van Rhijn. God bless you."

"She's over a hundred and has such spunk," Van Rhijn told Kane and Michelle. "Do you recognize her?"

"No," they said in unison.

"She's Bernice Flowers, and for three years back in the twenties, she was installed as governor of the islands. There are some old buildings in Charlotte Amalie where you can see her name on the cornerstones. . . . Come, step outside." He opened a door that led to a broad terrace overlooking a garden. It reminded Kane of the one at Windsor House, but on a smaller scale. There were beds of colorful flowers, shade trees, and concrete benches along the walks. Van Rhijn led them to a quiet little grove set apart from the rest of the garden. Kane noticed that there was a stone wall that extended around the vegetation . . . either to keep strangers out, or to keep confused patients from wandering off.

A female nurse—a native light-skinned woman, with a name tag that said *Simmons*—was sitting on one of the concrete benches within the grove.

"How is she today?" Van Rhijn asked.

"'Bout the same," Simmons replied with a West Indian lilt.

At first Kane didn't see the person they were talking about because her brown smock blended in so completely with the bark of the tree she was standing next to.

Christine Elvey was in front of an easel, painting a scene of flowers and trees from a small section of the garden. She was of medium height, with thick, gray-streaked chestnut hair that cascaded down her back. It was a style better suited to a younger woman, but with her strong features and high cheekbones, it made her look very Bohemian.

They walked closer to her and stood behind, admiring her work. She dabbed on colors with quick short jabs of her brush, then paused to mix paints on her palette. Kane privately thought the painting was all right, but it was no different from many others he'd seen dozens of times before in galleries.

He decided that Christine Elvey was a competent and talented artist but hardly a genius. Her work wouldn't be worth the kind of money that would make Ernesto and Sparky interested in her.

Although Kane, the doctor, and Michelle were very close to her, Christine hadn't turned to look at them. At first Kane thought she was too involved with her work, but as he looked more closely at her face, the vacant expression told him otherwise. He also noticed that her left hand hung limply at her side.

"She's had a stroke?" he said to Dr. Van Rhijn.

"Yes—a cerebral incident. There is some slight paralysis, but unfortunately it extends further than that." He tapped Christine on the shoulder and for the first time, she seemed to realize that someone was there.

"Oh, hello," she said, turning large, dark eyes on her three visitors.

"Hello, Miss Elvey. How are you today?" Dr. Van Rhijn asked, taking her hand.

"I'm fine, thank you."

"Some friends of mine would like to meet you." He gestured to Kane and Michelle. "This is Mr. Kane and Miss Mulhaney."

Christine looked at them blankly, a hesitant, shy smile touching her lips.

"They know a friend of yours . . . Senator Alan Mason," the doctor prodded.

"I'm sorry, I don't know anyone of that name," said Christine.

"I see," Van Rhijn said, glancing at Ben and Michelle and putting a finger to his lips so they wouldn't say anything. He turned back to the artist. Do you remember me? I'm Dr. Van Rhijn."

"I'm very pleased to meet you, Doctor," she said politely.

"Judy, come over here, please. This is your nurse, Clara Simmons."

"Hello."

"Do you remember Clara, Miss Elvey?"

The woman smiled vaguely.

"No, I don't."

"I see. By any chance, do you know who I am?"

161

"No, sir."

"All right," Dr. Van Rhijn said pleasantly. "What a lovely painting."

"Thank you."

"We shan't disturb you any longer," he said. "Have a nice day."

Christine turned away and began applying her brush to the canvas once more.

Michelle and Ben followed Van Rhijn back to the mansion.

The doctor shook his head. "I've spoken to her everyday since she came here, and she still doesn't know me. Every time I say hello to her, it's like the first time. The stroke has affected her memory in such a way that she cannot retain anything. It's as if her mind is a slate that's wiped clean after a few seconds. If I were to go back with you now and introduce you two to her again, to her it would be the first time she had set eyes on you."

They walked down the hall into Dr. Van Rhijn's office.

"How is she able to paint, then?" Kane asked him. "She has to remember how to hold the brush, how to mix colors . . ."

Van Rhijn nodded. "It does seem contradictory, doesn't it? There are three parts of the brain that function in different ways. To put it in layman's terms, the reasoning part, which we call intelligence, is the so-called 'gray matter,' which includes the senses; then there is the part of the brain that controls emotion, and the other main area is the brain stem, which directs involuntary actions such as breathing, digestion, and so forth.

"In Christine's case, the right hemisphere of the brain has been affected by her stroke, and has caused partial paralysis on the left side. In addition, there has been damage to the cerebral cortex, which affects her memory as well as her emotions. That's why she has that vacant stare."

"But wait a second, Doctor," Michelle put in. "You haven't really answered Ben's question. If she can't remember from one moment to the next, how can she paint?"

"There are different kinds of memory, Miss Mulhaney. There's data matching, which occurs when you come across someone you've met before. Your brain classifies the face and matches it up with a name. A whole process takes place that enables you to recall details about that person—how many children he has; what he does for a living; whether you liked him or not the first time you met.

"Then there are memories that are triggered by senses other than sight. The smell of perfume or cologne, for example, might bring someone to mind who wore the same scent.

"There is also another type of memory that the body absorbs through repetition. Tying one's shoelaces might be an example of 'rote' memory. This type of memory usually has been patterned so deeply into the mind that it is very difficult to destroy. People with amnesia, for example, can't remember their own names, but they can still dress themselves, use appliances, etc. In Christine's case, she is able to paint a lovely picture, but if you asked her tomorrow what she had painted, she wouldn't remember anything about it."

"Amnesiacs occasionally get their memories back, I understand," Ben said. "Will Christine?"

"I don't know, Mr. Kane. We'll just have to wait and see. I've spent my life studying about the mind. I've tried to find out what enables me to remember tons of useless information. To tell you the truth, the more I know about it, the less I understand it. Medical science is practically in the Dark Ages when it comes to this kind of thing. There are certain medications which have been developed in an attempt to reverse memory loss but no one knows what the long-term side effects are, and I hesitate to experiment on Christine. As long as she isn't bothered by her loss, I see no reason not to sit back and let nature take its course before attempting any extraordinary measures."

"There's something we have to tell you, Doctor," Michelle said, looking at Ben.

Kane nodded.

"We have reason to believe that there are two men who want to harm Christine Elvey."

She told him about the Suarez brothers and how they had tracked Christine to the deserted cabin.

"What could possibly be the reason?" Dr. Van Rhijn wondered.

"We've been trying to figure that out, but we haven't gotten anywhere," Kane told him.

"Do you really think she's in danger?' the doctor asked.

"I'm not sure, but I have some ideas about keeping her under close surveillance, just in case."

"I'll be happy to cooperate with you," Van Rhijn told him.

Michelle touched Kane's arm.

"Ben, what about Alan?"

Dr. Van Rhijn tapped the desk with a fingernail. "Senator Mason, you said, is an old friend of Christine's. Hmmm. Sometimes when an amnesiac sees someone from the past, it jogs the memory."

"I was just going to ask you if it would be all right for him to visit Christine." Michelle looked at her watch. "They should be docking at St. Thomas harbor just about now."

"By all means, have him come. It certainly won't do

164

her any harm, and perhaps it will do some good," Van Rhijn said.

"I'm afraid I'm more worried about Alan's reaction than Christine's," Michelle said sadly.

An hour later, Alan Mason nervously paced the floor in Dr. Van Rhijn's office. His omnipresent shadow, Miles, was sitting in the anteroom. Michelle, Mike, and Ben looked on as Van Rhijn explained Christine's condition. Mason was very upset.

"Doctor, do you realize what you're telling me? I loved this woman. She's the mother of my child. . . ."

"Umm, Alan . . . "

"No, Mike! I don't care anymore who knows. That's how I lost them in the first place."

"Whatever you say is strictly confidential, Senator," Van Rhijn assured him.

"Dr. Van Rhijn, I've spent a quarter of a century searching for Christine, and now that I've found her I can't believe she won't even know who I am."

"We don't know that for sure. I just want to prepare you for the possibility."

"May I see her alone?" Mason asked finally, when he had controlled his emotions.

"No, I'm afraid not. You see, if she does begin to regain her memory, it might be very traumatic. It will be a shock for her, and I must insist I be there—even though I tell you quite frankly, I feel the chance is very slight for that to happen."

Mason sank into a chair and cradled his head in his hands. He took a deep breath to steady himself, then looked at his old friend, Mike Mulhaney. "This is a tough one, old buddy," he said.

"I know, mate. Do you want me to go with you?"

"No, I've got to do this alone. All right, Doc," he said, rising, "lead the way."

Once again, Dr. Van Rhijn led the way to the garden. Long shadows spread across the lawn and the wind was a bit stronger, coming from the west and foretelling a storm.

Christine was still working at her easel when Dr. Van Rhijn walked over to her.

"Christine, you have another visitor—an old friend of yours is here to see you," he said gently. Do you remember Alan Mason?

She turned and looked at him. There was a long pause, and then the empty smile. "Hello."

"Christine, it's me . . . Alan," he said, reaching out and touching her shoulder gently.

"I'm sorry, I don't believe we've ever met."

She turned back to her painting.

Clara Simmons came over to her. "Christine," she said in a soft, low voice, "it's time to go inside now. It's going to rain."

The doctor and Alan Mason watched in silence as Christine obediently gathered up her belongings and headed back to the house, followed by Nurse Simmons carrying the easel. Mason drew a long, shuddering breath and covered his eyes with his hands.

CHAPTER 17

Ernesto Suarez decided it was a good thing that the thunderstorm broke when it did. The drenching rain kept people indoors, and there was less chance of his being caught by a police patrol. They would probably be holed up in a warm, dry spot, sipping coffee.

He was wearing ranger "invader" gear—black shirt and pants, stocking cap, and gloves made out of frictionless garlon. The new material had also been used in making his shoes, which absorbed all sound and made him feel like a cat on the prowl. He carried two grenades on his utility belt; one pound of semptex (the Czech plastic explosive), two three-inch slabs of specially treated rubber which could bond to the garlon shoes or gloves and enable him to climb any flat surface or scale the side of a building, and, of course, the .32 caliber German-made Munzak with silencer.

A bolt of lightning lit up the night, and he could see the Caribe Beach Nursing Home momentarily illuminated against the inky sky. He waited by the rear garden wall, blending into the shadows. His specially made watch—three tiny pinpricks of light on a black surface (one for the hour, one for the minute, and a revolving second sweep)—showed one second before 2 A.M. As the two dots converged, an explosion even louder than the recent thunder shattered the night.

Earlier, Ernesto had placed some of the semptex on the hood of a car in front of the Caribe Beach mansion, setting the timer for two to create a diversion. With the sound of the explosion and the subsequent fire in front of the building, he moved quickly and silently as a cat.

He scaled the wall easily and landed inside the grounds. Stealthily, he hugged the side of the building until he reached the rear entrance. Lights on the second floor were going on as some of the mansion's inhabitants hurried to see what was happening outside the front windows.

Ernesto tried the door. It was locked and probably alarmed. He touched it lightly and found it was made of wood reinforced with a steel plate—child's play. He reached into his pocket and pulled out what looked like silver-colored video tape on a small spool, then bent down and stretched a piece of the tape the width of the door. It was self-adhesive and formed a horizontal line about two feet from the bottom. He tapped each end of the tape three times and turned away, covering his eyes. In seconds there was a swishing sound as the magnesium strip, hotter than the core of the sun, cut through the wood and steel. He counted to five slowly, then turned to look at the door. It was still in one piece, except for a smoking strip where it was clear that the

168

magnesium tape had been.

Ernesto nudged the bottom section of the door with his foot, and it fell forward, allowing him to crawl into the building easily. He lifted the slab of wood and steel and replaced it in the doorway, in the unlikely event that someone might come by and see it.

He was now in a dark hallway which led to a stairwell. The patients' rooms would be on the upper floors. Christine Elvey's room was on the second floor to the right of the staircase. The stairway was well lit by a light bulb over the first-floor door and another over the door leading the second floor.

In the distance Ernesto could hear the sirens of fire engines on their way to put out the diversionary car fire. He pulled out the Munzak, attached the silencer, and shot out the bulbs over both doors. They imploded. Because of the silencer, it was as if they had been crushed by an invisible hand. Ernesto shut his eyes, knowing that his retina would retain the image of the staircase for a few moments and he could use the image to "see" in the dark.

He climbed to the top of the stairs and felt around for the doorknob. He opened the door slightly and winced when he heard a squeaking sound. He reached into a pocket and brought out a small aerosol spray can which contained a silicone compound that Ernesto sprayed on the door's jamb and hinges. He tried opening it again. This time it moved easily, without a sound. It was good that he had taken the extra precaution. Not more than ten feet away, with his back to Ernesto, stood a male nurse. He had just come out of a room and was walking down the hall to a front window to see what the commotion was.

Ernesto hugged the wall and walked backwards toward Christine Elvey's room. If the nurse turned around, Ernesto would have to shoot him.

He approached the room next to Christine's then fell to the floor as the door opened. An elderly black woman with wispy white hair and a cane stepped into the hall. Ernesto leveled the gun and watched her eyes. He was barely two feet away from her—all she had to do was to look down, but she didn't see him. In the black garlon he was just a shadow in the old lady's imperfect field of vision. She tottered down the hallway to join the male nurse at the large bay window overlooking the scene outside.

Ernesto crawled the rest of the way to Christine Elvey's room. He straightened and quietly turned the doorknob. He heard a click as the door unlocked and he slowly opened it a crack. The lights were off, but he could make out a figure on the bed. She was lying with her back toward him, her long hair flowing over the pillow. A white sheet covered her body. Ernesto stepped into the room and closed the door behind him. She was sleeping peacefully.

He raised the gun and took aim. There were little puffing sounds as the bullets spewed out of the silenced Munzak. The body on the bed twitched as each bullet hit home. There was no sound from the woman, who had probably been killed by the first shot.

But Ernesto didn't take any chances. He fired five more bullets into her body before opening the door again and retreating into the hallway. The nurse and the old lady still had their backs to him as he made his silent way to the staircase.

He opened the door and stepped into the stairwell which, without lights, was pitch dark. He couldn't take a chance on tripping over something. Ernesto pulled off his stocking cap and switched on the miniature battery-powered miner's lamp that was strapped around his forehead. He found the railing of the staircase and started down. Everything had gone according to plan

. . . so far. The tiny light guided him almost to the bottom, and then he heard a noise. someone was outside the first floor door to the staircase. There was no place to hide.

"I'll just go up and see how everyone's doing on the second floor," he heard a male voice say.

"Okay, Dr. Van Rhijn. It looks like the fire is out."

"I know, Miss Kerchee. I just want to reassure any of the patients who may have been frightened by all the commotion."

Ernesto flattened himself against the wall, raised the Munzak, and waited. Whoever stepped through that doorway would be a dead man.

The door opened, and then, surprisingly, closed part way.

"Oh, Miss Kerchee, please thank the fire patrol for me, won't you?"

"Yes sir."

The door opened again; and someone stepped through. Ernesto could see him clearly outlined by the light that was coming from the first floor hall. He didn't bother to flip off the switch on his little light. The man would never have time to realize that he was there. After him, Ernesto might have to take care of this Miss Kerchee, if she were still standing near the door, blocking his escape route.

He lifted the gun, and a shot rang out. For a millisecond, Ernesto didn't know what had happened. Why hadn't the silencer on the Munzak worked? The sound of the shot was reverberating in waves, deafening in the enclosed stairwell. Strange—he didn't even think he had pulled the trigger. . . . Pain was spreading from the base of his spine upwards like a white-hot poker. He opened his mouth to scream and wondered why the floor was coming up to hit him in the face. . . .

Ben Kane was standing on the second-floor landing

next to Ganja Grant. "Sorry, Skip," Ganja said, "but if I didn't take him then, he would have gotten the doc."

Kane nodded. "I know. It's too bad, though. If we'd gotten him alive, we could have sweated him and found out why they wanted to kill Christine Elvey."

Van Rhijn seemed to be in shock as he stared down at Ernesto's body. "I had no idea . . . I just wanted to come up and see that the patients were all right. . . ."

"Well, if Ganja hadn't been here, that might have been you," Kane told him.

Suddenly the doctor's face paled even more.

"Is Miss Elvey . . . Did he shoot Miss Elvey?"

"No, man. He put some holes in your sheets and pillows, and I think maybe he ruined a wig, but Miss Elvey is sleepin' like a log in another room," Ganja said.

"What are we going to do with him?" Dr. Van Rhijn asked the two men, indicating the body sprawled at their feet.

"Ganja will take care of Suarez," Kane said. "I'm going to—"

He didn't finish the sentence.

The door of the bottom landing burst open, and two men dressed in battle fatigues and carrying Uzi machine guns stormed into the small space.

"No one move. Everybody stay nice and loose. Drop that pistol, mister," one of them said to Ganja. "You too, Mac," he added to Kane. "You got any weapons on you, I want to see 'em."

The black man dropped his pistol. Kane reached into his ankle holster and placed his .9mm MAB on the floor next to Ganja's colt, cursing under his breath.

"I demand to know who you people are!" Dr. Van Rhijn said.

"I can answer that, Doctor." A tall, slim man in a white suit materialized in the doorway, every short

172

blond hair standing at attention.

"Weaver!" Kane said.

"You got it, ol buddy," Weaver replied cheerfully. "I work for the United States government, Dr. Van Rhijn." To the two goons, he added, "You can put the guns away for now, boys. Ganja Grant and Ben Kane are worth a lot more to us alive."

"I love your compliments, Weaver," Kane said acidly, picking up his gun.

"The man has a genuine talent for making you feel wanted," Ganja agreed.

"My men will help you dispose of this mess," Weaver said, looking down at Ernesto's body. "Kane, I want to see you in my Ultratech office in one hour."

"I've got things to do—" Kane began but Weaver cut him off. "Don't give me a hard time, fella. And remember, I don't like to be kept waiting. I also know how to turn the screws on you, you may recall."

He gave a mock salute and walked away.

Kane glared after him.

"You going, Skip?" Ganja asked.

Kane shrugged. "Yeah. Maybe I can pick Weaver's brain for once instead of the other way around. There are so many things here that don't add up." Kane thought for a moment. "I want you to get Chief and Miles and meet in front of the Ultratech building in Charlotte Amalie in an hour and a half. Get out the heavy artillery I have stored in the false-bottom chest— I want everybody loaded for bear." Ben spoke grimly.

Ganja nodded. "You got something in mind?"

"It's time we paid a visit to our friend, Sparky Suarez, in that gambling club of his. I want to give him the message personally about his poor dead brother."

Ganja smiled ferociously. "That sounds like fun, Skipper. I think Miles is getting tired of playing nurse-maid to Mason."

173

"Tell Mike to stay with Mason and bird-dog him until we get back. I'll see you later."

Seated at her desk in Ultratech's ultra-modern outer office, Suzy gave Kane a big smile and told him it was good to see him again. She had been Weaver's secretary as long as Kane had known him. An attractive woman of about forty, Suzy had long black hair that she usually wore in a tight bun. Big baby-blue eyes peered through tortoiseshell glasses that made her look efficient but didn't take away a certain sensuality that Kane found very stimulating. He had never made a move on Suzy—yet. It never seemed to be the right time, but some-day . . .

"Follow me, Mr. Kane," Suzy said, fluttering her eyelashes as she stood up.

"Anywhere," he told her.

She was wearing an Anne Klein silk blouse tucked into a tailored skirt. Both showed off her assets to best advantage. She had a very provocative walk, Kane decided. He wondered if Weaver and Suzy had ever gotten it on.

Kane knew Weaver had a number of offices in and around the Virgin Islands. Some of them, like Ultra-tech, were out in the open and known to the public. Others were in secret locations and known only to a few. Kane had once been blindfolded and taken by chopper to meet with Weaver. He was put in an elevator and seemed to descend hundreds of feet before the car stopped. Weaver's subterranean office had been one of the most luxurious Kane had ever seen.

The office located near Government House on Char-lotte Amalie was also luxurious, but not on the same scale as the other. The walls were paneled in dark, polished wood. There was a bank of video monitors on one wall and on another were two subtly lit electronic maps. One was a straightforward map of the Virgins; the other was a huge map of the world, broken up into various shades, from deep blue for the United States, Britain, and Canada, to lighter tones of blue for France, Italy, Germany, and Japan. The Soviet Union was a deep crimson, with its satellites different hues of red and pink. In the Middle East there was one island of blue—Israel—in a sea of pink. And in the Western Hemisphere, Cuba stood out with its deep red compared to its surroundings.

The Ultratech office was decorated in black and gray, with low-key recessed lighting—very high tech, very post modern. The carpeting was plush, practically ankle deep, and a cool shade of gray, with the seal of Ultratech—a large *U* over a *T* flanked by lightning bolts—in the center.

There were a couple of black desks in the room. The one directly opposite the entrance door was a very large U-shape. There were three large cast-iron elephants on the desk. Kane had noticed elephants in the outer office, too. Did that mean that Weaver collected the large mammals, Kane often wondered, or that he was a Republican?

On the left leg of the U-shaped desk were piled books, reports, containers of pens and pencils, legal-sized yellow pads, and in a prominent position, an autographed picture of Ronald Reagan and the First Lady in a dazzling chrome frame, which said: "To Weaver—Always the best, Ron and Nancy." They were in sailing clothes, and the President was standing next to a swordfish on the deck of a sleek yacht.

On the right leg of the *U*, Weaver had a Wang word processor, a large closed-circuit TV which was switched off at the moment, and an IBM computer.

Behind the desk hung floor-to-ceiling velvet drapes of a dark reddish purple, which Kane couldn't help thinking looked like the color of dried blood. He wondered if there was anything hidden behind the drapes. They resembled stage curtains covering up some elaborate mechanism.

Weaver's swivel chair was upholstered in black leather. There was a matching black-leather couch in front of the desk, and a smaller black-leather chair that Kane now sat on.

Weaver entered the room and handed Kane a glass filled with orange liquid. He was smiling broadly—always the perfect host.

"Screwdriver," he said. Made with Absolut vodka. That's your drink, right?" Kane accepted the glass without comment.

"Best screwdriver in the islands," Weaver continued. "Fresh-squeezed orange juice—none of that frozen concentrate crap. What are you staring at it for, Kane? Why don't you try it?"

"I'm not sure it isn't drugged," Kane growled.

"Drugged?" Weaver looked genuinely surprised. "What's wrong with you, ol' buddy? You gettin' paranoid on me? Why would the bartender in the commissary want to drug you?"

"Not him, Weaver . . . YOU."

"Me! Kane, how many oars do you have in the water? You're my best man. I depend on you, you know that. Why in the world would I want to hurt you? You're my friend, my pal, my ol' buddy. . . ."

Butter could melt in Weaver's mouth. Kane sneered. "With friends like you—you fill in the blank."

Weaver sighed. "Time out, old man." He held up his hand. "Look, Kane, I'm not running a popularity contest here. This is still a war. I'm not saying I have all the answers, but I try. Maybe you don't like my methods, but I do get results, buddy-boy. That's what our Uncle is paying me to do—get results!"

"No matter who or what gets in your way?"

"C'mon, Ben. Today, your ox is being gored. Tomorrow it will be someone else's. I can't afford to lose sight of the big picture. That's why that map is there for me to look at every time I raise my head. It's my job to see that our little enclave here doesn't show up on that map as part of the red tide. I want your help, Kane. I need you and your men on my team. I just wish you really understood how I feel about you guys." His voice dripped with sincerity.

"I understand, all right," Kane said, "but I don't like it. And I don't like you, either."

Ben reached into his pocket and pulled out a cigar. He started to undo the cellophane wrapper.

"Please don't smoke here. The smell stays in the carpet and drapes. Bad for my asthma," Weaver explained.

"Tough!" Kane lit the cigar.

Weaver shrugged wearily. "Okay then, smoke. The things I put up with in the line of duty . . ."

Kane wondered what Weaver's reaction would be if he knew the cigar was Cuban.

Weaver coughed ostentatiously several times, then sat behind his desk. "I have some things to ask you, Kane, and I would like some straight answers."

"No problem, if you agree to return the favor."

"All right, agreed." Weaver leaned back in his chair. "I had the feeling that something had happened to Mason. That's why I had the *Wu Li* followed, and that's what led me to the Caribe Beach Nursing Home. I followed you and Ganja. Was I right?"

"Mason is aboard the *Wu Li*, safe and sound," Kane told him. "How come you haven't had your men following us all along as a backup to protect the senator?"

"I was expressly prohibited from doing that by my superiors. Mason felt it was a waste of the taxpayers' money to have him under surveillance. *C'est la vie.*" Weaver sighed, then went on, "Now, tell me—who was this man that was killed tonight?"

"His name is Ernesto Suarez. I thought he was after Mason, but he actually wanted to kill a patient at the nursing home—an artist by the name of Christine Elvey."

"Why?"

"You got me," Ben admitted.

"What's the connection between Elvey and Mason?"

Kane debated with himself whether to tell Weaver about Mason's earlier relationship with the artist. He remembered Mason telling Van Rhijn that at this point he didn't care who knew about it. If Weaver could help save Christine from more attempts on her life, Kane was sure Mason wouldn't object.

So he divulged all he knew about the twenty-five-year-old affair. Weaver made notes on one of his legal pads.

"You assumed that these Suarez people were trying to get to Elvey in order to flush out Mason?" Weaver asked.

"That's what I thought . . . until tonight. When Ernesto tried to kill her, I had to assume that whatever these guys had against her had nothing to do with Mason. When you're angling for a big fish, you don't destroy the bait."

Weaver nodded. "Don't rule out revenge, though, Ben. Mason has stepped on a lot of communist toes. Look at it this way—not being able to kill Mason, they did the next best thing . . . killed someone he loves. That would be Gregor's style. What do you intend to do now?"

"I'm going to pay a visit to Suarez—the remaining Suarez, that is—and try to find the connection. I don't think it's as simple as you make it sound. And by the way, I can use some help on this one."

Weaver smiled.

"Sorry, Kane. That's not agency business. I've got to stay out of local affairs. I've already indirectly straightened out that business at the cabin at St. John's. The authorities won't pursue it any longer, but there's only so far they'll stick their necks out. I'll find a way to dispose of the gunmen's remains where they won't cause either of us any embarrassment."

"How did you know about that?" Kane wondered.

"Hank Brand has done some work for us on occasion," Weaver replied matter-of-factly.

Kane mulled that one over. Then he said, "Look, Weaver, just when do I get Mason out of my hair?"

"Fair question. We both would like to see him on his way. If Miss Elvey won't or can't help him locate his daughter, perhaps I can. That should help things along, and won't be in violation of any direct order. Of course, as long as Mason's here, there's always the chance that we can nab Gregor. Now *that* would be something to crow about!" Weaver's beady eyes positively glittered.

"Gregor is your business. Mine is running Caribbean Dreams," Kane snapped, getting to his feet.

"All right, Kane. You can go," Weaver said, with a wave of his hand. "I expect you to keep me informed."

"Don't hold your breath!" Ben replied. He looked around for an ashtray. Finding none, he nonchalantly ground out his cigar butt in the ear of the nearest elephant. "Have a nice day," he added. Before the door closed behind him, he had the satisfaction of seeing Weaver frantically trying to remove cigar ash from his prized possession, alternately dabbing it with a tissue and blowing at it. "Blow in her ear and she'll follow you anywhere," Kane said with a grin and stepped out of the office before Weaver could do more than turn an interesting shade of red.

CHAPTER 18

Michelle knocked on Alan Mason's stateroom door.

"Alan, it's Michelle. May I come in?"

"Yes, sure."

He opened the door and let her in. The sun was coming up over St. Thomas Harbor. Michelle knew that Alan hadn't slept all night, any more than she had. She had heard him pacing, and he was wearing the same clothes he had worn the night before. His eyes were puffy and red rimmed. "I heard you last night," she said. "I guess you couldn't fall asleep."

"No, I had a lot of thinking to do, and when I think, I like to walk around. I'm sorry if I disturbed you."

Michelle smiled. "That's okay. I've been up since the early hours myself."

"Is Ben back?"

"No. He took Miles, Chief, and Ganja over to Sparky Suarez's casino."

"Where?" Mason looked puzzled.

"Alan, sit down for a moment. We didn't want to burden you with this because of everything else that's happened. I mean, we all know how you feel about Christine, and when she didn't recognize you . . ."

Michelle sighed. Alan patted her hand and waited for her to continue.

"Alan, it looks like someone has been trying to kill her. Last night, a man named Ernesto Suarez tried to murder Christine at the nursing home."

"Oh, my God!" Mason's eyes widened in horror.

"Take it easy, she's all right. Ben and Ganja were there and they took care of everything. Suarez was killed, but Christine was safe in another room. This same Suarez and his brother, Sparky, were up at Christine's cabin in St. John's looking for her."

"But why?"

"That's what we'd like to know. Think about it, Alan. Is there any reason why someone would want Christine dead?"

Mason shook his head in utter bewilderment. "Michelle, I honestly haven't a clue. Of course, I don't know what she's been doing over the last twenty years, but I have no idea why anyone would want to hurt her. When I knew her, she was the most gentle and saintly woman I've ever met. I can't imagine anyone wanting to do her harm."

"Could it be some kind of vengeance against you? Have you gotten any threats? Any warning? Aside from Gregor, that is."

"Yes, I get threats all the time. Any official in the public eye receives threats, but they usually don't mean anything. I only took this Gregor business seriously because of my work on the Intelligence Committee.

Besides, if an enemy knew of my earlier relationship with Christine, wouldn't it serve their purposes better to kidnap her and use her as a bargaining chip? Why would they want to kill her?"

Michelle sighed. "I don't know. Maybe that's what Ben and the others will find out when they question Sparky Suarez. And there's another thing, Alan. We're trying to figure out how Ernesto Suarez knew Christine's whereabouts. I know you were on the phone yesterday. Did you mention it to anybody?"

Mason thought about it. "Yes. I called several specialists on strokes and memory loss. I wanted to be sure that Christine was getting the best care possible. I must have talked to ten or fifteen people asking them what they thought of Van Rhijn and his clinic."

"That explains it, then. The phones work on open radio frequencies. It's easy to listen in."

"You mean *I* put Christine's life in danger?" Mason asked, appalled.

"You couldn't have known. The important thing is that she's all right. How are *you* doing?" Michelle asked.

Alan sighed deeply. "I'll be okay. It was a terrible shock to me, seeing Christine like that. I thought yesterday was going to be one of the happiest days of my life. I had this fantasy about seeing Chris, and her throwing her arms around me as if the years hadn't passed at all. We'd go together to see Alana and I'd have a chance to make up some of the time I've lost." He covered his eyes with his hands. "I came so close . . . so close! If only I'd arrived a few weeks earlier."

Michelle watched him sympathetically, wishing she could be more helpful. To change the subject, she said, "Alan, what did those experts tell you about Dr. Van Rhijn?"

He pulled himself together. "They said he's one of the best in the field, and I should leave her where she is."

"Well, then, you now know for sure that she is getting the best possible care. Dr. Van Rhijn told us that patients who've had this type of stroke often regain their memories in time."

"I know that—it's what keeps me going. But Christine's my only chance to find Alana, and how much longer can I wait? I've had private detectives looking into her whereabouts, but I've never gotten one solid lead."

His expression suddenly changed. "Michelle, I think I should get Christine out of there. Now that those killers know where she is, they can come back."

"Don't worry. Ben spoke to the Marshal of the Virgin Islands. His name's Gordon—you met him at Windsor House. He's giving her around-the-clock protection."

"Thank God!"

"Look, why don't you try to get some sleep? As soon as Ben calls, I'll tell you what happened."

Mason nodded wearily. "I guess you're right. I'm not much good to anyone like this."

Chief Bukowski was driving a nondescript Ford van with "Armour Plumbing" painted on the side. Miles, Ben Kane, and Ganja Grant sat in the back and talked quietly among themselves. Each man carried modified M16s along with their regular weapons. They all carried three grenades apiece, while the Chief and Ben carried tear-gas cannisters in addition to their grenades.

It was still dark when they arrived in front of Slocum's, the cheap gin mill that fronted for the casino downstairs.

"We rush 'em, Skip?" Bukowski asked.

Kane thought about the narrow staircase and the dozens of innocent, well-dressed people who might be caught in the cross fire. The casino would be closing with the first rays of dawn.

"Let's wait them out. We'll have a better shot at taking Sparky alive if we can catch him outside."

They parked in such a way that they could see both the front and side exits of the building. For a half hour there was no movement. Then a couple who had obviously spent the night gambling (he was counting out a wad of bills) stepped out of the door.

Chief poured coffee from a thermos into Styrofoam cups. The hot, black coffee was a good idea. Kane felt the caffeine giving him a lift. Ganja refused the coffee and fished into his pocket for some "weed." Miles made a face as Ganja lit up, but didn't say anything. Kane knew that when Ganja smoked his namesake it seemed to sharpen his senses. His eyes might droop and his jaw might slacken, but the herb also seemed to turn Grant into a human killing machine, totally at one with his body and the universe.

"Look who just came out!" Bukowski said suddenly.

At first, Kane thought it was Sparky. He saw the tall, big-chested black man step out of the doorway and onto the street. The man looked at the sky as if to check the weather, and then walked slowly down the block.

"That was one of Sparky's goons, wasn't it?" Miles asked in his usual dull monotone.

"Damn right it was! That was one of the two guys who looked like bookends that you sat down at the table while I played out the hand. Miles, bring him back here," Ben ordered.

"Aye."

Miles scrambled out of the truck and caught up with Sparky's bodyguard near the corner. It looked as if Miles was asking the man for a cigarette. They stood together for a moment, and then it seemed to Ben that the man recognized Miles. He reached into his coat to bring out a gun, but he was much too slow for Miles. The thin man's hands moved so fast, they were only a blur, and the big guy was falling backwards like an oak chopped down with one swing of an ax. Miles actually caught him before he fell and, with a fireman's carry, brought him over to the truck.

Ganja opened the back door, and Miles carried the man in. He was unconscious.

Chief Bukowski took what was left of his coffee and threw it in the man's face. He coughed a few times, then coming out of his stupor, he wiped his face and looked up at the four men.

"Hey, what's going down? What's the beef?" he mumbled.

Chief slapped him hard. "I don't recall anyone saying you could jabber. You don't ask any questions, mister! You just answer them. Now, nod your head if you understand."

The man nodded.

"Where's Sparky Suarez?" Ben asked him.

"Don't know."

"Too bad," the Chief said. He moved out of the way to let Miles get closer.

Miles very methodically put on a pair of black leather gloves. The big man's face broke out in a cold sweat, remembering how Miles had knocked him unconscious with a blow he hadn't even seen. The guy was frightening—thin and gaunt, with a face that registered no emotion and eyes that belonged on a dead man.

"I think Miles is angry," Ganja said softly.

"Look . . . I'm telling you the truth!"

"Stand him up!" Miles said in that dull monotone. "I'm going to work on his face first."

The Chief got up and walked to the front of the van.

"Where are you going, Chief?" Ganja asked.

"I've just eaten, and I'd like to hold it down. I've seen Miles do this before. God have mercy on you, fellow," the Chief said seriously.

The big guy braced himself. His knees were turning to jelly, but he tried not to show any fear. He never saw

186

Miles's hand move. He was waiting for something to happen, and then he felt incredible pain in his nose and blood was pouring out of it. It was the shock of not seeing Miles move a muscle and his nose feeling as if someone had exploded a dynamite charge in it that made Suarez's goon start to scream.

"Now the left eye," Miles said methodically, like a surgeon explaining where he planned to make the next incision.

"No! I'll tell you what you want to know!"

Suarez's man was shaking like a leaf. He could be blinded by this maniac . . . or worse.

"That's a much better attitude," said Kane approvingly. "Sit down for a moment, Miles."

The big guy could see how reluctant Miles was to stop. He was definitely a psycho.

"Look, I just get paid to be a bouncer in the casino," the man babbled. "I don't need to take any shit for Suarez. You guys don't have a beef with me. I don't make enough to take this shit for anybody."

"Where is he?" Ben repeated.

"Honest, I don't know."

He saw Miles smile and start to stand up.

"No, I mean it! He walked out with Ernesto around midnight, and then came back, stuck around a couple of hours, and left, I swear that's the truth."

"But you have an idea where he is," Ben said.

The man looked at Miles nervously. "Yeah. You won't tell him? Jeez . . . somebody give me a napkin or something. I can't talk—I'm drowning in my own blood."

Ganja handed him a tissue, and he pressed it against his broken nose.

"Don't complain, man. Usually Miles doesn't just break it, he pushes it back into your brain," Ganja reassured him.

"All right! Where can we find him?" At this point,

Ben's patience was beginning to wear thin.

"He took two of the girls with him. He was real nervous about something. When he takes a couple of broads, that means he's going back to the compound. Sex gets his mind off things. Come to think of it, Ernesto was uptight, too."

"What do you mean, *compound*?"

"He lives about six miles from here in Bodersvaak. He's got this enormous house on six acres—"

"Hold it, man!" Ganja interrupted. "I know Bodersvaak. That place is a slum. All you've got there are little squat native houses and empty lots with weeds and rats as big as dogs."

"Yeah, except for Suarez's compound. He got the local politicos to bend the rules and evict at least twenty families. Then he had bulldozers come in and level the place. He's built a palace out there. He's got swimming pools, tennis courts . . ."

"How do we get there?" Kane interrupted.

"Hey, forget about it! Nobody could get in there. He's got an army guarding him. They've got cameras all over the place and around-the-clock guards with dogs. You'd have a better chance breaking into Fort Knox."

"Have you ever been inside?" Ganja asked him.

"Yeah, a couple of times."

"You're going to draw us a map and tell us what you know. Then you're going to be locked up in this van while we're inside. If you try to screw us, they'll be mopping you off the walls with a blotter," Kane told him.

Sparky called the room the "Hall of Mirrors." The walls around the king-sized water bed were mirrored, as was the ceiling. Sparky could watch himself screwing from any angle.

The two girls he was with tonight—he couldn't remember their names—were sleeping. He called the

188

blonde Whitey and the dark girl Blacky. It had amused him for a while to watch the entwining of their contrasting limbs as he made them go down on each other.

Then he fucked them both, his cock like a iron bar. Whitey protested when he didn't come; she said she was getting sore. Dumb cunt! He could hold off his orgasm for hours if he wanted to.

He thought about Ernesto while the blonde bounced on his *penga* and the black one sucked his nipples and rubbed her moist mound against his thigh. When the blonde complained again, he slapped her hard across the face and told her to shut up. This one liked pain, he knew. He felt her shudder and her pussy tighten as she came. He threw her off to the floor and lifted the black one on top of him.

This one rode him like a jockey on a stallion. She had her eyes closed and was murmuring to herself. Sparky watched the bounding of her tits and the flaring of her nostrils, and felt himself swell even larger in her tight channel. He could feel that she was close. He reached up and put his large hand around her neck. Her eyes opened wider as she approached her orgasm. She began riding him even faster and he thrust up to meet her, feeling his cock brushing against her womb.

She was moaning like an alley cat in heat, and he closed his hand slowly around the throat. He knew just how to time it, just how to close the windpipe as she exploded in ecstasy. He could be fully detached, still big as a bull and stimulated, but in full control over himself and the girl. The lack of oxygen was enough to make her light-headed, prolong her orgasm and sharpen it to a point she had never known before. He watched her eyes roll back in her head. A little more pressure, or a second or two longer, and she would be a dead *puta*. He could kill her and have her thrown into the sea without any problems. But this one had tried hard and she was a good fuck, so he decided to spare her life and let her keep breathing.

He waited until her orgasm was over and then rolled her off. She was unconscious. Soon she would drift into sleep. He had been fucking these two for three hours, and they were exhausted. He looked down at himself. He was still unsatisfied—his cock could be used as a battering ram.

Why hadn't Ernesto phoned?

Next time he would follow his own instincts. He hadn't liked getting mixed up with *Señor* Gregor in the first place. But Ernesto had insisted.

They had a million bucks worth of cocaine coming through to the island if they could come up with two hundred thousand in clean cash. They could cut the million of "blow" into twenty million dollars worth—even more if they could make a deal to convert it into crack.

Sparky had wanted to take the money out of their special stash. They could afford to do it and still have one hundred fifty G's left. But Ernesto had argued that it would take too much time before the deal could be closed with the people in New York. Maybe there would be an emergency and they would have to leave the islands in a hurry. He'd reminded Sparky what had happened in Cuba. If they'd had enough *dinero* then, they would not have had to serve time.

They had heard the street talk about Gregor looking for independent contractors to take care of a job on the Virgin Islands. He had offered a hundred thousand dollars to anyone who could find the American woman artist. Sparky had heard that people had come from all over to look for her.

They had called on *Señor* Gregor's representative, offering their services, and were told that when she was found, Gregor would pay an additional two hundred thousand for her murder.

"Look at the price he is offering!" Ernesto said. "It's

exactly what we need. It is a sign, no?"

But Sparky wasn't so sure.

They had gone to the cabin on St. John's. It was supposed to be an easy contract, but the woman wasn't there. Instead, they had found Ben Kane. Sparky scowled at the memory. Two times now Kane had made a fool of him. He and Ernesto had had to hide in the forest like frightened rabbits.

Then, Ernesto was to go to the nursing home and take care of Christine Elvey. That should have been easy enough. Yet it was hours since he had left, and still no word. Next time Sparky would follow his own instincts in spite of what his *loco* older brother said.

Sparky sat up on the bed and looked down at the blond girl lying on the white carpet. His eyes traveled down her slim back, noticing the slight protuberance of her spine, the tiny waist, and the flaring buttocks. Once again he felt the flare of desire. It was always like this when he was edgy. He reached with his toe and nudged her ass. He liked the feel of the rubbery flesh. She didn't stir. He kicked her hard.

"*Oww!*" she cried, waking up. She looked up at Sparky with a pouting expression, rubbing the spot where she had been kicked. "Why did you do that?" she asked.

Sparky pointed to a dresser in the corner near the door. "I have a box in the drawer of that dresser. Get it for me," he ordered.

The girl got up and walked to the dresser. In the top drawer, she found a small case and brought it over to the Cuban. He withdrew a small bag made of velvet and tied by a silk drawstring.

"What's in there?" she asked.

He ignored her. He lifted the silver crucifix from his neck and poured a fine white powder from the bag into one of the hollowed-out arms of the cross, then raised the crucifix to his nose and snorted the cocaine.

191

The girl watched intently. "How about giving me a taste, Sparky?" she pleaded.

The Cuban put a small amount of snow on his pinky, and transferred it to the girl's pert red nipple. Carefully, she lifted her breast so the powder wouldn't spill, but there was no way that she could get the breast to her nose.

Sparky laughed cruelly. He reached out and brushed the coke off her.

"Come on, Sparky," she whined.

"You'll have to work for it," he told her.

She understood immediately.

Sparky watched as she fell to her knees before him. Her hands fondled his erection and she rubbed it against her breast.

"*Muy bueno*," he said.

The coke was beginning to affect him. He felt the exhilaration beginning to build. Whitey's warm lips caressed his organ. He felt her breasts with his knees. His toe found her curly pubis. She ground herself against him, and he reached out and curled his fingers in the girl's hair. He came almost at once, and for the moment he was satisfied.

He tossed the girl a small glassine envelope filled with white powder. She quickly opened it and took it to the dresser where she cut two lines and snorted them quickly.

Sparky stared up at the ceiling. *What the hell had happened to Ernesto?*

192

CHAPTER 19

The Suarez compound was located about a mile off the main road. Ganja had been right about the squalor of the surrounding area. There were tar shacks without any plumbing facilities or electricity, separated by overgrown fields of weeds, burning tires, and rusting old automobiles.

As the morning sun began to light the countryside, the men in the van could see dark-skinned women carrying water in large bowls from a community well. The women were followed by a brood of small children holding on to their mothers' ragged cotton shifts. Most of the women were pregnant.

The Chief parked the van after tying up and gagging Suarez's bodyguard. He picked a spot in the dense brush of the tropical forest that lined the road. Once they were sure the van was well camouflaged, they picked up their gear and jumped out.

"Do you think he gave us good charts?" the Chief asked Kane, looking at the rough sketches of the compound the man had made for them.

"I think he understood that if we didn't come back, he'd rot in that van. There's no way anyone's going to see that thing, the way we've got it hidden."

"We've got no choice but to believe him," Ganja said.

"Let's not worry about it," Kane said.

He grimly strapped the M16 on his shoulder and led the three men through the forest toward Suarez's stronghold.

Kane had committed the sketches to memory. There was an electrified barbed-wire fence surrounding the grounds. Behind that, a track of cleared ground separated the fence from the landscaped area around the house. Guards with Dobermans patrolled this area. According to Suarez's man—whose name, they had discovered, was Armando—there were four guards with dogs who constantly circled the compound. Armando had also told them of surveillance cameras which had been placed at strategic points. He didn't know the exact location of all the cameras, but he had seen some in the trees and on specially made posts. One time, Armando had walked into the cinder-block guardhouse and had seen one of the men looking at six closed-circuit TV monitors. The surveillance center was on the second floor of the structure. According to Armando, there were always ten well-armed guards, in addition to the dog patrol, on the premises. Five of the guards were in various stations in the main residence. Armando thought there was a man on the roof, and at least two or three guards around Sparky. Another man usually guarded the front.

"Man, look at that place!" Ganja exclaimed.

There really wasn't much that they could see. Their line of vision was inhibited by a dense wall of hedges which, in turn, camouflaged the electrified fence. From their location they could see the square, squat, guard building and behind it, rising like the Matterhorn, Suarez's turreted "palace."

"You know what he must've patterned it after?" The Chief didn't wait for an answer. "That's exactly the way the Cuban presidential palace looks. The fool thinks he's Castro!"

"Any ideas, men?" Kane asked.

Attempting to get through the fence behind the hedge would hold them up too long, and give the guards with the dogs time to spot them. An additional handicap was not knowing where the cameras were.

"I hope we don't have to dig under," the Chief said.

"What about a chopper landing?" Ganja wanted to know.

In a pinch, Ganja had flown helicopters. He had no formal training, but he had a way with all mechanical things and could figure out how they worked in no time flat.

"Two problems with that. First, we don't have a chopper; and second, I wouldn't trust you to land the damn thing in one piece," Kane told him.

"Look at what we got over there, Skip," Chief said, pointing to a quivering in the hedge.

They watched as the hedges seemed miraculously to move to the side as if they were on wheels, exposing the inside of the compound.

"What the . . ."

"Damn! It's a camouflaged electric gate. There's a camera and a post right by the opening. See?" Ganja pointed.

"Probably a car going out to the main road. Ganja,

run down to the bend out of sight of the compound and hold him up. We'll be over in a minute."

As Kane spoke, a light blue Ford Fairlane came to a complete stop at the gate.

Ganja was already moving through the bush to a spot on the road beyond a sharp curve. As he turned, he could see the car start up again and the hedges close into a seemingly impenetrable wall.

Ganja took off his shirt and equipment and placed them on the side of the road, out of sight. He stood in the middle of the road, doubled over as if in pain, and waved at the car to stop.

"Please stop, mon. I got bad pain in stomach," he called.

Ganja hoped he fit in with the look of the natives of the surrounding countryside. He hoped the drive—or drivers—wouldn't look too closely at him and notice his combat boots. Poor, sick black folk from this side of the island didn't walk around in three-hundred-dollar foot gear.

Ganja made sure not to look up at the driver. For all he knew, the car could have had Sparky in it, and Sparky might remember him from the night they had pulled the card deal. He did focus, however, on the left front tire, making sure that he could leap out of the way if the driver decided to knock him over. The tire stopped spinning.

"Hey, what's wrong with you, mon? Too much rum?" The man had a Caribbean accent. It wasn't Sparky.

Ganja looked at him. He was a black man wearing a brown uniform. He stuck his head out of the car and scratched his nose as he looked at Ganja. He was one of the guards Suarez employed on the compound.

"Have some mercy on me, mon. I got a big pain in the belly. Take me to the hos-pe-tal, mon."

"No, I don't have time for that now. Get out of the

196

way before I knock you out of the way."

Ganja straightened himself up and placed his hands on the hood of the car. "Please, please, mon. I'm *dyin'*. If'n I don' get me to a doctor—"

"Get off my car, you dirty scum! I told you I got things to do. Get off or I'll run you down."

"Please, sir."

"That's it!"

The driver pulled his head in and cursed under his breath.

"Freeze!"

Ben Kane jumped out of the brush and landed next to Ganja, his M16 pointed right between the guard's eyes.

The Chief was alongside the car, his gun poking into the window.

Miles quickly opened the car door and threw the man to the ground, spread-eagled facedown in the dusty road. A quick pat turned up a Mauzer, which Miles tossed into the forest. There was a picture ID card which identified the man as Amos Turk.

Kane turned him over and placed the barrel of his gun on the man's forehead. "Don't even think about lying," Ben warned. "If I think you're lying, I'll below your brains out. Nod your head if you understand."

The man nodded his head slightly. His eyes were big brown pools filled with fear.

"How many men in the guardhouse?" Kane asked.

"Four," Amos Turk muttered.

"Kill him, Kane!" the Chief said. "We know there's always five in there."

"No, mon! I'm the fifth. I was going out for food. That's the truth . . . I swear!"

"How many in Suarez's house?" Kane asked him.

"Five. One at the front, three with Sparky, and a man on the roof with rockets."

So much for Ganja's helicopter idea, Kane thought.

197

"Ganja, I want you to go back in with him. Secure the guardhouse and open the gate for us. We'll join you there."

"Right, Skip."

Ganja strapped on his M16 and stood Amos Turk up. He pushed Turk back into the car. "I'm sure our friend will cooperate," he told Kane. Then Grant got into the back of the car and crouched behind the driver's seat. He carved a hole in the back of the upholstery with his long knife and poked the blade through until it was nudging Turk's spine.

"You give me away, brother, and you'll be in a wheelchair for the rest of your life. The only sex you'll ever have is gonna come from your tongue," Ganja warned. "Now, turn this piece of shit around and get to the gate. Let the camera see your face, and you tell them that you forgot something. You hip?"

"Don't worry. I don't want to get cut for Sparky."

"I ain't worryin'. You just play ball and you'll be okay."

He turned the Ford back up the road. When they stopped, Ganja knew they were at the hidden gate. He ducked farther down to make sure the camera wouldn't pick him up.

"What's up, Turk?" a voice called out.

"I forgot something. Open her up for me."

"Man, you always forgetting something," the voice on the intercom said in disgust.

Ganja heard the whirr of machinery as the gate slowly opened.

"Hurry it up. I'm getting hungry," the voice said.

The Ford started up slowly and then came to a dead stop. Ganja increased the pressure of his knife on Amos's back.

"Keep low," Turk said, "it's one of the dog teams."

Ganja heard the Doberman barking before he heard

the other voice outside the car window.

"Hey, Amos, that was quick," it said.

"No, mon. I forgot my fool wallet. I'm going down to get some cold cuts, and I don't have a thin dime."

"Well, they won't give it to you on looks alone. Jesus! What the hell is wrong with Gypsy?"

The dog was barking up a storm. Ganja knew Gypsy had picked up his scent.

Turk thought fast. "I guess he smells my cat. I had him in the car last night."

"Come on, Gypsy. Get down. Get *down*!"

The dog was on his hind legs, his muzzle peering down through the rear window at Ganja. Suddenly he was jerked away.

"I said come here and pipe down!"

"I'll see you later, Charlie," Amos said, starting the car.

Ganja waited a few moments and then raised up a little bit. "You did good, man," Ganja told Turk. "Over there where the trees are—pull over."

Turk did as he was told. Ganja climbed over into the front seat.

"Get out of your clothes, Amos. Fast!"

Ganja put on the man's shirt and uniform pants. He eased the brown hat over his eyes. Turk was about the same complexion and height, but the pants fit snugly. Turk put on Ganja's pants.

"I want you to crawl out the passenger side and keep going until you get to the trunk," Ganja told him.

He watched Turk get out and waited until the man circled to the trunk. Ganja hoped that from a distance it would look like Turk had stopped the car to look for something in the trunk.

"Get in!" Ganja commanded.

"Hey, look. I cooperated, mon!"

"I'm not going to let you give me away when I'm

inside. You either get into the trunk, or I'll knock you unconscious."

Turk thought it over and shook his head. He started to climb into the trunk. "Why did it have to be my turn to go out," he mumbled to himself.

"That may be the luckiest break of your life," Ganja told him, as he removed the handcuffs Turk had on his belt. "Hold your ankles," Ganja told him. He cuffed Turk's left wrist to his left ankle, and his right wrist to his right ankle. He took a piece of tape from his own pants pocket and slapped it over Turk's mouth.

"Can't have you kickin' or yellin'. That would be bad for your health . . . and mine."

Ganja closed the truck and got back into the car. He drove the rest of the way, about three hundred feet, to the guards' building and parked in a small clearing where there were two other automobiles of late-seventies vintage.

He got out of the car and walked toward the structure with his hat brim pulled low.

The building was made of ugly gray cinder block, two stories high. He tried the front door, but it was locked. That would have been too easy.

"Who's that?"

The voice jolted him. Then he noticed the speaker over the jamb. There was another of those infernal cameras poking out from a hole in one of the cinder blocks.

Ganja faked a coughing fit. "Let me in," he wheezed. "It's me, Turk. I forgot my wallet again." He started coughing again and deliberately doubled over to obstruct the camera's view.

There was a long pause . . . too long, Ganja Grant thought. He was about to blast his way in with one of the grenades when the voice came back.

"We're all hungry, and you're a shithead!" the voice

said with a note of exasperation.

There was a buzzing sound, and Ganja walked through.

He was surprised at the difference in temperature inside. It was at least ten degrees cooler. He closed the door behind him and gave a quick check for more cameras. He couldn't see any, and it didn't really make any sense to have them inside the building.

To his left there were three men involved in a card game. None of them looked up when he walked in. They were intent on their game, about twenty feet away, sitting at a card table in the small room. On the wall behind them hung a map. A quick look told Ganja it was a map of the grounds.

"Three kings!" one of the guards said, throwing down his hand.

All of them were dressed in the same uniform Ganja was now wearing. He walked over to the three men and was only a few feet away when one of them looked up. Ganja read the surprise on his face. The other two were still engrossed in the game.

"Hey, you're not Amos," the man said.

Ganja leveled the M16. "Nobody moves, nobody gets hurt!"

The three men looked at each other. They were Americans, or light-skinned Cubans. Each of them wore a sidearm.

"Everybody get up slowly, and we'll have a handcuff party. It'll be a good chance to get to know one another better," Ganja said. "I want to see all your guns on the table real quick . . . *now!*"

Ganja watched them. Two of the men were burly, with lobster-red skin and blondish hair. They could have been brothers. The other man, dark haired, thinner, and with shifty eyes, looked as though he was maneuvering something under the table. Ganja figured

201

he had an ankle holster that he was fooling with.

"Don't!" Ganja menaced, swinging the gun and bringing it level with the man's chest. The man hesitated, but the guard on the left thought he saw an opening. He had been about to place his pistol on the table. Instead, he turned it on Ganja.

A big mistake!

The M16 coughed once, and the blond was blown over the top of his chair.

"Son of a bitch!" the other red face bellowed, enraged beyond reason. He pointed his gun and Ganja put a third weeping red eye in the middle of his forehead.

The dark-haired man very slowly and very carefully put both hands on the table. "I have another gun in an ankle holster," he said weakly.

"Put it on the table and give me your handcuffs," Ganja told him.

The man placed the gun down ever so slowly so that Ganja would in no way think he was up to something. Ganja cuffed him to a pipe under the small slop sink. He took the man's walkie-talkie.

"Now you can holler, man, but if your friend upstairs hasn't heard the guns, he won't hear you. The only thing you'll achieve is a bullet in the head," Ganja said matter-of-factly.

In light of what the guard had seen, it carried more weight than an hour's worth of ranting and raving.

"I'll be quiet," he said.

"Good. Then you'll be just fine." He picked up the other two hands on the table and glanced at the cards. "Lucky I came in when I did. You would have lost to a flush."

Kane and the Chief were thirty feet from the hedge gate, covered by a large thicket of weeds.

Miles was farther back in the bush, doing push-ups and running in place in order to burn off nervous energy. He was like a watch spring overwound and ready to snap.

The Chief was aiming his M16 at the camera covered by foliage outside the gate. He prided himself on his markmanship, and Kane knew that if he didn't let him take the first shot, the Chief would be out of sorts for days.

"You've got to get it right in the lens," he told the older man.

"Damn it, Skip! I know. I was just about to pop it when you ruined my concentration."

"Sorry."

There was a tinkle of broken glass as the camera burst apart.

"There you go, Skip," the Chief said, looking up at Kane and smiling.

"Good shot, Chief."

He felt Miles behind him. The ex-SEAL settled in.

"When are we going to move in?" he asked Kane.

"There are four dog teams. I figure on the guy in the communication room to call one of the dog teams over to check out why his screen went dead. You take him if he shows up, Miles."

"No problem."

"What about the dog?" the Chief asked.

"What the hell is a dog?" Miles replied.

It took a little while, but finally the gate opened and a very tall guard with a dog on a leash stepped out. He walked over to the camera as the gate closed behind him.

Miles ran straight for him with no attempt at subterfuge or guile.

The Doberman sensed him coming. Its ears stood straight up and its body froze as it gave off a low growl.

"What's wrong, boy?" The guard turned to see what the dog was looking at. He didn't complete the turn.

Miles's straight-arm caught him under the chin and practically lifted him off his feet. The snap back of his skull made a sound like a tree branch breaking that Chief and Kane could hear even at a distance.

The Doberman stepped back a few paces and bared its fangs. Miles seemed to be doing the same thing to the dog. He bared his teeth and growled. The dog stopped in mid-bark. Its head moved to the side, looking at the man quizzically. Miles charged him. The dog made a brief attempt at getting set for a spring and then changed its mind as the wildman ran at him. It turned and ray away, barking over its shoulder at Miles. Its master lay on the ground, lifeless.

Kane and Chief joined Miles at the gate. Ben moved his hands around the hedges, looking for a seam.

"We're not going to force this thing. We'll just have to wait for Ganja. Let's pull this guy off to the side of the forest, in case someone else comes along before Ganja springs it open," he said.

"That leaves three dog teams to go," the Chief said.

"Yeah, but this team was probably the closest to the gate. If Ganja is able to get the thing opened, I didn't want this guard to pick us off or sound a warning to the others."

The Chief nodded and helped Miles camouflage the guard's body with the foliage. Kane watched them, making sure there was no one around who could sound an alarm.

When had killing become so easy, he wondered? He remembered the first time he had squeezed the trigger of a gun and watched a man die. His first week in Nam. It had been an old, crippled beggar who had come up to Kane and a group of his platoon asking for bread. Kane saw the beggar reach for something under the rags of his shorts where his leg had once been. He saw the grenade, stared, transfixed, as the man reached for the pin. Then, without thinking, Ben blasted him with a short burst from his automatic weapon. It had happened in the blink of an eye, and Ben's qwick action had certainly saved the lives of six men . . . but he had agonized over the man's death for many sleepless nights.

More killings had followed, but that was war.

From that, it was possible to consider what he had done in Nam for Weaver and the CIA as still part of an undeclared war. He thought he had put that part of his life behind him . . . until Weaver popped up again.

Kane took one of his cigars from his breast pocket and lit up. His thoughts drifted to Weaver. Kane had met a lot of guys like Weaver when he was in the Navy. They were hard-nosed and always convinced they were right. They'd go to any lengths to defend the freedom of America even if they had to take away the freedoms they were protecting in order to do it. If it weren't so ludicrous, it might even be funny.

Kane had just wanted to be left alone to take care of his business, but Weaver had maneuvered him into helping him by placing his entire operation in jeopardy. Why wasn't he furious at Weaver? He had every right to be. He thought hard about that and decided it was because Weaver was one person who didn't pretend to be something he wasn't. Weaver believed in what he was doing, and Kane had no doubt that whatever assignment he dished out to others, he would be willing to do the same assignment himself. What it came down to was that Weaver wasn't sitting in an ivory tower. He'd ask you to put your life on the line, but he'd be willing to do it, too. . . .

"He's tucked away, Skip," the Chief told him. "What do we do now?"

Kane took a long pull on his Havana. "Now we wait for the Ganja man to do his thing."

CHAPTER 20

If Turk had been telling the truth, the only person left in the guardhouse would be the man in the communications room. Ganja had received a pretty good layout of the place from Armando. There was a steel door which led into the windowless room. Inside, the guard watched the monitors for intruders.

Ganja had asked about air-conditioning ducts and had been told that there were steel grilles in the ducts that would prevent a man from entering the room that way. In one respect, the isolation of the room was a plus. Ganja was convinced that the sound of the shots a floor below had not been picked up by the man in the control room.

Armando had said that all the guards carried walkie-talkies to keep in contact with one another and with the communications room. Ganja hadn't seen a walkie-talkie on Amos Turk, but the three men downstairs each had one. He had made sure to remove the instrument from the guard downstairs before cuffing him to the pipe.

Ganja stood in front of the door. It was just as Armando had described it, solid steel with inside hinges. He thought for a moment about blasting it with a grenade, but discarded that idea. If the grenade didn't blow the door down, the guard would have a chance to call for help and he'd be a sitting duck in the guard-house, cut off from Kane and the crew.

How could he get in without having the guard send out an alarm? He remembered the man's words when Turk had spoken to him at the gate. He had chastised Turk for always forgetting things, and had said that he was hungry.

Ganja went back downstairs and out the front door. Once again he kept the brim of his hat low to escape detection from the door camera. He walked to the parking lot and opened the trunk of the car.

Turk was there, still bound and gagged as he had left him.

"Where's your walkie-talkie?" Ganja asked him after he had removed the tape from his mouth.

"Huh?"

"How come everybody has a walkie-talkie but you?"

"Mine was being fixed. I was going to pick it up when I got back," he told Ganja, looking puzzled.

"What's the guy's name in the communication room?"

"Roger."

"Did Roger know you didn't have the talkie?"

"No . . . What the hell is this to you?"

Ganja pulled out the knife and held it to Turk's

throat. "Why don't you say that again and give me an excuse to open your jugular. Talk!"

"No, Roger didn't know. He's always after us to take care of our equipment, and I'm always leaving mine somewhere. I dropped the damn thing, and it wasn't working right. One of the guys was supposed to go out and get us breakfast, but I worked out a deal with him. I'd take his turn and go out for breakfast if he'd fix my talkie."

Ganja nodded. He pulled the walkie-talkie he had taken from the dark-haired man out of his pocket.

"I want you to tell Roger that, and tell him that you need a few more dollars. You tell him that you're coming up to get it and to let you in."

"He won't go for that."

"He'd better. Your life depends on it." Ganja placed the instrument near Turk's mouth. "How do I raise him?"

"Press the side bar three times," Turk said.

Ganja did. In a second there was a crackle of static.

"Go ahead, Turk," was the bored reply. "When the hell are you leaving?"

"Roger, we're short a couple of dollars."

"Short? Why the hell are you short?"

"I can't seem to find a ten."

"What the fuck's wrong with you, man?"

"Hey, don't worry, Roger. I'll pay you back."

"Damn right you will! Come on up and I'll slip you a ten under the door." There was a slight pause. "Clay didn't have any money? What happened? Mac clean him out?"

"I guess."

"Hey, Turk, check out the front-gate camera before you come up. I lost the picture; and I can't get Paulie on the line. He's probably goofing off somewhere."

Ganja pulled the walkie-talkie away, disgusted. What

good was it if Roger was going to slip a ten under the door? Ganja couldn't get in that way. He was already thinking of something else for Turk to come up with. It would be taking a big chance. The guard in the communications room might definitely realize that there was something up.

He heard the crackle on the walkie-talkie again.

"Hey, Turk, when you go upstairs bring me a pack of smokes from my locker. It's open."

Ganja brandished the knife in front of Turk's face.

"Okay," Turk croaked.

Ganja replaced the tape over Turk's mouth and closed the trunk. Then he crossed to the building. The downstairs door opened just as Ganja got close to it. When he walked inside, the electric buzz stopped and the door closed. Ganja climbed the stairs to the second floor and rapped on the door.

"Just a second, man."

He heard the sound of heavy steel as a bolt was removed, and then the door opened a crack. Ganja didn't take any chances. He kicked the door and it sprung open in Roger's face, knocking him backwards onto the table that held the monitors.

Roger was a wiry young guy, not more than twenty-five, with long hair poking out from under his wide hat. He should have been at a disadvantage because of the unexpected attack, but his reflexes were razor sharp and he reacted with lightning speed. He rolled on the floor and pulled out his gun. Ganja ducked as the first shot sailed a few inches from his head. He dived on the fallen guard and managed to clamp a hand down on the man's wrist before he could get off another volley. The guard was very quick. He spun away from Ganja and leveled the gun again. The black man had one chance. He kicked out his foot and caught Roger's hand. The gun went flying in the air and clattered against the wall. Roger was up in a split second and running toward it. Ganja knew he could never get the M16 off his shoulder in time to prevent Roger's picking up the weapon. Instead, he pulled out his knife and tossed it just as Roger lifted his gun and turned it on Ganja. The knife hummed as it closed the space between the two men, doing cartwheels, until it lodged in Roger's chest with an audible thud. The guard's eyes opened wide. His tongue stuck out and spasmed, then he fell dead, the gun falling harmlessly at his side.

Ganja wasted no time in stepping over to the console and turning the switch marked "Front Gate." He noticed the video screen marked #1 was blank. That would be Kane's work, he thought.

He lifted the toggle switch and then looked at the other TV monitors. There was one covering the area around the front of Suarez's palatial estate. It looked as if no one was around. He wondered about the guard with the rockets on top of the building. They would have to take care of him first.

"Come in, Roger."

The voice came from a tiny square speaker on a shelf near the ceiling.

"Roger, come in!"

"Yeah." Ganja spoke in a hoarse voice, trying to imitate the voice he had heard when Turk had spoken to the communications-center guard.

"We've got something strange out here. I checked to see what the story was with Paulie. The damn front gate is open, and Paulie's dog is out here barking like crazy. Hey, Roger . . . do you read me?"

"Yeah, okay," Ganja said.

"Whaddaya mean, okay? Roger . . . ? Roger . . ."

Ganja put down the mike and dashed out of the room.

Kane, the Chief, and Miles were approaching the front door of the guardhouse. Ganja sped down the steps and met them. He waved for them to come forward into the guardhouse.

"This place is secured, Skipper. . . ."

"Good work, Ganja," Ben said.

". . . But we've got some trouble. One of the guards spotted the open gate. He tried calling the control room, and I had to cut him off."

"That could put three of them at our backs, Ben," the Chief said.

"Yeah—three behind us, and another five in the building." Kane thought about it. "The worst thing would be to get caught in a cross fire. We have to take the building and hold off whatever comes from outside. Where're the keys to the Fairlane?"

"Still in the ignition," Ganja told him.

"We need an escape hatch. Miles, get in the car and keep out of sight. When the time comes, you're going to have to get us out of there." Ben gestured to the large white house.

Miles looked disappointed, but didn't say anything. He would never question an order from Ben Kane. He turned on his heel, made sure the area was clear, and then made a run for the Ford. Ben watched him slip behind the wheel and duck down out of sight.

"All right, guys. Let's get out of here," Kane said.

They carried their M16s and circled around the back of the guardhouse. A second later, the area where they had been standing exploded with a roar, and flames engulfed the door and part of the guardhouse's first floor.

"What the hell was that?" the Chief asked, holding his ever-present stocking cap onto his head.

"That's the guy on the roof with the rockets. He must have gotten a call from the guard with the walkie-talkie."

There was another blast, and another section of the

guardhouse was wiped away.

"We've got to get that mother. Can you pick him off, Chief?"

"I got to see him first, Ben."

"You'll see him, but make it count. Ganja, you're with me. Chief, you'll have to keep the guards who were patrolling the gate off our tails while we're inside," Kane told him.

"Don't worry, Skip. I'll pin them down." He held up his gun.

"Ganja, let's go!"

Kane pulled the pin on one of his grenades and tossed it at the building. The explosion blew out the front door and all the downstairs windows. Ben and Ganja ran to a collection of big white rocks about fifteen feet from the blown-out doorway.

Kane knew he and Ganja were sitting ducks for the guy with the bazooka on the roof. He could picture in his mind the man's excitement as he aimed his launcher down at the two men using the boulders as cover. But he'd have to stand, giving the Chief that one vital shot. He head it—POW! And then a long scream as a body tumbled off the roof and fell dead onto the wooden porch.

The Chief stuck his head out from around the corner of the guardhouse. The building was spewing thick black smoke and flames as the fire started by the rockets burned out of control. The Chief smiled and raised his thumb up in the air. Ben returned the salute.

Their moment of relief was short-lived. Ben heard the staccato chatter of automatic weapons close behind them. The Chief made a run to join them at the boulders. He set up his gun and ducked down behind the rocks.

"Okay, Ben. I'll keep them occupied," he said.

Kane slapped him on the back and turned to the

213

estate. He tossed another grenade into the front, waited for the concussion, then charged forward with Ganja.

Sparky Suarez saw the two men dash from behind the big white rocks and run toward the building. He only saw the two for a second, but he knew who they were.

"That son of a bitch Kane!" he whispered under his breath.

There was no sound of shots on the floor below. That meant the first grenade had gotten Carlos.

The two terrified girls were huddled on the bed, hugging each other and crying. Sparky ran to the door and opened it. His three guards were standing near by, their machine guns being held with white knuckles. Sparky snatched one of the machine guns from the man closest to him. The man was tall, but not as broad as Sparky.

"Take off your shirt and pants, Chico," Sparky told him.

He hurriedly obeyed his boss's order.

"Now get in there."

He opened the door for the man. Once Chico was inside, Sparky locked the door with a silver key.

"Keep your eyes on the stairs," he ordered the other two as he got into Chico's uniform.

He heard shots from the guardhouse area. That meant he still had some men left. If Kane's people managed to get to the second floor, they would lose precious seconds trying to break down the bedroom door.

"Come out, Sparky. We don't want to kill you," Kane yelled from below. "Tell your men to put down their guns. We don't want anyone else to get hurt."

Sparky grabbed his two guards by their shirts. He stared directly into their eyes. "Listen to me! This man is a liar. He wants to kill us all. If he comes up here, we'll be killed. The only chance is for you to keep him away. You must hold them off! *Comprende?*"

"*Si*, Sparky," one of them said.

The other nodded.

"*Bueno!* I have an idea. While you keep them busy, I'll go down and attack from the other side. We'll catch them in the cross fire."

The two men nodded in unison.

"You have ten seconds," Kane yelled.

Sparky wondered what was keeping his other men. And how many people did Kane have?

He raced down the hall to a linen closet, which he opened with his silver key. For once, Ernesto had been right. His brother remembered how they had been caught in Havana and had wanted to make sure it would never happen again. In their "palace," they had built in some special touches. Now Sparky removed the Sheetrock panel and studied one of them. It was a very simple means of escape . . . a firemen's pole that led straight down to another door underground. He gripped the pole and slid down as he heard another explosion from one of Kane's grenades.

Sparky caught a whiff of something in the air. It wasn't a grenade that had exploded—it was tear gas. His people wouldn't hold out long.

He landed in another closet below the ground level of the house and stood upon the rubber mat which had cushioned his fall, regained his balance, and removed the dummy Sheetrock panel. He fiddled with the door in the dark and, cursing, finally got it open.

Above his head Sparky could hear the pounding footsteps of Kane and his men and the shouting of his own guards. He made sure there was no one in sight and then crossed over to a wood panel that covered a large pipe. He climbed in and replaced the panel, waiting for his eyes to become accustomed to the darkness. On hands and knees, Sparky crawled through

the inky blackness, ignoring the water that had collected on the bottom of the pipe and the bugs that
skittered over his hands and arms. He counted each
time he brought one knee forward. The tunnel was
thirty feet long. He knew he was coming close to the
camouflaged opening because it started getting cooler
and the dank, fetid air seemed just a bit fresher. It
wasn't his imagination—the tunnel was sloping slightly
upwards.

Sparky reached out and touched the metal plate at the
end of the tunnel. Two U-bolts held it in place. He
loosened the bolts and very slowly shifted the plate,
getting a faceful of dirt that went into his eyes and
mouth. He fought back the impulse to cough and,
instead, swallowed the dirt. He wiped his eyes and
stuck his head just a fraction through the opening.

From this spot he had a good view of what was going
on. One man behind a group of rocks was holding off
three of Sparky's guards. Kane and the other man were
apparently still inside the main building. He didn't
know how many more Kane had around the perimeter.

Sparky looked over his shoulder at the strip of
concrete where the guards parked their cars. Ernesto
had taken the Mercedes, and the BMW was in the shop.
That left two small Japanese cars, and a large Ford
Fairlane. He decided to make a run for the Fairlane. If
he had to bust through the front gate, the weight of the
larger car would be helpful. He took one more quick
look around before he pushed the plate completely to
one side and made a dash for the car.

Miles was in the front seat of the Ford, hunched
down behind the steering wheel. He watched the Chief
bottle up three of Suarez's guards because they stupidly
had rushed toward the house together. Now they were
behind the burning guardhouse, and as soon as one of

them stuck a hair out from behind the corner, the Chief would pin them back.

Kane and Ganja were taking a long time inside the "palace." With the firepower they had, it would have been easy to take out everybody inside, but their mission was to capture Sparky Suarez alive, and that was always more time-consuming and dangerous.

From the corner of his eye, Miles saw a blur of tan running toward the car. Somebody had spotted him . . . but how? Miles worked his automatic rifle off his shoulder. No, the guard hadn't seen him. The blur was probably just heading for the car in order to get away. When the door opened, Miles would blast him. He moved down even lower in his seat . . . and waited.

The man grabbed the door handle as he made sure there was no one around to take a shot at him. He half expected the door to be locked, but it wasn't. He had opened it quickly and started to slide in when he felt the barrel of a gun in his belly. Miles was ready to pull the trigger, but then he recognized that dark, ugly face.

Shit! It was Sparky Suarez!

The two guards ran down the staircase, their hands in the air. They had dropped their guns on the second floor and now, coughing and sputtering, they would have walked into hell itself in order to escape the lung-searing tear gas.

"Take these two and hold them," Kane told Ganja. "I'll flush out Sparky."

Kane slapped on a small carbon filter mask that was supposed to protect the eyes and lungs from the gas. It really didn't work too well. After a few minutes, it would be as if Kane had no protection at all. He'd have to work fast.

The second-floor hallway was thick with white gas. There were two bedrooms on the floor. Kane kicked in

217

the door of the first and dropped to his knees. It was empty.

The second bedroom looked more promising. The guards had left their guns in front of this one. Suarez was probably locked inside with the women Armando had mentioned earlier. Kane kicked the door and stormed into the room, his M16 rattling off shots in a drumroll of bullets. He aimed high, to discourage anyone in the room from doing anything but ducking. He wanted to take Sparky alive.

He saw someone on the other side of the room holding a rifle. Kane blasted through the smoke—and the image shattered into pieces. Damn! He had been shooting at a mirror image of himself! The whole damn room was mirrored!

Two girls were huddled together on the bed. They were both nude and they coughed and gasped for breath as the tear gas did its work. But no Sparky.

The look in the eyes of the black girl tipped him off. She glanced over at the closet a second before it burst open. A man jumped out, his pistol blasting bullets. Kane was ready for him. The M16 drew a line like a belt of blood in the area between his white undershirt and shorts. He was practically cut in two.

It wasn't Sparky.

"Where's Suarez?" he yelled at the girls.

They couldn't answer. They reached out to Kane and tried to clutch at him for support, but he brushed them aside and went to the window. It wouldn't open. Sparky was one of the few on the island with central air conditioning. Kane broke the window, pulled off his mask, and drew in a deep gulp of air.

He looked down below as one of the men the Chief had boxed behind the guard building tried to make an end run to the rear of the palace. The Chief cut him down like a mower in tall grass. The two girls were on either side of Kane now, taking deep breaths and trying to clear their lungs and eyes.

"Where's Suarez?" he asked them again.

"Gone. He left before. He left us here to die," the white girl gasped.

Kane saw the Fairlaine starting to move. What the hell was Miles doing? The car turned, wheels screeching, and raced to the front of the estate. It stopped on a dime right outside the front door.

Ganja ran over, poked his head in the car window and then looked up. He saw Kane and waved frantically.

"Miles got Suarez!" Ganja yelled.

Kane stepped over the body on the floor and ran down the staircase. The rear door of the car was open, and Kane dove into it, landing squarely on top of the unconscious Sparky Suarez.

Miles had the Ford moving again. The Chief was standing by, waiting for them. Ganja laid down a barrage at the guardhouse as the Chief moved to the front door. He jumped in beside Ganja and Miles.

"Get this thing moving!" Kane told Miles, and he was thrown back in his seat as Miles accelerated.

They had to go past the guardhouse and, for the first time, the two men in brown had a clear shot at them. A bullet shattered the rear window, another lodged in the car's roof.

"Crash the gate if you have to," Ganja told Miles.

"No need to. Look—it's open," the Chief said, pointing.

The gate was indeed still open, as it had been when Ganja flipped the toggle switch.

"Park the car here," Ben said. "That'll block them if they try to follow us."

Miles nodded, stopped the car between the two posts, and got out, followed by Ganja and the Chief. Kane pushed Suarez out the door. He was starting to come to.

"You better walk," Kane told him as he slapped his face.

"He'll be okay," Miles told them. "I just tapped him."

They doubletimed down the road to where the van was hidden. Suarez, fully conscious now, was cursing a blue streak. His eyes were daggers of hate aimed at Kane and his men.

The Chief darted to the rear of the van to open the two back doors and was surprised to find that they were already open. He half expected the inside to be empty, and Armando gone. But Armando was there . . . lifeless, his head in a pool of blood.

"What the hell is this?" Chief exclaimed.

Ben pushed past Suarez and took a look at the man on the van's floor. "He's been shot in the head."

"How very perceptive of you, Mr. Kane."

The voice came from directly behind them. The man who stepped from behind the trees carrying an Uzi machine gun was wearing a most evil-looking smile.

Suarez threw his head back and roared with laughter. "Very good timing, *Señor* Gregor," he said, taking the M16s from Kane and his men.

Kane and the rest of his crew stared in silent amazement at the master assassin.

It was Alan Mason.

CHAPTER 21

"What is this shit, Alan?" Ben growled when he could find his voice.

"Just keep your hands in the air where I can see them. Pat them all down for hidden weapons, Sparky. His little girl friend told me that Mr. Kane carries a .22 in his right pocket. Yes, that's it. Now, the ankle holster. Hmm, you're a regular walking arsenal, aren't you, Ben?"

"Skipper, am I dreaming, or what?" Ganja asked him. "Isn't this the guy we're supposed to be protecting?"

"You're right, Mr. Grant. You were protecting me from myself. You were doing too good a job of it, I'm afraid. I couldn't accomplish what I set out to do because of you people constantly around me."

"And that was to kill Christine Elvey," Ben said. Suddenly things were beginning to fall into a bizarre pattern.

"Exactly," Mason responded with that same evil smile.

"Then that fella that tried to kill him at Windsor House, that was a setup," the Chief said. His ears turned beet red as he realized how they all had been duped. "But how? That man took shots at him."

"Sure he did, Chief," Ben said. "He must have been especially selected because he followed orders to the letter. His orders were to shoot at Mason's chest. He probably believed he was supposed to kill Mason. He was hired by an associate, and he did exactly as he was told. But he didn't know that Mason would be wearing a bulletproof vest. Alan, here, knew he wouldn't be in any real danger, and he figured that would throw us off the track."

"Very good, Kane," Mason said. "Actually, I was hoping you'd all think poor Nicholas was the infamous Gregor and I would be given a free hand to look for Christine. Too bad . . ." Then he barked, "Don't even think about it, Miles! You're not *that* fast."

Sparky was patting Miles down and Mason sensed, correctly, that the thin man was poised for action. Miles glared at Mason and stayed where he was.

"Let's put them in back of the van, Sparky. I've improved the accommodations somewhat," Mason said.

Sparky dragged out Armando's body and dumped it unceremoniously onto the road.

"I had to waste this one, Sparky," Mason explained. "He was the one who led these Boy Scouts to your humble abode."

"He was no damn good anyway," Sparky agreed. He prodded Kane into the van. "C'mon, move!"

"Why, Alan? Why the need to kill Christine Elvey?" Ben wanted to know.

Mason shoved Ganja into the van. "That will give you something to think about during your ride to Mermaid's Chair."

"Mermaid's Chair? Why the hell are we taking them there?" Sparky asked him. "That's a good two-hour drive. We could take them back into the compound and kill them in a couple minutes."

"*I'm* not taking them, Sparky. *You* are! I have an appointment at the Caribe Beach Nursing Home with Christine Elvey." He looked at Kane. "My old buddy Mike and Michelle have arranged to have her released for the day, and I'm going to suggest we take a ride out to sea on the *Wu Li*. Actually, I'm going to tell them it was your suggestion, Kane. And somewhere on the ocean, we're going to run into one of those Bermuda Triangle phenomena. When I get picked up by the Coast Guard in my life raft, there will be no sign of the other three people on board . . . one of those unexplained mysteries that make good newspaper copy."

"You won't get away with it!" Kane said.

"You're wrong. A United States Senator can get away with just about anything."

"Why the hell Mermaid's Chair?" Sparky bellowed.

He was used to giving orders and not being ignored. Mason's lead-melting look made him seem actually to wither.

"Because, Mr. Suarez, these are the people responsible for your brother's death. I thought you might enjoy making them suffer in a place that no one will ever find and is completely equipped with the most modern and ancient torture implements. There's a curio shop near the beach called Jason's. Jason will assist you in making sure that Kane and his men's die slow, painful deaths."

"They killed Ernesto?"

Sparky's huge hands balled into fists as he went for Kane. A short burst over his head from Mason's Uzi stopped him cold.

"There'll be time for that later at Mermaid's Chair. You're wasting time, and I have to be going."

"I'm going to enjoy killing you," Sparky said to Ben Kane, reluctantly backing away.

The van the Chief had acquired from a plumbing concern contained a row of pipes and tools on both sides of the small truck, held by steel trays which jutted out about eighteen inches. An iron bar which had been welded into the body of the van ran the length of it on both sides parallel to the trays. Now Kane saw four nooses of equal size hanging from the bars: two on one side, and two directly across on the other.

"Your accommodations," Mason said. "A little less luxurious than what you're accustomed to, but functional nevertheless. The nooses should be just short enough so you'll have to squat through the whole ride. I hope Suarez is a good driver and doesn't go over too many bumps."

"Why the hell are you doing this?" the Chief asked him, bewildered. "We never did you any harm."

"No, but you thwarted my plans and you cost me time and people. I also happen to enjoy it," Mason replied coldly.

Ben realized at that moment that the man who might very possibly become the next President of the United States was completely insane.

Suarez laughed as he slipped the nooses around each of their necks. Apparently he was enjoying it too.

"Now tie their hands behind their backs. Tie them good and tight with what's left of the rope," Mason ordered. "As for you, gentlemen, don't think that you'll be able to untie each other. The nooses are far enough apart to make that impossible—but, of course, you're welcome to try."

Sparky finished tying them and looked up at Mason for further instructions.

"Take them to Mermaid's Chair and see Jason. I'll contact you then."

"What about my money for finding Christine Elvey?" Suarez asked him.

"I'm going to take care of her," Mason replied.

"Look, Gregor, I lost my brother. . . ."

Mason thought it over. "All right. We'll talk about it."

He looked at his watch. "Hurry now, you're wasting time." He opened the back doors of the van. As he got out, he said over his shoulder, "Oh, don't worry, Kane. I'll send your regards to the Mulhaneys."

Mason was right. The minute he left the van, Kane tried to reach Miles to untie his hands, but the nooses were spaced so that Miles was just out of reach. Mason—or Gregor—knew how frustrating that would be. Kane was on one side with Miles, and Ganja and the Chief were directly opposite them.

On St. Thomas, as on most of the Virgin islands, the driver of a vehicle sat on the right. That meant that Kane was directly behind Suarez's seat. If he'd had any mobility at all, he could have reached out and got his hands around Sparky's tantalizing throat. So near, and yet so far.

Things were starting to add up, no question about it. Alan Mason was the notorious Gregor. He had probably been a master spy since the war, but like many dyed-in-the-wool commies, he had fought Hitler and the Nazis. After all, Mother Russia was our ally at the time.

Mason might have been a mole even before he ran for office, Kane figured. It could well be that his try for the

225

White House was part of a diabolical Soviet plot that had been twenty-five or thirty years in the making. He was on the Senate Intelligence Committee, and the Foreign Relations Committee. Talk about letting the fox into the hen house!

That also explained why Gregor was so successful. Mason could direct his assassins using information that the CIA and other members of the intelligence community gathered. It would be child's play to kill a member of some hostile foreign government if you were privy to all the security arrangements. Gregor had been working for the enemy all along, and now they were shooting for the big prize . . . the presidency!

But why had Mason come to the islands in search of Christine Elvey? Ben tried to figure it out. She had to know something that could incriminate Mason, and ruin his presidential bid, something so devastating that he had to make sure she was killed before she regained her memory. Had Christine been blackmailing him? That would explain why he couldn't trust anyone else with the details. You didn't substitute one blackmailer for another.

Kane looked at his men. Like him, they were squatting on their haunches. Mason had made sure to shorten the nooses so they wouldn't be able to sit without choking themselves. Miles looked like he was sleeping; Ganja was holding up all right, but the Chief was cursing under his breath, very uncomfortable in the position.

"How you doing, Chief?" Kane asked.

Bukowski grunted. "From what I heard before, this is going to be the easy part of our trip."

Kane returned to the question of Christine. If she had been blackmailing Gregor, she'd probably been smart enough to put all the facts down someplace with instructions for someone to read the stuff in case of her untimely demise. What a break for Gregor that she'd had a stroke that wiped out her memory. The only problem was that Mason couldn't be sure it would never come back.

He had intended to use his friendship with Mike Mulhaney as a cover for his Virgin Island trip, but he hadn't counted on Weaver insisting that he be watched every minute. So Mason had decided to stage his own assassination attempt with Nicholas in order to throw them off the scent. With a little luck, Weaver and everybody else might have believed Nicholas was Gregor and that would have been an added bonus. Once Mason was president, he could do anything he pleased under the guise of national security, and his identity as Gregor would have been a distinct liability.

Now he was on his way to pick up Christine Elvey and take her along with Mike and Michelle on a jaunt on the *Wu Li*. Kane had said Mason wouldn't be able to get away with the murders of Mike, Michelle, and Christine . . . but he knew he was wrong. It would be easy enough. Mason wouldn't even have to pull the Bermuda Triangle story. Thanks to Weaver, there were already rumors about pirates in the area. He could make up a story about how they had come aboard and killed the three others while he managed to escape by jumping overboard or hiding. The story would be believed. If Mason wanted to, he could even have the American papers pick up the story and give him tons of free publicity back in the States. It might even make him look like a hero.

"Is everybody comfortable?" Suarez called back. "I hope not," he chuckled malevolently.

Sparky started to weave the van from one side of the road to the other, causing the men in the van to fight to keep their balance or have the nooses tighten around their throats.

227

Enjoy yourself, Kane thought. Sparky didn't realize it, but Mason wasn't going to let him live to ruin his master plan. When they had called him "Mason" in front of Sparky, they had sealed the Cuban's fate.

Mason was going to wait to kill Mike and Michelle, because he needed them to help him convince Dr. Van Rhijn to let Christine go for a sail with them. But then they'd be dead meat. He would kill Kane, Ganja, the Chief, and Miles and then get around to Suarez. Perhaps that was Jason's assignment at Mermaid's Chair? Armando must have recognized Mason when the senator opened the van. That's why he had gotten his head ventilated.

Mason had covered all the bases, all right, Kane thought gloomily. Anyone who could be a danger to him in the future had to be systematically eliminated. Why hadn't Mason just shot them all, Sparky included, when he came upon them at the van? Because that would have left half a dozen bodies, including Armando's, and would have started investigations galore. It was much better if they all "disappeared" in Gregor's torture chambers. Sparky was driving them all to Jason, who would kill them and tie things up in a neat package for Gregor. Except that left Jason with information. He would have to be killed, too . . . .

Wait! Of course! THERE WAS NO JASON!

"Suarez! I have to take to you!" Kane shouted.

"Shut up, Kane."

"Gregor can't let you live. You know too much."

"Is that right?"

"Yes, that's right! He knows that *you* know that he's Senator Alan Mason!"

"Just shut up."

"I'll shut up, all right, but you're never going to get to Mermaid's Chair. This whole ride is a setup."

"What the hell are you talking about, a setup?"

"Remember how he kept looking at his watch? How anxious he was for you to leave? You don't believe that he cared about you or Ernesto and wanted to help you get revenge, do you?"

Suarez wasn't answering.

"Don't you get it yet? He had all the time in the world to rig up these nooses. He came up with a plan to wipe all of us out."

"Sure he did. Give it a rest, Kane. You're just scared shitless about what's going to happen to you."

"Listen, you big moron!" Kane yelled. "Gregor planted a *bomb* on this van! We've been riding for about an hour— that's halfway. It's probably set to go off any minute."

"Bullshit!" Suarez said.

Chief nodded. "You're right, Ben. This trip just doesn't make any sense."

"Pipe down, both of you," Suarez said. You've got something planned."

"What the hell could we have planned? We're tied up like hogs for slaughter. Just stop this damn thing and take a look in the glove compartment, or under the seat. Your brother was carrying that semptex explosive plastic. One pound of that stuff has the explosive power of thirty grenades. Think of all the fun you're going to miss out on if we get blown up and you don't have your shot at revenge."

"I'm not listening to you," Suarez gnarled. He set his jaw and focused his concentration on weaving the van back and forth.

"Have fun, asshole. It's the last fun you're going to have," Kane told him.

He fought to keep his balance, but the rope tightened anyway. He coughed and struggled for air as the rope momentarily choked him.

Suarez steered the van back straight down the road.

Kane was convinced that he was right about the bomb, but the big baboon was too stupid or stubborn to check it out. What was the difference anyway? If Suarez did find the bomb, he wasn't about to show his gratitude by letting them go.

Without any warning, the van lurched to a stop along the side of the road. Sparky bent over and looked under his seat, then under the passenger seat. He grunted in satisfaction when he saw there was nothing there.

"Look in the glove compartment," Kane told him.

"I told you to shut up!" he said angrily, but he did open the glove compartment. "You're crazy, Kane. There's no bomb here."

"Then he put it under the van."

"There's nothing—"

"Damn it! Take a look! What the hell have you got to lose?"

"Don't give me no damn orders!" Suarez yelled.

He slid back behind the driver's seat and started the van. It moved forward about twenty feet before he stopped again. They watched him get out, and Ben could see him beginning to kneel down. His head didn't bob up at once, but they heard him then.

"Oh, shit!"

Then there was the sound of Sparky Suarez running down the road. Evidently, there was no time to do anything else. The bomb was set to go off any second!

Mike Mulhaney navigated the *Wu Li* out of St. Thomas harbor with Michelle helping on the sails. Christine and Alan Mason were talking quietly on deck.

Both Mike and Michelle had thought that Alan would have been encouraged by the news they had heard that morning. Dr. Van Rhijn had been beaming. It seemed Christine had been making progress with her so-called "short-term memory." She remembered the doctor and her nurse and some of the other patients at the home. She had even stared at Alan in a funny way. Van Rhijn explained that this might be the first step before all her memory came back. Surprisingly, Alan seemed depressed. Perhaps comparing the Christine he saw now to the girl he remembered was too much to take.

The little trip they were taking had been Alan's idea. He said he'd spoken to Ben about it and Kane had insisted that they use the *Wu Li*. Michelle had been worried about Kane, but Alan had assured her that his intelligence people were working closely with him and Kane was in safe hands. They were staking out Suarez's place, and those things weren't like in the movies. Sometimes you had to wait for days before your suspect showed up. At any rate, Alan had been in contact with him, and Kane had okayed the use of the *Wu Li*.

Michelle had been relieved to hear that Kane was all right, and Mike was very much aware of her feelings for the young man. He smiled to himself, thinking about how it would be to have Ben Kane as a son-in-law. At least she'd have a strong man to keep her on an even keel. Kane would run the yard along with Caribbean Dreams and he, Mike, would soon have a full crew of grandchildren. . . .

They were heading to a spot known as Honeymoon Bay on Water Island. Mike hadn't been there in some time, but Dr. Van Rhijn had said it was still as beautiful as ever. Mike remembered the times he had swum there off shore, diving with the pelicans and swimming with the flamingos. Those were warm, sticky-sweet memories. How did one live without good memories to fall back on in old age?

"Relax, Mike," Michelle said, moving up next to him. "From here on in, let the current do the work."

"She handles like a dream," Mike told her. "I didn't

231

believe Kane when he said he could sail her by himself if he had to. Now I can see what he meant."

Michelle rested her head on her father's shoulder and stared out at the beautiful, blue Caribbean. There was no water like it anywhere on earth, Mike had told her, and she believed he was right.

She glanced over at Christine and Alan. The senator was talking to the woman in a low voice. Christine was listening, but the blank expression on her face made Michelle wonder how much she was absorbing. Christine was wearing white cotton slacks, and a striped polo shirt, with a white kerchief tied around her neck. Her long, dark hair fanned out in the breeze.

"She must have been a very beautiful woman when she was younger," Michelle said.

"Girl, I wish you could have seen your mother," Mike replied, giving her a hug. "That woman was the sunrise and sunset all rolled into one."

"Am I like her?"

"Just like her, baby. Spitting image."

Mason walked away from Christine and stepped up to the small bridge. Michelle noticed that the woman continued to sit and stare off vacantly into space.

"How's it going?" Mike asked him.

Mason gave a sad shrug. "I've been asking about Alana, hoping I'd get some kind of response. But . . . nothing."

"I'm sorry, Alan," Michelle said.

"Yeah, well . . ." He looked out over the water. "There sure are a lot of boats around today, aren't there?"

"It's a busy channel," Mike explained. "It'll thin out as we move south toward Water Island.

"That's good," Mason said. "That's real good."

CHAPTER 22

"I hope one of you guys has an idea," Kane said grimly
to his three buddies.

There was dead silence.

"I see it's up to me." He sighed.

"That's why they pay you the big bucks, Skipper,"
Ganja retorted.

They tried to keep their tone light, but the underlying
knowledge of a powerful bomb about to explode under
their feet tended to put a damper on their repartee.

Kane was able to see over Ganja's head on the other
side. There were all kinds of tools on the shelf but not
one of them was sharp enough to cut through the rope,
even if he could reach it.

"It can't be much longer now, not the way he ran out

of here," Kane said. "At least if I could smoke one last Havana, it might not be so bad. . . ."

He looked over at the dashboard. "I've got an idea! Hurry up, Ganja! Take off your boot."

Ganja stared at him. "How the hell am I supposed to do that? And what the hell for?"

"Use your other foot and kick it off, or put it between my feet and I'll pull it off," Kane said excitedly.

Ganja managed to get the boot off. He wasn't wearing any socks. "Sorry, Lieutenant. I didn't dress my feet up for the occasion," he quipped.

"That's even better," Kane assured him. "Now put your foot over the seat and push in the cigarette lighter."

"The cigarette . . ." Light dawned. "Hey, yeah! I get it!"

"Come on, man. *Hurry!*"

Ganja stretched his leg until his bare foot reached the dash. He pressed in the lighter with his big toe. After an interminable ten seconds, the lighter popped out.

"Come on now, Ganja! You've got to bring the lighter over here between your toes. Can you do it?"

"I'll . . . try . . ."

"Come on Ganja. You can do it, man!" the Chief told him.

He wrapped his first two toes around the knob of the lighter and slowly withdrew it. If he dropped it now, they never would be able to get it again. It would fall on the front floor mats beyond their reach, and that would be the end of them.

"Hurry, man! Before the heat gets dissipated," Kane said.

"Good work, Grant," Miles added.

Kane turned around as far as he could against the slack of the noose and pushed his hands that were tied behind his back out towards Ganja.

"I might burn you, Skip," Ganja warned.

"Just *do* it, man!"

The cigarette lighter touched the rope and started burning through. The rope darkened at the spot where the red concentric circles of the heating element pressed. Pungent, dark smoke rose up for a few seconds.

"I've got to reheat it," Ganja said.

He maneuvered the lighter back into the hole in the dash. He found it wasn't easy.

"Come on, man. It's just like finding a port in a storm," the Chief urged.

Kane tried exerting all his strength to break his bonds, but it didn't help. Ganja got the lighter in once again. He pressed it and waited a few seconds. In the meantime, he flexed his toes.

"Cramp," he complained.

"Poor baby," Miles mocked.

Ganja threw him a dirty look. He got his toes around the knob of the lighter again and drew it out. The top was made of wood, but he hadn't grasped it squarely. A piece of hot metal was burning into his toe. The only indication of the pain he must be feeling was his clenched teeth and the sweat pouring off his brow.

"Forget about being gentle," Kane told him. "Push it down on the rope, HARD!"

There was a slight sizzling sound combined with the smoke and the smell of burning flesh. Kane gritted his teeth against the pain without a word.

"Damn! It's still not through," the Chief said disgustedly.

Ganja pulled the lighter off the rope. The heating element had cooled once again. Kane snapped his wrists apart. It seemed the whole business was held together by one stubborn strand. He gave one final desperate heave, and the strand gave way. He reached

235

up and slipped the noose off his neck.

"There's no time to untie all of you. I'm going to disarm the bomb," he hold them as he leaped out of the van.

He saw Sparky sixty feet down the road taking cover behind a tree, but couldn't waste time worrying about him.

In two seconds, he was under the van and examining the device attached to the muffler. It was a square pink package that looked like clay. The stuff was powerful, all right. Kane estimated there were about three pounds. He could see why Suarez had run.

The timing device was solidly implanted in the half-inch area that was a bright warning red. It was blinking without giving any indication when it would go. Kane tried to remember what kind of timing device this was. If it was a three-minute red, they'd be gone any second. If it was a five-minute red, he might have a minute, depending at what point Suarez had seen it and run.

He wanted to rip it off the muffler and toss it somewhere, but there was no telling if Mason had armed a release detonator. He'd have to remove the whole muffler.

THINK, KANE . . . THINK!

He climbed back up into the van.

"What's happening, Skip?" Ganja asked.

There was no time to answer. Kane poked through the shelves of plumbing tools. The best thing would have been a portable saber saw, but there wasn't any. He wondered if Mason had thrown out everything with a blade. He grabbed a heavy plumber's wrench instead.

"Hang in there, guys!"he told them, snaking out the door.

He clamped the wrench on the muffler and started yanking. The muffler was thin aluminum, but the job was seconds-consuming. He worked the wrench back and forth, turning and twisting the pipe. One side came loose. Kane eased it down on the ground.

The red light was still blinking like crazy. Definitely a five-minute timer, he thought. Thank God! He worked on the other side. He had the knack now and it came off easily. He placed it gently on the ground, checking to see that the muffler was between the tires, and then he scrambled back into the cab.

Shit! Had Suarez taken the keys?

No, he hadn't.

He turned the ignition and when it caught, he floored the accelerator. The van lurched forward ever so gradually, picking up speed. They were ten feet away . . . now twenty . . . now thirty . . .

The bomb exploded with a roar that shook the ground. The van seemed to be pushed forward by the force, and Kane saw bits of rock and trees go hurtling past. They had made it!

"Everybody in one piece?" Kane called out.

His men responded in various expressions of the affirmative. Then Kane saw something that made him groan.

"Hang on, boys—here comes more trouble."

Sparky had seen it all. Now he was standing in the center of the road like a matador awaiting a charging bull. But instead of a sword and cape, both his hands were wrapped around a very large and very dangerous-looking Magnum.

He got off three shots, breaking the front windshield in the process. Kane kept the pedal to the floor and at the last minute, Sparky stepped out of the way and rattled off four more shots.

"Son of a bitch!" Kane yelled.

He wheeled the van around and went after Suarez. Sparky smiled as he saw the van coming at him. This time he wouldn't miss. He had Kane in his sights and squeezed the trigger.

The gun jammed. There was no time to dive out of the way this time. Kane plowed into him and sent him flying off to the side of the road, then stopped the van and ran out, ready to apply the finishing touches. It wasn't necessary.

Suarez was dead.

Now at last Kane was able to untie his men.

Chief Bukowski tenderly rubbed the chafed area of his neck while Ganja and Miles tried to get the circulation going again in their fingers.

After he had put his boot back on, Ganja walked back down the road with Miles and took a long look at the large crater the bomb had carved into the ground. He and Miles looked at each other. Without saying a word, the two men knew each other's thoughts: *This time we made it. What happens next time is in the hands of the gods. Let's live life and if we die . . . we know that we did live.*

Kane turned the van around and picked them up. There was no celebration or back-slapping. They had had a job to do, and they were doing it. They were professionals and they expected to succeed.

Ben had originally set out to discover why Suarez wanted to kill Christine Elvey. What he had found out was even more chilling. He had to get into a town and use the first phone he could find. Was it already too late to save Mike, Michelle, and Christine?

They found a phone inside an ancient gas station where the pumps still had bubble tops. The owner, a mahogany-colored islander, ushered Kane into his office. Buried under greasy rags, calendars, service bills, and newspapers was the man's phone.

Kane got through to the Caribe Beach Nursing Home as the Chief filled up the tank of the van.

A nurse answered. It was the woman whose name sounded to Kane like a sneeze.

"Miss Kerchee, it's Ben Kane. Can I speak to the doctor, please?"

"Of course, Mr. Kane. Hold on for a moment."

Van Rhijn picked up the phone and started to pass pleasantries but Kane cut him short. He learned to his dismay that Mason and the Mulhaneys had left with Christine awhile ago.

"Did they mention where they were going?" he asked urgently.

Kane knew that if they had, Van Rhijn would remember it.

"Mr. Mulhaney mentioned about Honeymoon Bay."

"That's off Water Island," Kane said. That was a break. They had been driving in the direction of Water Island. It was due south from where he was standing.

"That's correct. Is anything wrong?" Van Rhijn wanted to know.

"There's plenty wrong, Doc. Tell you about it later. You've been a great help," Kane told him and rang off. Then he dialed Weaver's office in Charlotte Amalie.

As it rang, Kane noticed the station owner standing in the doorway. He was one of those blacks that could have been anywhere from fifty to eighty, and he looked apprehensive. They had filled up the tank and Kane was making expensive phone calls. Ben brought out his wallet and handed a hundred-dollar bill to the man. "That's for your trouble," he told him.

Kane was rewarded with a gap-tooth smile. "No trouble a'tall," the man said. He brought a chair over for him and, still smiling, backed out the door.

A female secretary answered and told Kane that Weaver was out in the field and couldn't be reached. Kane didn't believe her. He asked to speak to her supervisor, and she connected him with another woman, who sounded older but parroted the same message.

"You put on whoever is in charge of that damn office!" Kane snapped. Any patience he'd once possessed had now dissolved.

"Of course, sir," the woman said with forced politeness.

The next voice was male: cool and bored. "Mr. Morgan speaking. Can I help you?"

"No, Morgan, I can help *you*! This is Ben Kane. I'm working on something for Weaver and he's going to take it out on your ass if you don't hook me up to him. Don't bullshit me about not being able to reach him—I've seen that little doo-dad he wears in his shirt pocket that gives you a direct line to him anywhere on the Virgins."

"I won't 'bullshit' you, Mr. Kane. I *can* reach the director, but you'll have to tell me why."

"It has to do with Senator Alan Mason."

There was a momentary pause. When Morgan spoke again, he wasn't bored. "Just one moment, sir. We're patching you through."

"Weaver," the brisk, cheerful voice announced.

"It's Ben Kane."

"Kane, ol' buddy! Where the hell are you? We're at Suarez's compound, and one of the guards said he saw you drive off in a plumbing van."

"I thought the agency didn't get involved in local hassles," Kane said.

"As a rule we don't. But when I found out Gregor was involved, it changed the whole picture. It looks like you and your men handled things pretty well. We're here trying to pick up the pieces. Tell me, did you capture Mason?" Weaver asked him.

"Then you know that Mason is Gregor?"

"Yes, of course. After you left my office, I did some digging and learned all about Mason and Christine

Elvey. . . ."

Ben cut him off. "I'd love to hear all about it, Weaver, but I don't have the time. We haven't got Mason yet, and I'm afraid he's going to kill Elvey and the Mulhaneys, too, if we don't stop him. He's out on the *Wu Li* for a supposed pleasure cruise to Honeymoon Bay. He's going to pull something and kill everyone on board. Can you use one of your spy satellites and get a fix on the *Wu Li*? I'll do the rest."

"What spy satellites?" Weaver responded quickly.

"God damn it, Weaver! I've seen shots taken from those 'Eyes in the Sky.' You can photograph a license plate from a hundred miles up! The *Wu Li* is a lot bigger than a license plate. Get a couple pictures and give me the coordinates."

"Kane, if you're referring to our weather reconnaissance satellites that have been orbited under duly authorized permission of the friendly governments in this area, all we are interested in is hurricane warnings and cloud formations pertaining to weather." Weaver's voice sounded like a recorded message.

"That's what I mean," Kane said with disgust.

"Well, I could have a technician check the various meteorological photos, and if the *Wu Li* does appear . . ."

"You're wasting my time, Weaver! I'm near Brewer's Bay by the St. Thomas airport. I'm going to rent an amphibian and land in Mason's wake. When I call you back, you have those numbers for me!" Kane slammed down the phone and ran back to the van. The Chief, Miles, and Ganja scrambled in after him. Kane backed it out past the smiling native, who was waving the hundred-dollar bill and telling them to come back soon.

"How far are we from the airport, Chief?" Kane asked.

"Not more than ten minutes," he said. "We're not

241

flying, are we?"

"It's the only shot we have," Kane said. He remembered how much the Chief hated to fly.

"That just about makes my day," Bukowski said, slumping down in his seat and pulling his cap over his eyes.

Soon the airport loomed upon Kane's left. He bypassed the big hangars and terminals and sped down the road parallel to the western extension that had been construcved after a particularly gruesome crash had killed over a hundred North American tourists. Overhead, jets came in from San Juan and smaller craft made local hops from Tortola and the other islands. The International Airport in San Juan was an important junction for air traffic in the Caribbean. Kane passed planes on the ground from *Bahamasair, Prinair,* and *Liat.* There was also a whole fleet of flying boats.

Kane had previously used an outfit called simply Bob's Seaplanes. Bob Kalmus was an able pilot with three craft that he kept in good working order. His office consisted of a folding chair and a bridge table in a dusty hangar away from the bustle of the tourist planes. You found Bob's hangar by following little pieces of looseleaf paper pasted on walls with arrows that said: THIS WAY TO BOB'S SEAPLANES. Bob would sit behind his bridge table with his attaché case, sign people up for a flight, and then take out his captain's hat from the case and climb into the cockpit.

Unfortunately, Bob wasn't at his customary spot. Kane parked the van and read Bob's sign. He was out on assignment.

"Ganja, you better line up another amphibian. I'll call Weaver again," Kane said.

This time when Kane called Weaver's office from a phone in Bob's hangar, the secretary put him right through.

"All right, fella. We think we've spotted your floating bordello. She's at eighteen degrees, nineteen minutes, north latitude; and sixty-four degrees, fifty-eight minutes, west longitude."

"Got it," Kane said.

"Kane, don't do anything foolish! I'll be boarding a cutter here in the harbor and coming out there as soon as possible."

"I'll do whatever I have to do, Weaver. See you later."

Kane stepped out of the hangar and onto the runway. An old, twin-engine amphibian was taxiing out to meet them.

"Good! Looks like Ganja found us a plane," he said.

"I don't see him," said Miles. "It looks like there's only the pilot in the thing."

"Oh, no! I don't believe this," the Chief mumbled under his breath when he saw that the pilot was Ganja.

The door of the 1960-vintage Grumman four-seater opened.

"Where'd you get this crate?" Miles asked him.

"I couldn't find any pilots around, and this one was parked with the keys inside," Ganja said with a grin.

"Can you fly it, Ganja?" Kane asked him.

The Black man shrugged. "I think so. It don't look too difficult."

"Oh, my God!" the Chief murmured.

"Does it have gas?" Miles asked him.

"If this is the right dial I'm looking at here . . . I think so."

"Oh, my *God!*" the Chief moaned again. He had turned an ashen shade.

"Well, it'll have to do," Kane said. "Let's go. Everybody in."

"Can we discuss this, Ben?" the Chief asked weakly, hanging back.

"Inside, Chief!" Kane ordered.
"Oh, my *God!!*"

CHAPTER 23

Mason had never thought the channel would be so crowded with boats. It seemed impossible to have even a few minutes of solitude without some motor yacht going by, its passengers waving and tooting their horn.

The *Wu Li* was at a dead stop in the water. Michelle and Mike were below deck in the galley, and Mason and Christine were sitting together, looking out over the colorful scene.

"I find it difficult to believe that you don't remember me at all, Christine," he said to her.

"I don't," she answered simply.

"Why, just a month ago you sent me a letter. Surely you remember that? You warned me not to run for president."

"I really don't know what you're talking about." She smiled at him vaguely. "I'm getting a little chilled. Would you mind if I went below deck with the others?"

"By all means, let's go below deck," Mason said, scowling.

He stood up and looked around. For once, there didn't seem to be any other vessels nearby. He stepped over to the rail and looked down.

"Oh, Christine, come here a minute—take a look at the manta that just surfaced right near the boat. Too bad you didn't bring your paints—it would have made a terrific picture. The reflections on the water are just magnificent."

She came over beside him and looked down, and Mason moved behind her, glancing over his shoulder to make sure that Mike and Michelle weren't coming up the companionway.

"Bend over a little and you'll see it better," he urged.

She was leaning over the railing now, searching for the manta, oblivious of Mason.

He put his hands on her waist. "I'll hold you so you can get a better look," he said.

The table was set for four. Michelle had packed a large picnic basket before she and Mike had left, and Mike had made sure to put in one of his best white wines. Michelle was brewing coffee, and the aroma brought back memories of Mike's sailing days. Why was it that coffee always tasted so much better at sea? he wondered.

"Shall we call them down?" Mike asked his daughter.

"Let's give them a little more time. I feel so sorry for Alan." Michelle sighed. "He keeps trying to jog her memory, but it looks like he isn't getting anywhere. How is he ever going to find Alana?"

"If it was meant to be, he'll find her."

Michelle stood back to look at the table. She had brought a pretty red-checkered tablecloth that gave the room a sort of rosy glow. There was a large tossed salad in a wooden bowl, and French bread and roast chicken was warming in the oven of the galley.

"It looks great, Mike," she said.

"The secret for great-tasting food is to make it look good. We taste with our eyes, then with our noses, and only at the very end do the taste buds come in. By that time you've already decided how good or bad it is," Mike told her.

"I'll remember that. If I ever get married, I'm sure my husband will appreciate the tip," she said with a smile.

"What do you mean if!" I want a houseful of grandchildren, and don't you forget it!"

"Hold on, Mike. I'll be happy if—" She stopped when she saw Mason standing in the doorway. "Alan, is everything all right?"

"Sure," he said, smiling.

"Where's Christine?" Michelle asked.

"She's just fine. Don't worry about her."

Mike frowned. "Hey, Alan, you know we told Dr. Van Rhijn we wouldn't let her out of our sight. I'm surprised at you." He started for the doorway. "I'd better make sure she's all right. Besides, lunch is about ready."

"I told you she's okay!"

Mason reached behind his back and pulled out a snub-nosed Colt automatic from a concealed holster. "Stay right where you are, Mike!" he warned.

Michelle stared at him, open-mouthed.

"Have you gone crazy?" she asked.

"What kind of foolishness is this? I don't think it's funny. Alan, not with that poor woman topside probably not even remembering where she is," Mike said, continuing to walk toward Mason.

Alan stepped back to let him pass, then clubbed him

hard on the back of his head with the butt of the gun. Mike groaned and fell heavily to the floor.

Michelle gasped and ran over to her father. She touched the back of his head, then stared at her bloody hand. Mike was unconscious.

"You bastard!" she hissed.

Mason reached down and grabbed Michelle by her hair. His face was a twisted mask of rage. "You do what I tell you, or your father is a dead man. I'll pump lead into him right now and feed him to the sharks. Do we understand each other?"

Michelle couldn't believe what was happening. This couldn't be Alan Mason! This couldn't be the warm, sensitive man who was her father's old, trusted friend.

"Do we understand each other?" he repeated, pulling her hair even harder.

"Yes," she answered, gritting her teeth.

"Fine. Now you're going to do a little job for me. Get into the radio room," he told her.

But Michelle didn't move.

"Ben never did tell you to take the boat out, did he?" she asked. "You planned this to get us out on the water. Why? Why are you doing this to us?"

"Don't worry about your friend Ben Kane. He and his merry men are dead by now."

"I don't believe you!" Michelle gasped.

"Suit yourself. I didn't plan to hurt you and Mike, but I needed you to help me get Christine released."

"Alan, I don't understand. Has the fact that Christine lost her memory made you crazy? You've got to get hold of yourself. Put down the gun, Alan. We can talk about it," Michelle said, trying to reason with him.

Mason threw his head back and laughed. "No, my dear. My great love for Christine isn't the root of my *madness*. All I wanted from Christine for the last twenty-five years was to find her and kill her! But enough talk! I know you know how to use the radio, and so do I. Don't try anything, or Mike will be used for target practice."

He grabbed her arm and dragged her into the radio room.

Michelle, in a daze, sat down in front of Kane's sophisticated gear, turned on the system, and waited for Mason's instructions.

"I want you to send out a general distress saying that the *Wu Li* is being attacked by pirates," he said.

"You *are* crazy!" Michelle snapped.

Mason slapped her across the face. "Just do it! Weaver used the pirate dodge for his benefit—now I can use it for mine. Get on that radio! NOW!"

Michelle pushed the red button which was used for emergency situations and spoke into the mike. "This is the *Wu Li*, U.S. Registry Number 6214, out of Barracuda Reef. We're approaching west of Honeymoon Bay. . . ." She hesitated for a second. Mason turned and pointed the automatic through the open doorway at Mike's head.

". . . We're being boarded by pirates. Repeat . . . the *Wu Li* is being boarded by pirates. We seek assistance. We seek . . ."

Mason shut off the radio.

"That was fine," he told her, smiling in fatherly fashion.

"Ohhhh . . ."

Mike was trying to sit up, rubbing the spot on his head where Mason had slugged him.

Michelle ran over to him. "'Are you okay, Dad?" she asked, worry deeply etched on her face.

"Yeah, I guess so," Mike mumbled.

He looked up and saw Mason's gun pointing at his face.

"Alan's insane," Michelle whispered to him. "He just had me radio for help, saying that we were being boarded by pirates!"

"Did he?" Mike said thoughtfully.

"Get on your feet, Mike," Mason told him. "We're going up on deck."

"Why?" Michelle wanted to know.

"I have a feeling the 'pirates' are going to make us walk the plank," Mike told her grimly.

"No! He said he didn't want to hurt us," Michelle cried.

"I lied." Mason smirked.

It wasn't the prettiest takeoff in the world, but somehow Ganja had gotten the Grumman up into the air. Kane settled in the seat next to him as Miles and the Chief gave each other nervous looks in the back. The floor of the cockpit was littered with cigarette butts and gum wrappers. The leather seats were ripped, with white tufts of stuffing coming out, along with a rusty spring here and there. If the plane's windows had ever been cleangd, it had to be during the Kennedy era. Twice the engine sputtered and the Chief was sure they were going down, but Ganja cursed under his breath, monkeyed with the controls, and got the plane to behave itself.

"The clutch sticks," he announced.

They made it over the land mass and out to the ocean. Miles told the Chief to take a look down below. The channel was filled with all different varieties of watercraft.

"No, thanks," the Chief told him. "I'm keeping my eyes closed until we land—*if* we land!"

Kane found a book of charts under the seat and started reading them.

"How fast can you push this tub?" he asked Ganja.

"This is about as fast as she'll go without looking for trouble," Ganja replied.

"This is fine," the Chief piped up.

"How come you took off your headphones?" Kane asked their makeshift pilot.

"The tower kept telling me we were in an unauthorized flight pattern," Ganja said cheerfully. "He was getting me nervous."

"Oh, my God!" groaned Bukowski.

"I'm sorry I asked," Kane said, studying the charts. He checked Ganja's compass on the instrument panel.

"Just keep her headed west and south. We'll be coming to Water Island pretty soon. Then hug the coast."

"Okay, Skip."

Kane got up and walked out to the passenger area. "How are you holding up?" he asked the Chief.

Bukowski was sitting with his eyes tightly shut. His knuckles were white from holding on to the armrests, but he said, "Fine and dandy. If that bastard harms a hair of my little Michelle's head, I'll skin him alive!"

Kane gave him a reassuring pat on the shoulder, though he felt far from confident about Michelle's safety. Miles was standing, looking down at the water below. Kane had no idea of what altitude they were flying, but he knew that Ganja was trying to stay low to keep out of the flight patterns of larger planes heading into St. Thomas.

"There's Water Island," Miles said, pointing to a gray-and-green mass down to the right. Ganja maneuvered the amphibian so that the plane was over the coastline.

There were still a lot of boats around—too many, Kane hoped, for Mason to pull anything. But as they headed farther south, the traffic would thin out.

"Keep your eyes peeled, Ganja. We're in the area now," Kane told him.

Ganja lost altitude sharply. Kane and Miles braced themselves as they heard the engines of a jet that sounded much too close.

"It's okay. It just seemed a lot closer than it was," Ganja reported.

The Chief didn't say a word. His eyes were still shut, and he was sweating profusely.

Kane had heard a metallic sound coning from the small head in the back of the plane. Now he opened the door. A bright yellow air tank that had fallen off its perch rolled past Kane's foot. The bathroom had long since outlived its original function. It was now a changing room for passengers. Kane saw a woman's scuba outfit and a spear gun hanging on a hook, and a pair of men's scuba trunks.

"Miles, check out the tank," Kane told him as he brought down the spear gun, and cursed when he discovered that the firing mechanism was broken right off.

Miles turned the bottom valve and let out some air. He checked the nozzle and the top dial.

"Seems okay, Skip," he said, standing it right-side up.

Ben found the straps for the tank under the woman's wet suit.

"I figured they had some of this stuff aboard," Miles said. "Why have an amphibian if you aren't going to do some diving? Too bad the spear gun doesn't work."

Kane thought regretfully about the gun Suarez had used on the van. After hitting the Cuban, he should have gone back and picked it up. When they confronted Mason, the senator would be armed while they would be barehanded. Lousy odds any way you looked at it.

"There she is, Skip!" Ganja yelled excitedly.

Kane raced back to the cockpit and looked where Ganja was pointing. The *Wu Li* was off in the distance, floating by herself with no other craft around.

"Take her up high and let's circle for a minute," Kane said.

"Okay, Skip. Hang on, everybody."

"Oh, my God . . ."

"Let's go. *Move it!*" Mason commanded.

He was behind Mike and Michelle on the open staircase that led up to the deck. Michelle was in front of Mike, and Mason poked his former friend hard in the back.

"Get going, Mike!"

They all heard the sound of the amphibian's engines at the same time.

"Hold it! Stay where you are," Mason commanded.

He reached up, grabbed a handful of Michelle's hair, and yanked her hard. She fell back down the stairs to the floor below.

"Bastard!" Mike yelled, lunging at Mason.

"Try it!" Mason said, putting the gun squarely between Mike's eyes.

Mulhaney backed off.

"Both of you get into that stateroom," he said, pushing them along.

He opened the first door he came to and pushed them both inside.

"Let's have the keys, Mike," he told him.

Reluctantly, Mulhaney handed the keyring over.

"Let Christine come down here with us," Michelle pleaded.

"Don't worry—you'll be joining her soon enough, deep down in that beautiful bright blue water!" Mason laughed to himself. He heard Mike and Michelle gasp simultaneously as he closed the stateroom door and locked it from the outside.

Then he went up to check on the plane. He hadn't counted on such a quick response to Michelle's Mayday. If the plane was just joy-riding and in the area by coincidence, that was one thing; but if it was there in response to their request for assistance, then he'd have to change his plans. He had originally decided to put a bullet in each of their heads and toss them overboard, then wait until he heard the sound of an approaching craft, shoot himself in the arm, and come up with a story of how he had fought the pirates, trying to save the life of his old friend and Mike's daughter. He'd even taken a bullet in the arm for his trouble. Then he'd dive into the water and pretend to be drowning. He didn't have all the details worked out yet, but he knew that once the rescuers were on the scene, he'd be well prepared.

In fact, he'd been looking forward to devising a story that painted him a hero. He could use it to get his presidential campaign rolling. But this airboat arriving too soon would spoil that scenario.

Now he would have to kill Michelle and Mike in the cabin. He'd still give himself a superficial wound and spin a story about how the pirates had mistakenly left him for dead.

Mason stuck his head out on deck and looked around. The plane wasn't in the sky any longer—it was floating on the water about fifty yards to starboard. What the hell was it doing there?

If the bastard didn't move soon, he'd have to utilize the second option and shoot the Mulhaneys below. He could always say the pirates had killed them and left just after Michelle made her distress call. Yes, and they were in a white motorized yacht. There had to be hundreds of those within a ten-mile radius.

Mason didn't like the way the plane was just sitting there. It looked like some giant bird of prey waiting to pounce on its target. Then he smiled to himself. If they wanted to play cat-and-mouse games, he had just the ticket.

He crawled onto the deck on hands and knees, staying low until he reached the .35mm cannon that Kane had had installed in his honor. Slowly he worked the heavy canvas off the big gun and saw the neat stack of twelve dull brass shells in the rack next to it.

Mason made sure he kept his head down as he maneuvered himself into position behind the gun. He lifted one of the shells, placed it in the breech, and locked it. Then he set the sights for fifty yards and lined up his target. The blowing up of the amphibian would just be another dastardly act by those missing pirates.

Suddenly, as if sensing impending danger, the amphibian started taxiing away from the scene.

Mason was sure the occupants of the plane hadn't seen him. He was also convinced now that it wasn't responding to the distress call. Maybe it was some horny couple looking for a secluded spot somewhere to knock off a piece. They probably resented the *Wu Li* being in the area as much as Mason resented them.

He watched the wake of the amphibian as it taxied to a distant spot off toward the horizon. Good riddance! Mason thought.

He went back to the companionway leading below, opened the door of the stateroom—and waited. Of course they would expect him to step in so they could jump him. He swung the door open wide and looked in. Mike and Michelle were hiding behind the door.

"Suit yourself. If you want me to put holes in Mr. Kane's stateroom door, that's okay with me," he warned.

Mike came out first, with Michelle behind him.

"Let's get back up on the deck, shall we?" Mason suggested pleasantly.

He could shoot them here and then throw them overboard, but why exert the energy to carry the bodies up to the deck if he didn't have to?

"Will you at least tell me why?" Mike asked him. "Tell me what the hell this is all about?"

"I'm Gregor," Mason said, with a self-satisfied smile.

"I don't believe you!" Mike was aghast. "You're no spy. Hell, I served with you in the war! I *know* you!"

Mason shook his head. "We were comrades in arms then, Mike, because it served the needs of my country

255

. . . the Soviet Union."

"What the hell are you talking about? You're an American, just like me!" Mike blustered.

"No—my real name is Gregor Korelenko. I was born in a small town near Moscow, educated in the Pravistuk Institute, and trained in espionage since the age of seven. I'm only one of hundreds of operatives who have assumed American identities and have infiltrated all levels of your society."

"You couldn't have," Mike said weakly. "It's not possible!"

"Oh, but it is, Mike. On a personal level, I'm sorry to have to kill you, but the ideals of world order, world peace, of no class distinctions must take precedence over sentimental feelings of friendship."

"What kind of peace? What kind of world order? What kind of idealism made you kill a poor innocent woman suffering from a stroke? Or killing two innocent people like my father and me?" Michelle cried.

Mason sighed. "I don't expect you to understand," he said. "And believe me, Christine was no innocent! But you two are wasting time. Get up on deck!"

He marched them up the steps and to the railing in the bow. The seas were empty. He had lost sight of the amphibian.

"Face the water. It will be easier that way," he suggested.

But Mike turned around. "I want you to look me in the eye when you kill me," he said defiantly.

"Me, too," Michelle said. She glared at Mason, her chin quivering ever so slightly.

He shrugged. "Suit yourself."

He lifted the gun and pointed it between Mike's eyes. "Sorry, old buddy," he said.

A bright yellow air tank went flying across the deck. Eight inches higher, and it would have hit Mason on the head. Instead, it landed squarely between his shoulder blades, knocking him forward into Mike. He pulled himself away and whirled.

Kane stood on the other side of the deck, his lean muscular body, wet from his swim from the amphibian, glistening in the Caribbean noonday sun.

"Kane!" Mason said in disbelief.

He raised his gun for a shot, but Michelle grabbed his arm and the shot went awry. Kane was no longer standing in the same spot. Where the hell had he gone so quickly?

Mason pushed Michelle and Mike out of his way and ran to the opposite side of the deck. No Kane. He turned and saw Mike Mulhaney charging at him. Mason swerved out of the way and got off a quick shot. Mulhaney went down. Michelle screamed and ran toward the entrance to the hold.

Mason ran after her, grabbed her by the throat, and dragged her to the center of the deck.

"Where are you, Kane?" he called out. "Come on out, Kane, and show yourself. If you want your girl friend to be killed, that's up to you."

"Don't listen to him, Ben! He's going to kill us all anyway," Michelle screamed. "He shot my father. He's GREGOR! You have to stop him. This maniac might become president!"

"Shut up!" Mason barked. He smacked her hard with the back of his hand.

They were standing over Mike Mulhaney's body. Michelle tore herself away from Mason and dropped down to cradle her father's head in her lap. Mason crouched down next to her with the gun at her temple.

"I'm going to count to three, Kane, and then she gets it. One . . ."

Kane dropped from the boom over Mason's head. He landed on Mason's shoulders and wrestled him to the ground. The gun fell from Mason's hand and clattered to the deck. Ben punched him, catching him with a glancing blow on the jaw. Mason's head snapped back. He cursed and took a wild swing at Kane that missed completely. He managed to pick up the gun, but Kane kicked at his hand, and it spun off the bow into the water.

Mason caught Ben's bad leg and twisted, and Kane went down hard, banging his head on the teak deck. He shook his head to clear the cobwebs.

Michelle screamed, and Ben looked up just in time to see Mason charging at him with the heavy scuba air tank. He ducked to the side as Mason, using the tank as a club, missed Kane's head by inches and crashed the tank onto the deck.

From his position under Mason, Kane countered with an uppercut that caught his adversary in the pit of his belly. There was a whoosh sound as Kane's punch emptied the older man's lungs. Mason doubled over, and Kane hit him flush on the chin with everything he had. Mason went down . . . and stayed down. His legs twitched reflexively, and then he stopped moving completely.

Kane ran over to Mike and Michelle. "How is he?" he asked.

"He's still alive," Michelle answered through her tears, "but he's bleeding badly. We've got to get him to a doctor, Ben. And it has to be right now if we're going to save his life!"

CHAPTER 24

Kane dashed down to the communications room and called Ganja on the radio. They had agreed that they'd keep the amphibian out of sight until Kane had a chance to deal with Mason. Now Kane wanted Ganja to transport Mike to the nearest hospital. He kept trying, but there was no answer. Seeing the way the amphibian was maintained, he wouldn't have been surprised if the plane's radio was down.

"Ben! Ben! Come quickly," Michelle called suddenly.

He hustled up to the deck and followed her outstretched arm. A large Coast Guard cruiser, the *U.S. Scorpion*, was bearing down on them. There was a figure standing on the bow, Kane could tell, wearing a white suit that, even at a distance wasn't regulation Coast Guard.

For the first time in his life, Kane was happy to see Weaver. He called out to him, telling him to bring a stretcher. Weaver boarded, along with another man carrying a black bag, and two seamen carrying the stretcher he had requested.

"This is Dr. Rosen," Weaver said. "I asked him to come along in case there were any injuries. Since you asked for a stretcher, I thought there might be."

"Damn glad you did, Weaver," said Kane.

The doctor was already bending over Mike, taking his pulse and then his blood pressure. He directed the two seamen to place Mulhaney on the stretcher. They strapped him down, then carried him off to the cutter, an anxious Michelle following them.

"Let me take a look at this one," Dr. Rosen said. He made a move toward the still unconscious Mason, but Weaver stopped him by placing his hand on the doctor's shoulder.

"We'll handle it from here, Rosen," he said.

The doctor didn't argue. Kane got the impression that he was one of those people who found it paid to be deaf, dumb, and blind. That was probably the reason Weaver had called on him.

They waited for the doctor to leave the *Wu Li*, and then Weaver knelt down and reached for Mason's carotid. He looked up at Kane.

"He's still alive. Did you do this, ol' buddy?"

"He was about to kill Mike and Michelle. Christine Elvey wasn't on board—he probably killed her, too. I connected with a roundhouse."

"From the top, Kane . . . and slowly," Weaver said. "I'm all ears."

Kane saw him touch something in his coat pocket and knew that everything he said would be recorded for posterity. He told Weaver how Ganja had landed the amphibian nearby and how he had swum, using the scuba equipment, to the *Wu Li*. He described the fight with Mason. Weaver listened to the whole story, nodded once or twice, then asked if Mason had given any reason for his actions.

Kane had said, "No. I'm hoping you have an explanation, Weaver. Why did Gregor need to kill Christine?"

"We'll have plenty of time to discuss that later," Weaver replied.

Kane started for the communications room. "I have to call Ganja on the radio again. I couldn't raise him before. Maybe now I'll have better luck."

"Don't bother," Weaver told him blandly. "Your motley crew are safely aboard the cutter. You can join them now, if you like."

Kane frowned. Something didn't sit right. Why weren't Ganja, Miles, and the Chief standing on the *Scorpion's* deck if they were aboard?

"Weaver, why do I feel you're not leveling all the way with me?" Kane asked, narrowing his eyes.

"What on earth do you mean?" Weaver was the picture of innocent curiosity.

"If my people are okay, how come they weren't on deck to greet me?"

"They're being debriefed, Kane. This isn't one of your run-of-the-mill drug-smuggling cases," Weaver explained patiently. "We're talking about an influential member of the United States Senate. You just don't take a situation like this lightly."

"All right! I want to see them. And I want to see how Mike and Michelle are doing."

"Of course. Go on board. I'll tend to Mason and take him into custody."

After Kane boarded the *Scorpion* he was immedkately met by a lieutenant who asked him to follow him below.

261

Two seamen were walking close behind him. When they stopped in front of a door the lieutenant reached into his pocket and pulled out a key.

"Are my men locked up?" Kane asked incredulously.

The lieutenant opened the door and Kane saw Ganja, the Chief, and Miles, sitting at a table playing cards . . . or trying to play cards as best they could with handcuffs on their wrists.

"What the hell *is* this?" Kane exploded.

He turned to see that the two seamen had their guns drawn and pointing straight at him.

"You're under arrest," the lieutenant told him briskly. "Now let's have your hands for the cuffs. Don't make any trouble," he said, slipping the cuffs on Kane's wrists.

The two seamen unceremoniously pushed Kane into the room.

"I think it's the Skipper's turn to deal," the Chief said, giving him a wry smile.

"What happened?" Kane asked. "What the hell's going on?"

The Chief did the talking. "We were cooling our heels in the amphibian waiting to hear from you, Skip, and the next thing we know we're being boarded by the Coast Guard. Weaver's standing there on the bridge like the tin-horn dictator he is and he's telling the sailors to put us in the brig. So they did, and here we are."

The "brig" was really a stateroom that had been modified as a sort of holding pen. The porthole in the room had been covered with a steel grid. The door had no knobs or locks on the inside and could only be opened with a key from the outside. Despite those touches, the room was fairly pleasant, with bunk beds, a table, a large head that contained a shower stall, and a closet. Ben opened the closet. It was empty.

"How long are we going to be locked up, Skip?" Ganja asked him.

Kane shook his head, dazed. Who could know what that maniac, Weaver, might have in store for them next? But he tried to reassure them.

"It won't be long—probably just until we get into port."

He told them what had happened aboard the *Wu Li*. Ganja yelled, "ALL RIGHT!" when Kane described how he had flattened Mason. They all grew very quiet when Ben told them that Mike had been shot.

Michelle sat next to the bunk in a small stateroom, holding her father's hand. Mike seemed to be breathing easier now. He seemed to be still unconscious, but Dr. Rosen had explained that the pain-killers were making him sleep.

When Michelle had asked if Mike was going to make it, Rosen just adjusted the intravenous and said it was too early to tell. From what he could see, Mike Mulhaney appeared to be in excellent health, and that was a big factor in his favor. The doctor told her that they wouldn't be able to come up with a definite prognosis until they were able to get him to the St. Thomas General Hospital for X-rays.

When they docked at St. Thomas, an ambulance was waiting for them. The same two seamen who had carried Mike onto the *Scorpion* put him in the ambulance, then followed Michelle inside the cramped van and rode with her all the way to the hospital and up the elevator.

Michelle was very surprised and a little hurt at first that Ben Kane hadn't shown his face, but decided that Weaver was keeping him busy for some reason.

Awhile later, after Mike had been taken to Emergency, Dr. Rosen walked into the hospital room, where

263

Michelle was waiting, with a big smile on his face. "I've got very good news for you, Miss Mulhaney," he said. He was carrying Mike's X-rays, and he placed them on the light box.

"The shot seems to have missed all the vital organs. The bullet entered the lower left quadrant and exited right through the body. There might be some internal bleeding, and we'll have to guard against infection, but I feel safe in saying that your father is going to be all right."

For what seemed to be the first time in hours, Michelle started to breathe again. The moment the doctor left, she buried her face in her hands and began to sob with relief. When she was able to compose herself, she looked around for a phone to call Ben.

Where would he be? Had they let him take the *Wu Li* back, or was he on the *Delphi*? It was strange that Ganja, Miles, or the Chief hadn't come by. There was no phone in the room. Perhaps there would be one down the hall.

She tried turning the doorknob. That was odd—the door appeared to be locked. On impulse, she ran to the window and pulled the brightly colored curtains apart. She gasped when she saw the bars.

They had been docked now for over an hour. Kane paced the floor like a tiger at feeding time, all kinds of thoughts racing through his mind.

What if Weaver wasn't the gung-ho patriot he appeared to be? What if he was in on the whole thing with Mason? No—that didn't make any sense. Weaver wouldn't have let him guard Mason if they were working together.

Could Weaver be bought? Why had Weaver sent everyone off the *Wu Li* and insisted on taking care of Mason alone? Was their incarceration Weaver's idea?

The Chief said he gave the orders for them to be placed in the brig . . . but maybe the orders came from higher up.

"If I get my hands on that scumbag, Weaver . . ." the Chief growled, seeming to read Kane's thoughts.

"You'll have to wait in line, man," Ganja told him grimly.

Miles sat still, staring at the wall. His dark, brooding eyes radiated steely, cold anger.

The door opened suddenly and the young lieutenant, flanked by the two armed seamen, walked into the room. The seamen removed Kane's handcuffs.

"Well, it's about time!" the Chief said, standing and holding out his hands.

"Not you, mister. Just Kane. The rest of you stay put," the lieutenant told them. "This way, Mr. Kane."

"I don't leave without my men," Ben Kane said.

"Mr. Kane, my orders are to bring you to Mr. Weaver's office. But my orders don't say *how* you have to arrive. If you want it to be unconscious, that's all right with me."

"If you touch the commander, you'd be making a big mistake," Miles said in his dull monotone. He slowly stood up and stared at the lieutenant. The young officer took a step backwards.

"Easy, Miles," Kane warned. "We don't want to hurt anybody. They're just following orders."

"Ben, why don't you jawbone with Weaver? The sooner you see him, the faster we can all get out of this shithole," the Chief said. "At the very least, you can get some news about Mike."

"Go on, Skip. We'll be all right. It'll give me more time to clean out these suckers," Ganja joked, picking up the cards.

"All right, lieutenant," Ben sighed. "Take me to your leader."

CHAPTER 25

When Kane arrived under escort at the Ultratech offices in Charlotte Amalie, Suzy gave him a big smile and made small talk as she showed him into Weaver's private office. The imposing map of the world with its red and blue lights gave the office an eerie quality until Suzy turned on the recessed lights. She softly closed the door behind her as she left.

Kane settled himself in the leather chair. When he heard the door opening, he whirled around, expecting to see Weaver.

But it was Michelle who entered.

"Oh, Ben!" she cried, and ran into his arms.

They finally broke their long embrace, and Kane said, "How's Mike? What happened?"

"He's going to be fine," she told him. "The doctor said there are no serious internal injuries. In a week or two, he'll be his own surly self." She tried to smile. "What happened to *you?* I thought I'd see you when we docked."

"Weaver, that's what happened. He picked up Ganja, the Chief, and Miles and threw them into the brig. After I got off the *Wu Li*, he had me thrown in there with them."

"And I was locked in a hospital room," Michelle told him. "Ben, what the hell is going on?"

Kane shrugged. "I expect we're going to find out any minute now."

"I *hate* that bastard, Weaver," Michelle said, putting her hands on her hips. "He's such a slime!"

"Yeah. But on the other hand, by bringing a doctor with him on the cutter, he probably saved Mike's life," Kane pointed out.

"True, but if it weren't for Weaver, we wouldn't have had any shooting in the first place. Mason could have done what he wanted without dragging all of us into it." She thought about what she had just said. "I don't really mean that—I didn't want anything to happen to that poor lady. She was on deck, and then when we went back up . . . she was gone. He must have thrown her overboard." She shuddered, and Kane had just put his arms around her again when Weaver walked in. He walked right past them without saying a word and took a seat behind his desk. He was carrying two manila folders in his hand.

"I'd like both of you to sit down, please," he said.

"You have some explaining to do, Weaver!" Kane barked angrily.

"No problem, Kane. All in good time. How's your father, Miss Mulhaney?"

"He's going to be fine," Michelle snapped. "No thanks to you!"

"My, my . . . everyone's so touchy today," Weaver

said, arranging the papers.

Kane leaned over, palms flat on the surface of Weaver's desk. "Why were we held in custody, Weaver?"

Weaver shook his head sadly. "You and your friends face some pretty serious charges, I'm afraid, ol' buddy. The way I see it, a judge could give you twenty or thirty years. . . ."

"What the hell are you talking about?" Kane exploded.

"Ben, ol' boy, you *cannot* go and steal an airplane, fly in unauthorized air space, show reckless indifference to human lives, and expect to walk away without paying a penalty."

"What?"

"And you, Miss Mulhaney—you and your father signed a release for the day for one Christine Elvey, whose body was washed ashore on Water Island a half hour ago. You were responsible for the well-being of that poor woman, and you are now under investigation for her death."

"Weaver! What kind of shit is this?" Kane bellowed. "You know exactly what happened on the *Wu Li*. You know why we had to take that amphibian. You should be pinning medals on us instead of treating us like criminals."

Kane leaned closer to Weaver. "I'll tell you what, Weaver—you put us on trial and we'll tell our story about Gregor and your phony pirates. The press will have a field day, and we'll see who the jury believes. Come on, Michelle—let's go back to jail. It's a hell of a lot better than having to waste time with this scum!"

Michelle and Kane began walking toward the door.

"Sit down! Both of you. Let's all take it easy, okay?"

Michelle and Kane exchanged glances, then turned and reluctantly sat down.

Weaver clasped his hands together. "No one said anything about a trial. I just wanted you both to know the seriousness of these charges. Hey . . . we're all

269

reasonable people, we can work things out to our mutual satisfaction. The truth of the matter is, Mason is dead," he told them.

"What do you mean *dead*? You saw him. Yeah, I knocked him unconscious, but he sure as hell wasn't dead."

"These things happen, Ben. A blow to the head can have devastating repercussions." Weaver shook his head sadly.

"Bullshit! If he's dead, it's because you killed him!"

Weaver said coolly, "I doubt there will be many tears shed at his passing. You see, if he'd lived, he would have alerted many of his confederates that we were closing in on them. He also would have been a terrible embarrassment to many organizations who unknowingly supplied Mason with information which he used to assassinate and subvert. There was also the possibility that, had he lived, he might have found a way—using his enormous influence—to escape any prosecution whatsoever. I think you'll agree that his passing is no cause for great sorrow."

"Weaver, what are you getting at?" Kane asked warily.

The president of Ultratech opened the two files he had brought into the room with him and took out three typewritten sheets. He looked from Kane to Michelle and smiled.

"I know that both of you have been under a great strain. That's why I had you placed in rooms where you could rest and not be disturbed by anyone. I'm sorry you were handcuffed, Kane. Obviously, someone misinterpreted my orders. I'll personally deal with that matter. And I'd like you to know that your crew is resting comfortably at this moment at the Hilton as guests of the St. Thomas Chamber of Commerce.

"These papers I have in front of me contain the full story of what went on aboard the *Wu Li*. I think you will agree with the account there *exactly as it is written*. All you have to do is sign on the bottom line."

He handed the papers to them.

"What is this? It's just a pack of lies!" Michelle said after she had quickly skimmed over the pages.

"You'll never get me to sign this crap, Weaver," Kane said angrily.

Michelle shook her head. "Where did you get this from?" She read aloud, "*We were attacked by six men wearing masks. They shot my father, Mike Mulhaney, and proceeded to toss Christine Elvey into the ocean after breaking her neck. . . .*"

"Mine says that I saw Alan Mason fight one of the men, that he was knocked unconscious and then tossed into the ocean. Are you out of your skull, Weaver?" Kane asked.

"Nope . . . and you both WILL SIGN," Weaver said confidently. "I think you might like to know, Kane, that after this incident, the waters will be swept clear of pirates and there will be no threat to any of your charter boats."

"Now isn't that fine and dandy," Kane said sarcastically.

"There *were* no goddamn pirates!" Michelle snapped.

"If that was the case, why did you send an emergency SOS to all ships in the Caribbean?" Weaver countered. "Do you have any idea what the penalty is for sending a false report? I think your shipyard might find itself without an insurance carrier if it came out that you were incompetent enough to do such an irresponsible thing."

"But Mason made me do it!"

"C'mon now, Miss Mulhaney. Do you expect me to believe that a United States Senator, a man who was favored to be the next President of the United States, would hold a gun on you and force you to break the law? Do you think that's what the people of this great country of ours want to hear about one of its heroes? Isn't it better if the late Alan Mason can be remembered defending his friends against pirates, the way he de-

271

fended this country from its enemies?"

"What about Christine Elvey? Her death gets white-washed, too?" Kane asked bitterly.

"Yes . . . Christine Elvey." Weaver thought a moment about the woman. "When you left my office the other day, Kane, I did some checking. I ran Miss Elvey through our computers under both her married and maiden names. There was nothing on file. That's pretty strange, considering we usually have *some* information on virtually the entire population. Just for the hell of it, I thought of checking the pre-tech files."

"What the hell is a 'pre-tech file'?" Kane asked.

"Everything was transferred onto main-frame computers in the sixties. Whatever we had in the dossiers was painstakingly entered in the data banks. As a matter of fact, the dossiers before 1965 should have been destroyed. But I contacted one of my people in Washington, and tucked away in the archives, he found a file for Miss Elvey.

"Obviously, the file had been overlooked when it came time to transfer data to the computers. It made very interesting reading, I can tell you. Elvey was under surveillance for espionage activities. She was a communist sympathizer who signed leftist petitions in high school and was involved with a Marxist-Leninist Club in college. She graduated from those activities to seduce various members of Congress who lived in her home state of Missouri. She then went to Washington and served as a secretary for one of her boyfriends. We believe she was blackmailing him at that time."

"You're making this up," Michelle gasped.

"No way. The man she worked for eventually committed suicide. He left no note, but it was believed that Miss Elvey—who had the key to his apartment—might have taken everything that could have incriminated her before our people arrived. She was kept under constant surveillance from then on, and continued using her charms to infiltrate the halls of Congress through her bedroom."

"I'll be damned!" Kane said.

"There was a report on file from one of our operatives saying that he had uncovered evidence that she was blackmailing her victims into helping the careers of certain unknown political hopefuls and extending their influence far beyond the norm. In the next-to-last report, we find that one of these guys was a man who was just beginning a brilliant career in politics."

"Alan Mason," Kane said.

"Yes, Alan Mason. Incidentally, the individual who filed that report was found dead three weeks later."

"You're saying that *Christine* was working for the Russians too?" Michelle said. "And she had never been married to Mason's old friend, I bet. And of course, there was no daughter."

"You got it. She must have done a good job for Mason, because he wound up with some very important friends who took him under their wings."

"But none of this explains why Mason would want to kill her," Kane said.

Weaver shook his head. He reached into his desk and handed Kane a sheet of paper.

"Take a look at this, Kane. You see, Elvey became afraid that when Mason's career took off, someone higher up might decide that she knew too much. It dawned on her that the slave masters in Moscow were looking for some very important results from their boy Alan. She knew the way they think. As long as she was alive, they couldn't be sure she wouldn't blow the whistle on them. One day, she learned that KGB agents were waiting for her in her apartment, so she took off and left the country. She eventually settled in the Virgins and started to realize at last that this country is a great place to live. She buried her past and tried to make a new life and identify for herself as an artist. After a while, the KGB seemed to forget about her—bigger fish to fry, I guess.

"We've managed to piece the rest of the story together. She read in the paper that Mason might be our next president. She had changed so much that she couldn't let that happen. She sent him a letter saying that if he won the nomination, she would expose him. She also said that she was no fool and that a copy of the whole story was being left with her lawyer and would be made public if something happened to her. That's what you're reading now, Kane."

"How did you get hold of this?" asked Ben.

Weaver smirked. "That's *my* business. Mason couldn't move until he got rid of Christine. The whole operation to make him president hinged on it. He couldn't risk her regaining her memory, so he had to kill her."

"Good Lord!" Michelle said softly. "She looked so sweet."

"From where I sit," Weaver said, "she saved this country from an even bigger mistake than Jimmy Carter. She knew what she was doing when she warned Mason. I think, under the circumstances, that stating she was killed by pirates is preferable to exposing her as a person who spied for the Russians twenty-five years ago."

"What do you want us to do?" Kane said quietly.

"Like I said before, I want you both to sign those affidavits. I'll depend on your patriotism to persuade your people to go along with the story, Kane. And your father's, too, Miss Mulhaney."

Michelle sighed.

Kane thought it over.

"Give us a couple of pens," he said resignedly.

CHAPTER 26

The Rainbow Keg Inn had ben adorned with brightly colored Chinese lanterns and streams for the occasion. The big sign which was draped from one end of the building to the other spelled out its message loud and clear: WELCOME BACK, MIKE MULHANEY.

It had been ten days since Mike had been wounded, and his friends on Barracuda Reef wanted him to know how much they had missed him. The party, which had started at seven, was now in its fifth hour without any sign of winding down.

Ben Kane was in a reflective mood. He watched Ganja win the limbo contest ("I always said the man was a snake," the Chief wisecracked) and tried to pay equal attention to Jessica and Michelle, both of whom were looking particularly alluring that evening.

Dr. Van Rhijn had been invited and was astounding the group of people at his table with his extraordinary memory. Kane had overheard him quoting an entire chapter of *Gone with the Wind* verbatim—Van Rhijn had asked the person making the request if he wanted the book or the movie version.

Lord Philip had cornered Kane and asked if he had heard anything about the world chess match, wondering if there was a player in the world who could beat Karpov. Kane politely told him he hadn't heard a thing.

Now he walked out of the Rainbow Keg and made his way to the water. He looked out over the dock at the boats dancing on the bright, rippling waves. Behind him, he could hear the bass sounds and drums of the reggae calypso band. He took a deep breath and patted the pockets of his blue blazer, looking for a cigar. He stripped off the cellophane, struck a match, and got it started.

It was a comfortably cool evening. There was the heavy, sweet smell of tropical fruit in the air. Kane watched some frolicking brown pelicans splashing one another in the moonlight before they got down to the serious business of fishing.

"Mind if I share the rail with you, Ben?" Mike Mulhaney asked.

"Welcome aboard," Ben said, smiling.

Mike stood next to Kane, leaning his elbows on the top iron bar.

Ben handed him a cigar and lit it for him. Mike had his stomach taped heavily, Kane knew, and he walked a little more slowly than before, but from all indications, the Patron Saint of Barracuda Reef would be as good as new in no time. Mike took a deep drag on the cigar.

"That's a good one, Ben. I've got to sneak them now. Michelle nags the life out of me."

Ben drew another cigar out of his pocket and stuffed it into Mike's breast pocket. "That's for later," he said.

They both stared out at the water in silence. A small, brown-skinned youngster who should have been home sleeping was fishing ten yards from them. The native boy, using a bamboo pole, had something nibbling on the hook. He pulled up a bony plated boxfish, and his smile lit up the dock. They watched him run off.

"How are you feeling, Mike?"

Mulhaney laughed. "I swear, Ben, I'm going to get me a button that says *Just Fine, Thanks*, and point to it all day long."

Kane smiled. "Sorry."

"Oh, not you, Ben. I'm talking about the people who ask about my health but just use that as an opening gambit to find out about the pirates."

"You, too?"

"Man! I'm not happy about lying like this. And I don't like the idea that every paper in the damn islands makes Mason out as the greatest hero since Rambo, either."

"I know," Ben sighed. "I guess it's the only thing to do, though."

"Was his body found yet?"

"No. Gordon and his men have been figuring the tide. They think it'll wash up on the beach any day now."

"Something eatin' you, Ben? You don't look like you're enjoying my party," Mike said, looking closely at the younger man.

"I'm just trying to figure it all out," Ben said. "This is the garden spot of the world, Mike. People here should be able to live their lives in peace. I thought the war was over in Nam . . . but it's not. It's around us every day, everywhere we look."

"You can sit it out, Ben. You could tell Weaver or

anybody else to take a hike, and the hell with the consequences."

"Yeah, I could, but it wouldn't really change anything. Behind the curtains of paradise are the Four Horsemen . . . and they're not going away unless somebody works at it. Like it or not, we're all combatants in this war."

The two men watched the clouds scudding across the velvet sky, silent for the moment.

"I'm glad you weren't hurt bad, Mike," Kane told him at last.

"Yeah—real lucky this time." He put his arm around Kane's shoulders. "How about you and me getting a couple of beers and going back on in?"

"You go ahead, Mike. I'll be along in a few minutes. I just want to finish my cigar," Ben said, staring off into the soft darkness.

The Russian looked at Weaver's map. "You are still keeping score, I see. This time I think a little more red since I been here last." He smiled and a large gold front tooth glinted in the light of Weaver's office fluorescents.

"The game has a way of shifting, doesn't it? How's Havana?" Weaver asked him.

"Hot. And Castro is still making six-hour speeches . . . and I sit on the reviewing stand soiling . . . and sweat is running down my back like river."

"We'll be back there one day, Alexei, you can bet on it."

"You live in a dream, Weaver. Now, what is so important to call me to the Virgin Islands?"

Weaver leaned back in his chair. "I have a deal to make with your bosses in the Politboro."

"Weaver, Weaver, my friend, I tell you many times I am small functionary in Soviet Mission to Cuba. You amuse me by thinking I am big spy. Me . . . Mr. James Bond."

"You are Alexei Mikorski, in charge of espionage for the Caribbean. You report to Boris Poolov who is the number-two man in the KGB. You have a minimum of one hundred and twenty agents whom you control through the Soviet missions of twelve Caribbean nations. Shall I go on, Alexei?"

The heavyset Russian shrugged his shoulders. "Is pure speculation . . . not based on fact. But I am flattered that you think my government would give such a responsibility to a poor peasant like myself."

"To business then, Alexei."

Weaver's eyes narrowed. This was a side of him few people ever saw. His clothes, his hair, the breezy-cool manner . . . all disguises masking the real Cord Weaver, a calculating Machiavelli with an iron will and bulldog tenacity.

"I am always interested when you talk business," Alexei told him.

"We have Gregor Korelenko," Weaver said, watching Alexei's face.

The man never moved a muscle.

"I am not familiar with the name," the Russian said.

"Then we have nothing more to say to each other. I'm sorry you made the trip for nothing. I'll have a plane take you back to Havana."

Weaver stood up.

"I don't want to appear stupid, Weaver. Let me think for a minute if I have ever heard . . . Yes, I do believe I remember the name from somewhere."

"How about the name Alan Mason. That ring a bell?" Weaver asked.

"I do not know many Americans. Tell me about this man . . . Korelenko. If it is the person I recall, he was killed on some boat."

"It appears that he survived."

The Russian smiled. "That is most fortunate."

"Not for you, Alexei."

The Russian leaned back in his chair. "If the man is a Soviet citizen, he is probably most anxious to go home to Mother Russia."

"*Very* anxious."

"Well, we have to think of his worried family and friends. What kind of comrade would I be if I would not help a countryman return to the Motherland?"

"That's quite touching, Alexei," Weaver said drily.

"Is settled then. I will pick up this man and take him with me." Alexei stood up. Weaver stayed where he was.

"I'll be happy to give him to you. You know, Alexei . . . we have six American patriots who are rotting in East German prisons," he said casually.

"You are referring to the Hamburg Six? They are convicted spies who infiltrated a friendly state to gain secrets for their capitalist CIA bosses."

"Korelenko for the six," Weaver snapped.

"Out of the question!"

"Good evening."

Alexei started to walk to the door. Weaver pushed a button on his desk. "Send a car around for Mr. Milorski," he said into the intercom.

Mikorski paused. "Weaver, you know that you are asking too high a price."

"I don't think so."

"You are a fool!"

He walked out the door and slammed it behind him.

Weaver smirked. The Russian would be back. He would carry the bluff all the way to the plane and then he would come back.

Weaver looked at the large map of the world on the wall opposite his desk, his expression deadly serious.

One day, the colors of the map would change.

It would be all blue . . . BLUE . . . *BLUE*. . . .

Kane watched the lights of a boat far off in the distance. The sound of a distant fog horn could be heard echoing through the stillness of the dark night.

He smelled Michelle's perfume before he felt her cool hands cover his eyes.

"Guess who?" she whispered.

"The most beautiful woman in the world."

He removed her hands and turned to her. She smiled at him and touched his face with her fingertips.

"Mike said you were out here. I missed you. Are you okay?"

"Sure."

"You look sad."

"Not sad, just thoughtful. How's the party?"

"It's a lot of fun . . . but I can think of something that might be even more fun."

She wrapped her arms around him and drew his lips down to hers. Their kiss was long and passionate and left them both breathless.

She was wearing a tropical silk gown that rustled seductively as she moved. Kane's hands explored down her back and cupped her firm buttocks. She moved closer to him, pressing herself against him.

They kissed again, their tongues darting.

"Ben, remember you told me to hold that thought when you came barging into my room the other day?" she asked huskily.

"You mean when you pulled off the covers?"

"Um, hmm . . . Well, I've been holding that thought for a long time."

Kane grinned. "What exactly do you have in mind?"

"Let's sneak up to my room," she whispered.

"Somebody'll see us, Michelle. There's a party going

on right downstairs from your room."

"I know that." She rubbed her body provocatively against his. "That makes it even more exciting, don't {ou think?"

"That's just the kind of excitement I had in mind," Kane said.

She took his hand and began leading him back toward the Rainbow Keg.

Get ready to follow Ben Kane and his Caribbean Dream super luxury fleet into their next high-speed adventure against The Facility, a posh island "retreat" whose real mission is world domination in . . .

KANE'S WAR #3:
DEATH WAVES